SINS *of the* FATHERS

Also by James Scott Bell

FICTION

Deadlock

Breach of Promise

The Darwin Conspiracy

Circumstantial Evidence

Final Witness

Blind Justice

The Nephilim Seed

*City of Angels**

*Angels Flight**

*Angel of Mercy**

A Greater Glory

A Higher Justice

A Certain Truth

Glimpses of Paradise

NONFICTION

Write Great Fiction: Plot & Sturcture

*coauthor

SINS *of the* FATHERS

JAMES SCOTT BELL

ZONDERVAN™

GRAND RAPIDS, MICHIGAN 49530 USA

ZONDERVAN™

Sins of the Fathers
Copyright © 2005 by James Scott Bell

Requests for information should be addressed to:
Zondervan, *Grand Rapids, Michigan 49530*

Cataloging-in-Publication Data is available from the Library of Congress.

ISBN-10: 0-310-25330-6
ISBN-13: 978-0-310-25330-3

LCCN: 2005004287

Interior design by Beth Shagene

Printed in the United States of America

05 06 07 08 09 10 11 12 /❖ DCI/ 10 9 8 7 6 5 4 3 2 1

For Nate

† † †

Our fathers have sinned, and are not;
and we have borne their iniquities.
Lamentations 5:7 KJV

Everybody's got their dues in life to pay.
Steven Tyler, "Dream On"

SINS *of the* FATHERS

PROLOGUE

† † †

Ollie M. Jones would be the first one the cops would talk to. The fact that he was spattered with blood no doubt had something to do with it. His white jersey with the blue Royals across the front was a canvas of dappled red, certain to catch the attention of the responding police officers.

But Ollie would look back on it and know it wasn't the blood that nabbed the gaze of the young LAPD badge, the one with the dark eyes and bull shoulders. It was the screams that did it.

Ten minutes after it happened, Ollie was still screaming, unable to keep the horror silent.

◆ ◆ ◆

Tara Lundgren thought she heard the sound of several metal bats making contact with several balls simultaneously. That's the way she described it to the reporters from the three local news stations, plus the CNN guy.

"I was standing right here"—Tara indicated with her arm one of the park's four baseball diamonds, the one in the northeast corner—"watching my son's game, when I heard the shots. Like I said, it sounded like bats hitting balls, but then I thought to myself, it didn't really, because a ball hitting these aluminum bats goes *ping*, and this sound was more like *whap*. Then I heard the screams, and I turned around like this"—Tara did a forty-five-degree pivot—"and I saw the people running. And I thought, no, it couldn't be happening, it has to be a joke. But it wasn't. Dear God, it wasn't."

• • •

At the hospital, Robert Landis blocked the homicide detective's path.

"Sir," the detective said, "the doctor says it's all right—"

"I don't care what the doctor says. You can talk to him tomorrow, if he's able, if he wants to, or you can—"

"Sir, listen to me, I understand completely—"

"Do you?"

"I do, sir, I do. I have two boys of my own."

"He shot my son in the chest! While he was playing baseball! What kind of a sick . . . why don't you just shoot *him*?"

"Sir, if you'll let me talk to your boy, we can put together a case, we can make sure this guy gets put away."

"No," Robert Landis said. "Kill him. You have to kill him. You have to make sure of that."

"If you'll let me see your boy now?"

Robert Landis erupted in tears.

• • •

"How many?"

"As of now?"

"Yes."

"Six."

"Six." Syl Martindale's breath left her, turning her chest into a vice. "Six kids dead."

"Five boys." Reesa Birkins swallowed. Hard. "One adult."

"Why, why, why?"

Reesa placed a hand on her friend's arm. "That's beyond us. I can't understand it, I can't. I just have to look to God to—"

"God?" Syl sat straight up, jostling the coffee cup on the kitchen table. "What are you *talking* about? My best friend just watched her only child die in the dirt in front of her."

• • •

Chamberlain Mills, vice president of KNX Newsradio, 1070 AM, delivered his nightly editorial the following evening.

"And now the scourge of violence has come not to another school campus, but to a public park, a place once thought safe in the daytime, a place where families could picnic or watch baseball games under blue southern California skies. That dream is now shattered. What is our answer? We must start with a deeper understanding of the cause of all this violence. How, we must ask, can a thirteen-year-old boy murder six people in cold blood? And what are we to do with mass murderers who have not even reached puberty? These are deep and troubling questions for our society. We must seek understanding above all else. Only then do we have a realistic hope for a solution."

◆ ◆ ◆

"We're going all the way on this one," District Attorney John Sherman told the reporters. "This is it, the line in the sand. We can't let this keep happening. What we need here is not some wishy-washy understanding of sick minds. What we need is punishment for monsters. I don't care how old they are."

◆ ◆ ◆

And in the lockup at the Van Nuys jail, a four-by-eight reeking with the smell of ammonia and urine and sweat and old clothes, he sat alone, barely hearing the sound of cop footsteps and radio-static voices over intercoms, looking at his hands. For hours he would look at them, wondering if they were like his father's hands, or would be when he was all grown up. And he would think about what he'd done and wonder even more, part of him at least, why he didn't feel a thing about it. Not a single, solitary thing.

PART I

✝ ✝ ✝

ONE

✝ ✝ ✝

1.

Lindy Field gunned her Harley Fat Boy, snaking through the congested Los Angeles traffic in the Cahuenga Pass. She'd bought the bike for days like this, when she was late getting downtown and the LA freeway system was pulling its asphalt-glacier routine.

Well, for that and because she just didn't see herself as a car person. Inside all the best defense lawyers, Lindy believed, was a hog engine revved to the limit. She could not abide the lawyers who putt-putted around the criminal courts, doing deals when they should have been chewing prosecutors' rear ends.

The way she used to. Maybe the way she would again, if the chips fell right for a change.

She made it to the Foltz Criminal Courts Building five minutes after her planned time of arrival and took off her helmet. She could feel her tight, sandy blonde curls expanding. Security gave her red leather jacket with the Aerosmith patch on the back a skeptical once-over. They probably thought she was just another family member of some loser defendant here in the city's main criminal court center.

Of course, Judge Roger Greene's clerk, Anna Alvarez, knew her. She'd called Lindy to set up the meeting, the nature of which was still a mystery to Lindy. Anna stood at her desk in the empty courtroom and greeted Lindy like an old friend.

"Hey, there she is. Been too long."

"What is this place?" Lindy looked at the walls. "It seems somehow familiar."

15

"Yes, it's a courtroom. A place where strange lawyer creatures can sometimes be seen."

Lindy hugged Anna. "If a strange lawyer is what you want, I'm your girl."

"Good to have you back."

Was she back yet? *You need a case and client for that, don't you?* Lindy breathed in the familiar smell of carpet and wood and leather. Yes, familiar, yet oddly out of reach.

Anna took Lindy back to Greene's chambers. Greene embraced her like a father welcoming his child home as Anna returned to her desk.

Judge Roger Stanton Greene was fifty-seven, lean, with a full head of black hair streaked with imperial gray. Very judicial. Greene served in Vietnam as a Green Beret. Came back, finished first in his class at Stanford Law.

And he was one of the better judges in town. Actually fair toward people accused of crimes. That he continued to be reelected in law-and-order Los Angeles was something of a miracle. Lindy had tried a few cases before him as a PD, and he always seemed to be looking for ways to cut her a break.

"You look wonderful," Judge Greene said.

Lindy tossed her helmet on a chair. "You're a great liar, Judge. Ever think of going back into practice?"

He laughed. His chamber was filled with books—not just law, but all sorts of subjects. Greene was one of the most learned men she knew.

"So how long's it been since you've tried a case down here?" Greene asked.

"A year. A little more."

"Get some skiing in during the off time?"

"I don't ski when I'm on meds. I tend to run into trees."

"Was it rough?"

Lindy inhaled deeply. She knew he was referring to her crash-and-burn after the Marcel Lee verdict, when she went from rising deputy public defender to thirty-two-year-old washout. "Yeah, it's been rough. But I beat it back with ice cream and Kate Hepburn movies. You'd be surprised what a little *African Queen* can do for the spirit."

"Who's handling the Lee appeal now?"

"Appellate Division. Menaster."

"He's good. If there's a way to get the thing reversed, he'll find it." Greene did not say it with much conviction. That was understandable. The days of frequent reversals were over. The fair citizens of California, demanding easy answers to a complex crime problem, were initiative happy. They passed laws that promised instant, get-tough results. They elected politicians and judges who strove to come down harder on crime than Torquemada. They passed bond measures to build more prisons to warehouse an ever-swelling population of hard timers and three-strike losers.

And if a kid like Marcel Lee got tossed into that fetid swamp, so what? One more they wouldn't have to worry about being out on the streets.

Lindy felt that sensation that took over her skin whenever she thought of Marcel. *Fever skin*, her mother used to call it, when every pore felt sensitive and exposed. She couldn't will it away, so she settled into a chair like a swami lowering himself onto a bed of nails.

Greene sat behind his desk. "You have an office?"

"I pay a guy for a mailing address in the Valley, and the use of his library and conference room."

"Hard to get started again?"

"Only thing I know for sure, making it on your own as a lawyer is not about competence."

"What's it about?"

"Overhead."

Greene nodded. "And getting clients."

"Oh yeah. I've heard of those."

"Why don't you do one of those lawyer commercials? Like that guy who used to have his clients say, 'He got me twenty million dollars.'"

"Right. I can see it now. One of my guys pops onto the screen. 'Lindy Field got me twenty years.'" It felt good to be talking plainly again.

Greene swiveled in his chair, smiled. "So you want to know why I wanted to see you?"

"Comic relief?"

"An assignment."

"Cool. *Court-appointed* means county pays."

"It's a juvenile matter."

An involuntary groan escaped Lindy's throat. "Judge—"

"Just hear me out."

"I don't want to do juvenile again."

"I understand. But there's something about this one. Does the name Darren DiCinni mean anything to you?"

Lindy's jaw dropped like a law book falling from a shelf.

"That's right," Greene said. "The one who killed those kids at the baseball game."

Lindy tried to wipe the shock off her face. Was he actually asking her to rep the thirteen-year-old whose face was all over the news?

"Won't the public defender handle it?"

"There's a conflict."

"How?"

"The boy's father, Drake DiCinni, was repped by the PD's office for something that got dismissed a year ago. So they can't do it. Even if they could, I'd want you."

Lindy closed her eyes for a moment, trying to keep the office from closing in around her head. "But there are so many others you could tap."

"I know this is not your average juvi case. But you have a way with them."

"Had."

"You still do. You don't lose that touch, Lindy, no matter what. And this kid's going to need special handling."

"He said God told him to kill the people?" That's what she'd read in the *Times*.

"Right."

"He connected to some cult or anything?"

Greene shrugged. "I only know what's been reported."

Lindy paused, then shook her head slowly. "I just don't think I'm ready for something this heavy."

"There's one more thing. The deputy handling this is Leon Colby."

The name hit her like a spear. It took a long moment for Lindy to remove it. And then she felt the old wound, the one shaped like Marcel Lee. Colby prosecuted the Lee case, sent the boy away for life.

"This is some kind of weird *Twilight Zone*, right?" Lindy put the heel of her palm on her forehead. "I'm going to be getting out of this universe soon, right?"

"I know what you must be thinking."

"Really? You know? From on high?"

Greene said nothing.

"I'm sorry," Lindy said. "That was a rotten thing to say."

"It's okay. I completely understand. Why don't we just forget it?"

Yes, forget it. Leave now before you change your mind. Leon Colby? Why had Greene even considered asking her?

Maybe because he knew the thought of Colby coldly scavenging the bones of another kid almost made her gag.

"Hey," Greene said, "there's a great play at the Taper. Have you seen—"

"I'll see him," Lindy said. "Once. And I'm not promising anything."

"Lindy, you don't have to—"

"Don't press your luck, Judge. Where is he now?"

2.

The last time Lindy was in Men's Central Jail was during the Lee case, right after Marcel attempted suicide.

Why wouldn't he? This was no place for juveniles. That was the whole reason for having Juvenile Hall. But when the kids were tried as adults, Los Angeles threw them in Men's Central, downtown, where they spent twenty-three-and-a-half hours a day locked in windowless four-by-eight-foot cells.

Death-row inmates at Quentin had it better. Career criminals at Pelican Bay were on easy street by comparison. All those guys got ample time each day for showers, phone calls, and a walk in the corridor in front of their cells. Not the juvis in Men's Central.

Lindy remembered when the *Times* did a story on the horrible conditions behind the steel door of Module 4600 at Central, which guarded the two tiers of twenty-four cells where the juvis were housed. Four, five, or six to a cell. Some of the local politicians jumped on it and beat their chests for change. It gave them a couple days' publicity.

And change did happen. For a time. Most kid-adults were taken to Sylmar, a juvi lockup, and that seemed to make everybody feel good. But pretty soon the bottom line snapped its jaws tight around the situation: it cost more to put kids out there.

So little by little, the warehousing of juvis in Men's Central—isolated from the adult population, of course, but crammed inside those cells that had only a toilet and what the county had the temerity to call bedding—little by little, the dumping of kids no one had any sympathy for returned. And without the *Times* making hay, the politicians kept quiet.

There was no rousing plea to be kinder to juvenile criminals.

He didn't look like Lindy had pictured. When he was marched into the interview room, shackled and in his orange jailhouse jumpsuit, he was a lot smaller than she thought he'd be. Lindy estimated he was about her height. Which wasn't good for him. If he got sent to prison—and Lindy knew that was the most likely outcome, even if Clarence Darrow came back from the dead to defend him—Darren DiCinni was not going to last long. He'd be fresh meat, tossed into a pit of ravenous lowlifes with nothing left to lose.

"Twenty minutes," the deputy sheriff said as he put Darren's hands in the desk cuffs. The jail classified juveniles as K–10s, highest security, and kept them isolated. The deputies claimed it was because juvis did crazy things, to prove themselves to the older inmates. Darren was also a "high power" inmate, one with notoriety and media coverage. He needed to be protected from prisoners who might want to make a name for themselves by taking out a celebrity killer.

She tried to read his face. Who was Darren DiCinni, besides some teenager lost in oversized coveralls? Who was this boy sitting on the steel stool on the other side of the wire-mesh Plexiglas in the green interview booth, accused of an abominable crime? How did he get to this place?

She always asked herself these questions about new juvenile clients. They were only a step or two removed from childhood, yet they did evil things.

Why?

He did not look at her.

Lindy leaned toward the talk holes in the Plexiglas. "Darren, I'm Lindy Field. I'm your attorney."

His eyes did not move. He was staring at the floor like some sort of comic-book character who could cut through stone with laser beams shot from his eyeballs. Lindy suddenly had no trouble believing he had killed six people in cold blood.

"I'm here to talk to you about your case."

No change.

Lindy had handled bad ones before, ones with attitude, with chips on shoulders the size of buses. But she'd always managed to penetrate the barriers, at least a little bit, to a level where she could communicate.

Some were tougher to get to than others, that was all.

Darren DiCinni was going to be one of the tougher ones.

"Look, you don't have to talk to me now, but at some point we're going to have to get together on this thing. The DA isn't going to look out for you. The cops aren't. Your lawyer is, but you've got to give me something. Remember, anything you say will stay with me. I won't talk about it with anybody else."

That was always the first move. Establish trust. Cast yourself on their side.

DiCinni didn't move.

There was something strange here.

Despite his inner fires, Darren DiCinni didn't have a bad-boy aura. His light brown hair was trimmed and neat. He was a skinny kid too, stuck in that awkward stage between child and young man. His hands and wrists looked as if they could slip right out of the shackles, like toothpicks from a wedding band. And his face, cool and impassive, was almost translucent, like baby skin.

Darren DiCinni was not, at first glance, like the tattooed and scarred outlaws she was used to. Nor was he trying to be.

But the peculiar thing was, he wasn't some tragic innocent, either. A few years ago, another young, skinny kid had shot up a school down near San Diego. He looked so young, so impossibly young to do such a thing.

DiCinni might have seemed that way too, except for those eyes. And that made him impossible for Lindy to peg.

There was a reason he did not fit into any apparent slot, and Lindy had to find out what that was. She had the feeling the answer would be her—and DiCinni's—only hope of getting a more favorable sentence than life in prison without the possibility of parole.

"Darren, I'm going to talk to the DA about your case. I need to get to know you just a little. I want you to know you can trust me."

Nothing. Those lasers burned into the floor.

Maybe there was a competency issue here. Maybe DiCinni wouldn't have the capacity to help with the defense, and she could get him into a mental facility, keep him out of prison.

"You gonna talk to me today, Darren?"

She waited. And then, slowly, DiCinni shook his head. He still had not looked at her.

Lindy wanted to reach through the glass and grab him, shake him. She wanted to rouse him out of his stupor, force him to pay attention, make him realize he was dangling over a gorge by a string. And, she realized, to make him help *her*. She didn't want to lose another one like she lost Marcel Lee.

"Please, Darren. Let me help you. That's what I'm here for, that's what I do. I went to law school and everything. I had seven years with the public defender's office. Will you just give me something to work with here?"

DiCinni looked up. She now could see his eyes were brown speckled with flecks of green. They were still shooting hot beams, but with something added. A probing.

She let him look.

Then Darren DiCinni started rattling his desk cuffs. Violently.

"Darren—"

The metallic clatter got louder.

"Stop, Darren."

He did not stop.

The deputy charged over and slapped Darren's back. "Cut it out."

"I wanna go back," Darren said. His voice was high, like a choirboy's.

"Darren, you have to talk to me," Lindy pleaded.

He glared at her with a mix of defiance and confusion. The deputy began to undo the shackles.

"Darren, wait."

The deputy looked at Lindy with disdain. "Says he's through, he's through."

Lindy put her hand on the Plexiglas. "Wait a second."

But the deputy already had the desk cuffs off. Darren got up quickly and didn't look back as he was led away.

Outside Men's Central, the harsh glare of the LA afternoon sun hit Lindy's eyes like a police interrogation light. The kind cops used to coerce confessions in those old B movies. *Why don't you just admit it, Lindy? Come on, you know it, we all know it. You lost your chops when they put you in the psych ward. You don't have what it takes. Your father knew it all along, didn't he? Tried to tell you. What've you got to prove, Lindy? Give it up. You can't help anybody, especially this kid who rattles chains at you.*

She had to get to her bike. The growl of her Harley was the only thing that could drown out her thoughts this day. But she knew, with a harsh, prophetic certainty, that no sound was going to help her this time.

Two

† † †

1.

The moment she realized she was waking up, Mona Romney cried out in her mind.

No, oh please no, dear God, don't let me. Don't let me wake up. Let me die, dear God, let me die.

But her consciousness fought, dragging her toward wakefulness.

Where am I? I don't want to be here. I want to go back.

She felt a coldness on the other side of what she determined were sheets. The lights were too bright. She wanted to go back to blackness, but her body would not let her.

The bright light was from sunshine streaming through the window.

Make it stop! Make the light go away!

She wanted to yell at somebody to close the curtains, but she had no voice. Her throat felt thick and her tongue was a sand weight on the bottom of her mouth.

Why do I want to die? She struggled to remember.

"Honey?"

The voice drifted into her ears, unwelcome.

"How you feeling? Can you hear me? You been out a long time."

Brad. Her husband. Loving Brad. Faithful and strong. She wanted him to go away. She wanted to scream at him to go away.

She felt his hand on her forehead, stroking it. She wanted to jerk away from him but her body was too heavy with drowsiness. That was it. She remembered now. They'd given her a sedative. She'd been some kind of hysterical.

25

She was home.

No, no! I don't want to be here. I don't want to be anywhere Matthew is not.

"Babe, it's me. I love you so much."

Go away.

"I've been praying all night. I was on the floor in the living room on my face, just crying out to God. I'm so tired."

She opened her mouth and a guttural, wordless groan spilled out.

"Yes?" Brad was a fuzzy blur next to the bed. He was holding her hand, squeezing it. "You want to say something?"

Mona swallowed. It was an effort, like pushing a wide rock down a narrow dirt hole. But she was going to speak, she had to speak or she'd go crazy. She was probably crazy anyway, and always would be.

"What is it?" Brad whispered.

"Don't."

"Don't what? Are you uncomfortable?"

She squeezed his hand with all the strength she had, which was not very much, but enough to make his hand tremble in hers.

"Don't. Talk about . . ."

"Yes?"

"God."

"But—"

She squeezed his hand harder. "Ever."

She released him and he stood up. Stiff. She could tell. She knew when something hit her husband hard. Like when he got the news his dad had died. How he stood stock-still with the phone in his hand, like a granite statue titled *Man with Mouth Half Open*. Or when his former business partner served him with a lawsuit. That time it was *Man with Hurt on Face*.

Now he was stiff like that again. Wet clay fashioned into a kind, loving, Christian husband whose wife was telling him not to bring up the name of God in front of her.

Oh how she meant it.

Matthew Romney was only eleven years old. And he had one of those sunny outlooks that gets turned into a Disney film. His pitching arm had made him one of the stars of the league, but he had a side Mona was sure only she could fully understand. He was sensitive like her. He felt things deeply. He told her once, when she was tucking him in and it was just the two of them, that he wanted to make people feel better when they hurt. Because that's what she did for him.

He was eight years old when he said that.

Now he was dead.

And now her husband was standing there, and she had hurt him. Or maybe just confused him. She didn't care.

For a moment, that scared her.

But then she did not care that she was scared.

"Go away," she said and then mustered the strength to turn her back to him and bury her face in the pillow.

2.

"Lindy, good to see you." Leon Colby had all the sincerity of a showroom smoothie. The only difference was he was bigger than any car salesman she'd ever seen, at least six foot six, and he still had that linebacker's body. His hair was short and in his glasses he looked like a very large Ivy League professor. No wonder juries loved him. He possessed that aura of power and intelligence combined with a certain charisma that made superstars in any profession.

That's why the buzz around town was that he would make a good run at becoming the first African-American district attorney in LA history.

Lindy felt her hands go clammy even as she tried to breathe steadily. Power flowed downward from Colby to her, and she knew it.

"Been what, a couple years?" Colby said. "Coffee?"

"No thanks." Lindy sat on one of the hard chairs in front of Colby's desk. She noticed it was almost pathologically neat. Even the small pad of Post-its was set so its lines were parallel with the desk edge. She couldn't help comparing it to her own "desk"—a kitchen table that looked like a Dumpster behind a stationery store.

"So how you doing?" Colby said, turning and grabbing a small coffeepot from the credenza.

Better than Marcel Lee, thank you very much. "I'm okay."

"Good. 'Cause I heard about . . . that you were in . . ."

"I'm fine."

"Well, good, it's good to be fine." He picked up the file folder sitting on his desk. Like all DA folders, this one had a form printed on the outside, with lots of boxes for checking off as the case progressed from arraignment to sentencing. It appeared Colby had made no check marks on this one. Yet.

"So Greene assigned you to Darren DiCinni," Colby said.

"I'm going to handle the arraignment. After that, I don't know."

Colby opened the file and gave it a cursory look. "Maybe we can work something out."

She had prepared for this moment and pounced. "I'm going to want a suspension of proceedings."

Colby closed the file. "What for?"

"A 1368 hearing."

"Mental competency exam?"

"You got it."

"You're dreaming."

"Am I?"

"Come on, Lindy. You have to show he is unable—*unable*—to understand the nature of the proceedings. Houseplants understand the nature of proceedings."

Cute. "The statute also says he has to comprehend his own status *and condition* in those proceedings. You haven't even seen him."

"I haven't seen Paris. Doesn't mean it isn't there. And just because he claims God talked to him doesn't—"

"We are going to have a 1368."

Colby didn't flinch. "That just gives me more time to prepare for trial. And make no mistake, Lindy. This case is going to trial. Unless . . ." He raised his eyebrows, as if to signal it was now Lindy's move.

"You have an offer?"

"He's going to have to do time. A lot of it."

"You don't even know his background."

"We don't let murderers off because of background."

"This kid needs help."

"Based on what? Have you done any background on him?"

Lindy felt like a hostile witness skewered to the witness chair by Leon Colby's almost legendary cross-examination skills. She cleared her throat. "We haven't come close to doing a full probe on this one, but when—"

"Want me to make it easy for you?"

Lindy waited. He would make it easy for the jury too, unless she came up with something soon.

"This is no climate for mercy," Colby said. "People are sick of this kind of thing, no matter what age the killer is. You want soft gloves? Forget it."

"There's a risk for you taking this to trial."

"Get serious, Lindy. The only factual issue is going to be mental state at the time of the shootings. You got something I should hear about?"

"It'll come."

"Let's see." Colby looked at his fingers as if they were a crib sheet. "You can't go for duress. The Cal Supremes ruled that's no longer a defense for murder. Maybe you could try to nullify premeditation-deliberation, keep it from the special circumstance of 'lying in wait.' But *People v. Hillhouse* says just walking up to a victim qualifies as 'lying in wait.' Here you've got a kid walking up to a whole field of vics. You want me to go on?"

"Fascinating." And scary, because Leon Colby was brilliant. Lindy had researched him during the Lee case. Colby was second in his class at UCLA Law after finishing up an all-American football career for the Bruins. Only a blown-out knee kept him from getting millions in the pros.

And while Colby was getting the glory at UCLA, Lindy was slogging away in the night program at little Southwestern Law School, working during the day at Target. The difference in legal pedigree was not lost on her. In the world of criminal law, he was best in show. She was a night-school mutt.

"Now, you might be thinking some kind of insanity defense," Colby continued. "The *God told me* thing. We all know how successful that defense is. Al Sharpton has a better chance of being elected mascot for the Ku Klux Klan. So where does that leave us?"

"We got a thirteen-year-old kid who I've seen up close and you haven't. No jury is going to want to toss him to the wolves."

"You think? You think after all the gang killings and—"

"There's no gang connection here."

"Close enough for government work."

"I can't believe you said that. Since when is *close enough* a legal standard?"

"I'm talking about perception, Lindy, about people being fed up with the streets going to juvis with guns. You want to get some sympathy going for this kid? Good luck."

"Neither one of us knows jack about this kid. How can you sit there and say anything?"

"Because we're holding all the cards here, and they come up L-WOP."

"Life without parole? That's your deal?" Some deal. L-WOP was the harshest sentence for murder short of lethal injection. Served in a maximum-security prison. Where Darren DiCinni wouldn't last five minutes. And who would care? Prison rape was an issue the public or politicians didn't want to look at. The harsh picture of what prisons had become was too disturbing, too disruptive for California dreamin'.

Lindy's hands closed around the chair arms. "You can't send this kid to state prison for life."

"Who says?"

"There was a case, a couple of years ago. *In re John J.* or something. Had to do with juveniles going to state."

Colby smiled as a father would to a child who was delving into issues well beyond her understanding. "That case was depublished by the Supremes. There's no authority on it now, and we're going into this thing without any reservation. We think the Court of Appeal will back us up, if it comes to that."

The words that formed in Lindy's mind caused pain. But she knew she had to say them. "What sort of deal can we talk about?"

She almost did not look at his face when she said it. But when she did, she thought she saw something like pity in his eyes. Because he did hold all the cards, and they both knew it. A plea bargain was the best she could expect on this, and that was true most of the time anyway. Even though every citizen is supposed to have a right to trial, the fact was, judges would hold a trial against you at sentencing time. If you didn't plead out, you'd face a much harsher penalty if the jury came back with a guilty verdict.

The justice system was a rigged roulette wheel.

"Murder second," Colby said.

Lindy clenched her jaw. "Reverse remand." A juvenile tried in adult court could, with the prosecution's cooperation, be remanded back to the juvenile system. If a client got a sentence of fifteen to life under juvenile law, he would go to the California Youth Authority and not state prison. When he turned twenty-five, he could get out.

"Not gonna happen, Lindy."

"Why not? What's so all-consuming about a thirteen-year-old who—" Lindy stopped her own words, pistons firing in her mind. "Wait a second. This is about you, isn't it?"

"Me?"

"About you becoming DA."

He paused momentarily before answering. "I take the cases as they come."

Lindy pointed to the top of Colby's filing cabinet, at the little statue of a blindfolded woman holding the scales of justice. "When did you stop believing in that? When did it become a matter of winning at all costs?"

Now the darkness in Colby's eyes seemed to take over his entire form. "If you're trying to soften me up, you're doing a lousy job."

"No," Lindy said. "I'm not going to soften you up. I'm just trying to get you to do it right this time."

"This time?"

"Marcel Lee was convicted on a lie, and you know it."

Colby looked at her with the cool menace that quarterbacks who opposed him must have seen countless times. "This meeting is over, Lindy. I'm going to see to it that this monster goes away forever."

3.

"Are you a monster?"

Lindy stared at Darren DiCinni through the Plexiglas in the jail's interview room.

Darren's face held the same, expressionless gaze as before. But she thought her words got his attention this time.

"Yeah, that's what the prosecutor says, that's what the whole town, the whole world, is saying about you. You got anything to tell me to make it otherwise?"

Darren DiCinni shook his head.

It was communication of a sort, a step in the right direction.

Lindy took another step. "You care what happens to you?"

Darren looked at her a moment, shrugged.

"At least let me tell you what's happening. Will you let me do that much?"

He said nothing.

"All right. The DA wants to make an example out of you. He wants to treat you as an adult and get you a life sentence, without possibility of parole. That means you'll go into the adult prison population and never come out."

"Can't they just kill me?"

There was his voice again, a child's voice. The innocence of it made Lindy want to scream. What kind of world is this? What world turns out a kid who, just a few years past Barney stage, goes out to shoot down children with a rifle?

Lindy wrestled her insides to the mat. "No, Darren. You don't have to worry about that. You're a juvenile, and in this state we don't put juveniles to death, even when they're tried as adults."

"I want them to."

An iciness gripped her. "You don't mean that."

"Tell them."

"Tell them what?"

"I want to die. I want them to do it to me. Tell them."

Lindy looked at his face. His smooth skin wasn't even forming pimples yet. But he wanted to die. And thousands of people out there would be happy to shove the needle into his arm. "You're not going to face the death penalty. But they can put you away for life. In prison. With hardened adult criminals. I can't let that happen to you."

He seemed to be thinking about this, ideas tumbling in his immature brain, conjuring confusing images. "You called me a monster."

"That's what the DA's calling you."

"You think I'm a monster?"

"No."

"Why not? You don't even know me. Maybe I am."

She wanted to tell him that he was too young to be a monster, to be consigned forever to that fate. Did she believe it? Maybe some were born this way. Maybe she'd been wrong about juveniles all along. One big sap.

"Help me to help you," Lindy said.

Darren DiCinni shook his head. She could perceive him retreating into his skinny shell.

"Darren?"

No answer this time. And despite five more minutes of trying, she pulled no more words from him.

4.

It was nearly dark when Lindy returned to her mobile home in Box Canyon in the westernmost part of Los Angeles County. Box Canyon was the last outpost of soon-to-reach-retirement-age hippies, bikers, and a smattering of folks who remembered when they could actually hunt in these hills.

And a solo lawyer who needed money.

As she got off her bike, Mr. Klinger called to her from over the fence.

"Hey, fancy lawyer!" Emil Klinger was well into his eighties, a former Catskills comedian who'd done some character work in B movies in the fifties. He lived next door and usually wore a white undershirt and suspenders, as he was now. Thatches of white hair marked his shoulders and chest like scrub brush.

"How you doing, Mr. Klinger?"

"My urine is pink."

It was Emil Klinger's passion to share his physical dissolution with Lindy at the start of every conversation.

"You taking your medications?" Lindy checked up on him regularly, to make sure he was getting the attention he needed. He didn't have family close by.

"Marry me and find out."

"You know I would, Mr. Klinger, but it would make my cat jealous."

He shrugged. "Ah, s'okay. At my age there's six women for every man."

"That so?"

He shook his head ruefully. "What a time to get odds like that. Can you make a will for my son?"

"That's not my specialty."

"He doesn't care for specialties. He's an idiot. But a paying idiot."

Actually, a simple will sounded good. Anything simple that paid sounded good. "Okay, have him call me."

"You got it, baby. And then I'll call you myself." Klinger clucked a couple of times.

"I'll drop by later to check in on you. But no hanky-panky, right?"

"What's to hank or pank? I went from Why not? to Why bother? years ago."

Lindy went inside her trailer. Her cat, Cardozo, greeted her with a sophisticated *mew*. He was a black-and-white she found half dead in the hills of Box Canyon. She nursed him back to health and named him for Benjamin Cardozo, the great Supreme Court justice whose opinions Lindy loved reading in law school.

"What a day I've had. Wanna get fat? I'll get the ice cream, and you can pork out on some of those salmon treats you like. Whaddaya say?"

Cardozo blinked.

"So am I ready to take on another case?"

No answer. But Cardozo was listening.

Lindy got the mocha almond fudge from her freezer and started spooning some into a bowl. "Or am I still crazy and should go into another line of work? Like price checker at the Everything's-a-Dollar store. Think I could handle that?"

Cardozo padded over to her feet.

"Oh really? You want me to get out there again? Go for it? Look who's talking. When's the last time you caught a mouse around here?"

Lindy grabbed a few salmon treats and doled one out to Cardozo.

"Okay, kid, we'll figure this out together."

Her cell phone chimed. She saw a familiar number on the LCD. Great. Not the call she wanted right now, but she'd have to deal with him sooner or later.

"Hi, Sean."

"Hey, babe, you picked up. That's a good sign." His voice was honey rich, easy on the ears. Seductive. That and his matinee idol looks made it easy to understand why he was such a hot TV reporter in a town full of eye candy.

"You're just lucky, I guess," Lindy said.

"Good to hear your voice without the knives in it." Two nights ago Sean McIntyre took Lindy to Geoffrey's in Malibu, overlooking the Pacific Ocean, then back to his apartment for another stunning view. Then he had tried to view something more, pawing at her clothes and kissing her until she socked him in the jaw and left.

"So when can we go out again?" Sean said.

"I thought I made it clear—"

"I called to apologize, okay?"

"I'm about to go to bed."

"Care for company?"

"You are a piece of work."

"That's what my publicity says."

She paused, fighting urges within her. Hang up? Keep talking? "Your publicity also says you're not wanting for female company, so—"

"Whoa, we're not talking about other women."

"I am."

"Lindy, I know I've been out with a lot of women the past couple of years—"

"No kidding. Who was that last one, that anchor woman?"

"Sahara Davis?"

"Yeah. What kind of name is Sahara anyway? She should be dating Lawrence of Arabia."

"The Sahara's in Africa."

"Don't get technical."

"Can you really blame me for the other night? That I find you attractive? Come on. We've been going out a month and we haven't even . . ."

"Even what? We *talked*, remember? Talking is a good adult thing to do. And then we walked on the beach, you kissed me."

"Yeah, but come on, *a month*."

"Sean, I've given up casual sex, okay? It doesn't work. It's like the Thighmaster of human relations."

"Come to New York with me."

"Sean—"

"Did you hear me say *New York*? I'm going to be interviewed on the *Today Show*. About my reporting on the Dixon murder. It could mean a network gig."

"Sean, you're a great reporter—"

"I know."

"But I need to give this a rest for a while."

"Look, I'm sorry it happened. What can I say? I had a little too much to drink, I admit it."

"A little? You were doing shooters like breath mints and then you grew four arms and used them all on me."

"I can be incredibly charming once you get to know me."

Lindy said nothing, believing him and not wanting to believe him at the same time. *Remember the anger.* She honestly didn't know what he did to her. She only knew that part of her wanted to keep him and not let him go. But another part was shouting, *Stop, idiot!*

"All right," Sean said. "I'll go to New York alone. But don't be getting hooked on anybody while I'm gone." His jaunty tone had an edge.

"Have a nice trip."

"I intend to."

He hung up. That bothered her no end. The least he could have done was let her hang up on *him*.

That night Lindy dreamed of death.

5.

First came the children.

In Lindy's dream they were running and screaming, dozens of them, in some sunlit field. A billowing surge of terrified kids, boys and girls, some in baseball garb, others in variegated ragtag clothes that gave the impression of a Dickens novel run amok.

A dark, unseen terror chased them. From the hovering perspective that only dreams afford, Lindy sought desperately the source of the fear.

She saw a black forest behind the field, one that belonged in fairy tales. Or nightmares.

She moved toward the forest, knowing who it was, who was in there, knowing she'd meet him coming out. Darren DiCinni would have a gun, and in the dream she glided low to avoid being shot.

Moving closer and closer now, the screams of the scattering children fading behind her. Without having to look behind she knew that a raft of cops was pulling up to the scene.

Was she going to warn DiCinni, or just look at him?

Would he say anything to her, or she to him?

Bad things lived here, in this gloom where gnarly fingered trees came alive at night.

Lindy didn't want to go in, but she couldn't stop herself.

A shadowy figure started to materialize, from deep within the forest, and it was running toward her.

She opened her mouth to scream, but no sound came out.

Stop, stop, stop she wanted to say, but she could utter no words.

The figure came closer. He was holding a shotgun.

Pointed at her.

He was going to kill her, and she couldn't move. Her feet became sandbags.

And then, on the edge of the forest, where the light from her world met the shadows of his, the killer emerged and now she did not scream but opened her mouth wide and silent.

It was not Darren DiCinni.

It was Marcel Lee.

And then, powerless to stop them, Lindy was assaulted by image after image from a tortured past.

She saw Marcel, running with a gang at seventeen, trying to get out. Now accused of murdering a cop.

I ain't do it, Ms. Field . . .

She saw his eyes again and knew he wasn't scamming. She could tell, after six years of looking into juvi eyes.

She shouldn't care. She told herself in her mind, in her dream, she shouldn't care so much about a client. But she always did. And Marcel's mother, who told Lindy she trusted her with her son's life.

She saw the police witness, Officer Brandon Scott. She saw his eyes again, lying eyes. Like in the song.

And Leon Colby. He had to know his wit was lying. But he didn't care. And in her dream, he didn't care again.

She saw Marcel Lee, going away to do life in Quentin. And his mother, crying and screaming in the courtroom. At her.

Why'd you let 'em do it? Why didn't you stop 'em?

In her dream, Lindy's heart bolted out of her chest, bloody and beating, and fled into the dark place.

The dark place was Elmwood, the psych facility where they'd taken her after weeks of barely any sleep, after downing half a bottle of pills to kill the ghosts.

She saw Marcel's face again, only it wasn't his face, it was Darren DiCinni's face now, and he looked at her, wild-eyed and hopeless.

And that's when the guns in shadowed hands opened fire, filling his body with holes, his blood spraying her.

6.

"I can't do it," Lindy said.

It was 8:14 Tuesday morning. Darren DiCinni's arraignment was scheduled for nine. Lindy's stomach was churning. She could see the corner of the *Times* building through the window of Judge Greene's chambers.

Greene, as always, spoke calmly.

"Is this you talking, or is it Marcel Lee?"

Lindy shot him a look, saw the astonishing understanding in his face.

"Both," Lindy admitted.

"Then take it. Take the case. You have to put the ghosts to rest."

"They never rest."

Greene laced his fingers behind his head. "The thing about fear is that you don't get rid of it by will. And you can't sit around and wait for it to leave. It won't. What you do is act. Right in the face of it. And then it slowly loses its power."

Lindy rubbed her hands over the worn leather briefcase on her lap. "I don't know what I'd do if I lost another one."

"But you're not going to lose this one."

She looked at him, wondering what he could possibly mean.

Greene leaned forward, putting his elbows on his desk. A pewter representation of the Ten Commandments sat to one side. Lindy always wondered what the ACLU would have thought had they known. She carried an ACLU card herself.

"Here's what you do, Lindy. Go down there and plead him not guilty. Then make a statement to the reporters. Speak from your heart. Presumption of innocence for everyone. A bedrock of our system. The facts aren't fully known. You know the drill."

Lindy waited.

"Then you tell Colby you're willing to plead guilty in return for disposition to a mental institution. They'll offer you the twenty-five-to-life deal. You insist on minimum security and you'll take it. Everyone comes out ahead. The state is spared the expense of a trial, you make a great deal for the boy, everyone knows your name."

For a long moment Lindy saw it unfold just as Greene had said. "What if a mental is really what he needs?"

"If you can get Colby to go along with that, it would be a double victory."

"I still don't know. Let me get him through arraignment and—"

"Do it, Lindy. I know you can. And I'll be right here if you need me."

For the first time in a long time, Lindy felt like crying. She wanted to let everything out, find some footing in life again. She wanted to do it in front of Roger Greene, the one man who could understand what she was going through.

But she saw it was 8:44, and she had a boy waiting for his arraignment for mass murder.

Just get through the next hour. One step at a time. Isn't that what they told you, over and over, in the hospital? One step at a time. Five minute increments, and you're done.

But a cold tentacle of dread wrapped itself around her heart, squeezing the life out of any incipient hope for conclusion.

THREE

† † †

1.

As mother of one of the victims, Mona Romney was allowed a seat in arraignment court, along with the press, which was well represented. Several reporters asked her for a comment, but she refused. She was not ready to talk to reporters, or anyone else for that matter. She was here for Matthew, for his memory. And to see that justice was done.

She was grateful that a man like Leon Colby was handling the case. He seemed like the kind of lawyer who would fight for justice, wouldn't let any defense lawyer get the better of him. Yesterday she heard her husband speak to him by phone. Brad expressed his approval of the man, told her about his reputation. He'd taken on tough juvenile cases before, built his renown on them.

Mona knew nothing about the defense lawyer, save that she was a petite woman with aggressively curly hair. When this woman, this Lindy Field, entered the courtroom, dressed in a gray pantsuit and carrying a briefcase and motorcycle helmet, Mona's spine tingled with electric suspicion. She gave the lawyer a long look from the second row of the gallery.

Was she one of those tricky lawyers, the kind who'd do anything to win? The type who would hide evidence, lie to the court, mislead a jury?

She recalled the Menendez case, the one where the two brothers who'd blown away their parents had a feisty woman representing them. She tried a lot of things to get them off, but the jury came back with a solid guilty verdict.

This woman reminded Mona a little of that feisty lawyer. She looked smart. But Leon Colby was smart too. And truth   didn't that matter? Wouldn't that rise to the top in Colby's capable hands?

Mona closed her eyes and willed it to be so.

On the way in, Mona saw other parents who'd lost boys to the killer. They looked like she felt, empty and worn down. They were all still in shock. Up to the last minute, Mona wasn't sure she'd even come to the hearing. But she had some inner need to do *something*. If she didn't come, she would be letting Matthew down. She could do this for him and maybe fill the void that gaped in her heart and soul.

She sat in the chair nearest the wall and exchanged terse introductions with a woman named Dawn Stead. Her boy Jared had been on the Royals, Matthew's White Sox opponents that day. She seemed like she'd be nice enough in other circumstances. But now neither one of them was in the mood for talk. Mona couldn't have managed anyway. Death was a fist inside her throat, choking the words.

Mona was so tense her shoulders cramped. Her son's murderer was going to be in this room, not fifteen feet away from her. She didn't know how she would react.

Once, when Matthew was three, he busied himself collecting leaves and sticks from eucalyptus trees, arranging them carefully in a pattern in the sandbox. Two boys, five or six years old, looked on. Mona thought that was nice. But then one of them kicked the sand, scattering Matthew's labor. The other boy joined in the destruction. And Mona saw Matthew's eyes grow wide with shock at the random violation.

Mona's reaction was intense, instant, savage. Only the fact that she had to run from the picnic table to the sandbox, and was given a momentary pause to reflect, kept her from physically throttling the older boys. She wanted to hurt them, cause them pain. She was not rational. She did not *want* to be rational. She wanted to hurt the ones who had hurt her child.

Sitting in court, remembering that day, Mona's chest tightened and she had trouble breathing normally. She wanted Brad with her, and she didn't want him. Would things ever be normal again? Would life relent, give them a break?

And then, at nine o'clock, the defendant was brought in.

Mona gasped. She had seen him the day of the shooting, but only in a flash and far away. He had seemed huge then, but maybe only because of all that was happening around her. Maybe her mind had built up his monstrosity, adding layers to her memory.

But this was a boy, not much older than Matthew, and he was dressed like a criminal.

Because that's what he was. He was one of the boys from the sandbox, grown older and harder and more evil. And despite his age, he had to be stopped. He had to be punished. He had to be put away for the rest of his life for what he did.

Mona realized she was holding on to the arms of the courtroom seat so hard her fingers were curled into claws.

The judge, Darlene Howard, looked like a grandmother, and Mona did not want a grandmother's softness anywhere near this case. Even though this was only a brief hearing—*arraignment* was the word—it felt to Mona like a setting of the tone. She did not want the killer's lawyer to get anything for her client, if anything was possible.

"The People of the State of California versus Darren DiCinni," the judge said. "Counsel, state your appearances."

"Good morning, Your Honor. Leon Colby, deputy district attorney, for the people."

"Lindy Field, Your Honor, for the defendant Darren DiCinni, who is present in court. At this time we will waive a reading of the complaint and statement of rights and enter a plea of not guilty."

Not guilty. How could this lawyer even mouth those words? Contempt began to boil inside Mona Romney. This lawyer was an enemy to Matthew's memory. She could not be allowed to get the killer off the hook, in any way.

The judge asked Darren DiCinni to stand up. "Mr. DiCinni, did your lawyer explain the charges against you?"

Mr. DiCinni? Mona squirmed. How could the judge call him that? *Mister?* That kind of respect should be reserved for good people, not murderers.

The killer looked at his hands.

"Your Honor," the killer's lawyer said, "I explained the charges and proceedings to my client, but he has not communicated with me about his plea. This is an issue I will take up at a 1368 hearing."

"Is that really called for here, Ms. Field?"

"I believe it is."

"Mr. DiCinni," the judge said, "is there a reason you are not communicating with your attorney?"

Nothing. Mona could not see the killer's face, but it had to be defiant, unrepentant.

"I am addressing you, young man," said the judge. "I want an answer. Why aren't you talking to your lawyer?"

No response.

"Your Honor," Leon Colby said, "the people will not object to Ms. Field's withdrawing from the case. We want the defendant to have counsel he can cooperate with. We don't believe a 1368 hearing is called for."

"Your Honor, I do not believe Mr. Colby is the one who should be deciding who withdraws and who doesn't. I am Mr. DiCinni's lawyer for this arraignment, assigned by Judge Greene. I would request that a 1368 be set, at which time the permanent counsel issue can be settled."

The judge glowered. "All right. Mr. DiCinni, you need to understand something. You are not going to get away with this act in my courtroom. You are going to speak when you are spoken to, do you understand?"

The killer, of course, said nothing. Mona's contempt grew like a fireball, a flare from the sun of her hate.

"Speak up, young man. Do you understand?"

The killer shrugged.

"On the record, Mr. DiCinni. Yes or no?"

"I guess," the killer said.

"I will take that as a *yes*. And how do you plead, guilty or not guilty?"

Another shrug.

"I will enter for the record a plea of not guilty." The judge was clearly ticked off now. "The court accepts the plea. Defendant's motion for a 1368 hearing is granted. I can't figure out if he's all there or not, so let's let the experts decide. Next case."

What? What just happened? It was moving too fast. All Mona could gather was that the defendant was granted something. *What? What?* And why didn't Leon Colby say something?

Dawn Stead said to Mona, "And so it begins."

"What?" Mona said.

"The defense lawyer's gonna try to get the kid off on an insanity deal."

"Off?" The word pecked at Mona's chest. Off? As in walking out of the courtroom? As if he had never killed her son? "But she can't."

Dawn's smile was rimmed with cynicism. "Just watch her try."

2.

Lindy felt a hand on her arm.

"What's your hurry?" Sean McIntyre smiled, his perfect white teeth reflecting sun. His dark brown hair was worn short and spiky, not enough to call attention to himself but enough to announce his cutting-edge status in the world of local crime reporters. Under his tight blanket-stitched turtleneck Lindy could make out the impertinent pecs and biceps he worked so hard to maintain.

"What are you doing creeping around?" Lindy didn't want to talk to him, not now. She wanted to choose the time and place.

"This is a public parking lot, last time I looked."

"So?" She was poised with her keys, seated on her Harley, ready to go. At least she'd slipped the other reporters. She wasn't ready to make a public statement on the case yet. She wasn't ready for Sean McIntyre, either. Too much emotional fodder in the blender at the moment, thank you.

"So here I am, standing with Lindy Field, who's got the hottest case in the country, and I'm thinking, I'm the one reporter who deserves an in."

"What makes you think—"

"Because I'm the one who knows where Lindy Field likes to park her bike. Guy like that deserves a comment, doesn't he?"

"Call my assistant."

"You don't have an assistant."

"Exactly." She pointed her keys toward the ignition. Sean snatched them away.

"Hey!" Lindy pawed the air.

Sean flashed more teeth. "Just a quick interview, huh? Chance for me to say I talked to the defense lawyer in the DiCinni case. Exclusive."

"Give me my keys."

"Couple questions. You don't even have to be specific. Just so I can say—"

"What part of 'give me my keys' don't you understand?"

"What I don't understand is why you are not returning my phone calls."

A car on Hill Street honked an L.A. insult at someone. It zapped Lindy's skull. She felt dazed. That was the word, especially around Sean. Did she want to see him or not? Maybe, but she was afraid. Afraid of what she might allow herself to do if she kept seeing him. Afraid that, with Darren consuming her thoughts, now was not the time to get romantically involved with anyone.

Lindy brought her leg over the seat and stood her ground. Sean was about six-one, a decided advantage. "Quit acting juvenile."

"Like your client?"

"He's only my client. Temporarily."

"You sure about that?"

"Off the record?"

"On."

"Keys."

Sean shook his head. "Do you know you drive me wild? What is it about you I find so captivating?"

"Hand them over." She swung her helmet at his shoulder. It bounced off with a loud *fwap*.

Sean's smile disappeared.

"Give me my keys."

"Take 'em then." He threw them at Lindy, hitting her in the chest. The keys fell to the asphalt. "What happened to you?"

"Me?" Lindy was incredulous as she bent down for the keys.

"What did I do to you that was so bad? We had a good thing going."

They had, hadn't they? Lindy couldn't remember that many bad moments. Sean had been there for her after a disastrous breakup, and in the short time they'd known each other treated her kindly. Until the night of the meandering hands. But he was a *guy.* Wasn't that the natural progression?

His tone softened. "Lindy, let's give it another shot, huh? I've got some wine cooling at home, we can put on some music, watch the stars come out."

"This is L.A., Sean. You can't see the stars."

"I meant on *Entertainment Tonight.*"

"Maybe another time."

Sean shrugged. He also let his face reflect an obvious self-satisfaction, with a half-smile that said *I know something you don't know.*

Lindy willingly took the bait. "What?"

"Oh, nothing." Sean scuffed the ground with his Italian loafer. "Just a little inside information about the DiCinni family, that's all. Maybe where the kid's father is. But you wouldn't be interested."

"Cut it out. What do you know, if you think you know anything?"

"Hey, maybe I don't. Maybe I'm not the best crime reporter in L.A. Who needs me, right?"

"Sean, tell me what you know."

"Sure."

She waited.

"Tonight. My place. Shall we say seven thirty?"

3.

Sylvia Martindale, known to all her friends as Syl, was Mona Romney's best friend. They'd met in junior high school, back in the days when it was still called junior high school. They'd been cheer-leaders together at Grant High School, and even though they went to different colleges—Syl up to UC Santa Barbara, Mona to Cal State

Northridge—they remained like sisters, writing all the time, then emailing, and always calling on the phone.

It was Mona who became a Christian first, in her senior year, during an outreach by the college group at Word of Life church. At first Syl was skeptical, but accepting. She told Mona this phase would probably pass. Mona was always going through phases, like her Sting phase in 1983, and her Bon Jovi phase in 1990.

But it did not pass like all those other things. It stayed, and Mona stayed in church, which was where she met Brad, and where they were married, and where they dedicated Matthew as a baby.

It was during the dedication, in fact, that Syl came to church and decided to stay herself. That day had been one of the best of Mona's life.

Now they were together in the dark shadows of Mona's worst phase, the season of mourning for Matthew that threatened never to end. Mona allowed Syl to drive her to the beach, to Zuma, just to sit together and talk and listen to the waves. In high school, they had come to this beach often, sunning themselves and studying the various lifeguards on display.

But Zuma, with morning fog hanging over the beach like a shroud, seemed empty of all good memories. Even the sound of the water, which usually soothed, grated today. Mona kept up a good front for her friend, not wanting to disappoint. Syl, seeming to understand, kept words short.

They loved each other enough not to worry about silences.

Syl had one of those instant cabana things that came out of a bag, and she propped it on the sand in about a minute. Mona had beach chairs and a radio, and each had a book to read. Mona had snatched the old paperback at random from her shelf. Turned out to be one of Brad's military thrillers. Mona didn't care. She wouldn't be reading today.

"Remember that lifeguard on number seven?" Syl pointed, through the mesh of the cabana, at the wooden tower to their left.

"There were lots of lifeguards," Mona heard herself say, her voice sounding distant.

"I mean the one that day who came out and posed. Remember? He had this tanning oil all over him and those muscles, and he knew we were scoping him, I know he knew, and he pointed out to the ocean like this." Syl held her arm up in the fashion of a bodybuilder showing off his bicep, only with the hand turned outward so the index finger could point.

"Oh," Mona said. "Yeah."

"It was so funny, but he was built, wasn't he? And we started giggling like crazy."

"Right."

"And couldn't stop."

"Mm-hm."

Syl sighed. "I actually think he had his eye on you. He walked in front of us a couple of times."

"Did he?" Mona looked out at the gray veil over the ocean. A few scattered people sunbathed along the beach. It was early yet.

"What was the name of the guy in our English class, the one who wanted to be an astronaut? You remember him?"

"You don't have to do this, Syl."

"Do what?"

"Not talk about it. I can talk about it if you want."

Syl reached for Mona's hand. "Only when you're ready."

"I don't know if I'll ever be ready." Mona expected hot tears to burst from her eyes, but they didn't. Not yet. She was as cold as the ocean mist.

"I know," Syl said. "I just wish I could do something to help."

"You're doing it."

"I pray so hard for you."

Mona nodded, but the words passed right through her.

"I just wonder sometimes"—Syl looked at the waves—"why God . . ."

"Allowed it?"

Syl pushed the sand with her foot. "That's what I wonder."

"You're not the only one."

They sat in silence as the waves beat the shore.

Finally Mona said, "Maybe the world's a farce." The words sounded stark and strange, like someone else had uttered them. Some other person living in her skin.

She felt Syl's hand, still holding hers, tremble a little. "You don't really believe that."

Mona took her hand away and in that moment felt a slipping away, a slight yet perceptible sensation of change. She was different, the world was different, and her place in it was not the same as it was even minutes ago.

A breeze hit her then, and with it came the smell of dead kelp. The beach was covered with it. Mona put her head down and closed her eyes, and tried to keep dread from entangling her with thick, rotting strands.

4.

"First thing we do," Sean said, "is open a nice bottle of wine. Does a fine Chard sound good?"

Lindy shook her head. "No way, Clyde. I'm not going to fall for that again."

"What?" Sean put his arms out in a gesture of feigned virtue.

"You know what I'm talking about. You're not going to get me drunk."

"Lindy, me? I'm wounded."

She breezed past him, letting her briefcase scuff his leg, and went to the living room of his spacious apartment above Sunset. Sean McIntyre lived like the rising star he was. His immaculate, trendy digs were not some standard single guy's hovel, but the orderly arrangement of an accomplished seducer. Lindy knew she shouldn't be here, at night, amid bomber-jacket brown-leather furniture, Erté prints, and a killer view. But she needed something he had. Information.

One thing Sean seemed to have, like a sixth sense, was a dependable line on information about crime in L.A.

Plopping on the couch, Lindy snatched a copy of GQ off the glass coffee table. "You leave this literature around where people can actually see it?"

"Hey, I've got a spread in there." Sean entered, carrying a single glass of white wine. "What can I get you to drink, Lindy? Tap water?"

"Nothing for me. This isn't a social visit, if you'll recall."

He sat next to her, keeping a respectable distance. "Can't we just relax a little first?"

"No."

"Don't beat around the bush, Lindy. Just tell me how you feel."

She flipped through the magazine, finding the photos of Sean without a problem. Apparently the periodical had been thumbed frequently to this spot.

Lindy nodded. "Makeup does wonders."

"Funny." Sean put his feet up on the coffee table. He was wearing dark socks to go with his slacks. His casual silk shirt was two buttons open at the collar. "Do I look like an animal to you?"

Lindy tossed the magazine on the table. It hit the edge and fluttered to the floor. She made no move to retrieve it.

"So how did you land this plum assignment?" Sean asked.

"Plum?"

"It's national news. Your face is going to be everywhere."

"You think I care about that?"

"Don't all lawyers care about that?"

She turned, pulling one leg up on the sofa, and faced him. "Were you born cynical, or did you develop it all on your own?"

Sean winked. "Which answer will get you to spend the night?"

"Can we get down to business, please?" Lindy opened her briefcase and pulled out a legal pad.

Sean sipped his wine and smiled. "I'm here to serve."

"So you know where Darren's father is?"

"Yep."

"And that would be . . . ?"

"Nearby."

"Okay, wise guy. Just tell me."

"Now look, Counselor, you don't think I'm just going to give up this choice nugget out of the goodness of my heart, do you?"

"Your heart has goodness?"

"Maybe you choose not to see it." He leaned toward her and actually bobbed his eyebrows. It was like he was sixteen years old.

"Can we get back to the matter at hand?" Lindy said.

"We never left it. We're discussing this piece of valuable information. I'm a reporter. Maybe I want something in return. *Quid pro quo*, as they say."

"What you want I'm not giving."

Sean put his hand over his heart in feigned shock. "You make me sound like such a tramp."

Lindy smiled and almost nodded.

"Look, I already apologized for being a jerk, what more do you want?"

"I want to know where DiCinni's father is."

"Then give me the inside story."

"What inside story?"

"On your client. What makes him tick and all that soft stuff they eat up on *The View*. This is the biggest crime story of the year. Maybe I can get a book deal out of it, a shot at a network show."

"I told you, I don't know if I'm going to rep him."

"Right, the whole Leon Colby thing."

"What Leon Colby thing?"

"You don't have to explain. I wouldn't blame you."

"You don't think I can handle it?"

"*You* don't think you can."

Boom. He was right. The aura of self-doubt emanated from her. Was she ever going to get past it? If she was going to be a lawyer, she would have to, or she'd be no good for any client.

"How about this," Sean said, "just to show you my good intentions: I'll give you what I have. You follow up. If you take the case, you help me out from time to time. A little insight here, a little there. I'm a reasonable man."

She pondered this a moment. "Okay. I'll give you what I can. But I can't reveal confidences. You know that. So we'll do this on my terms. I say how and where we talk."

"Agreed."

"Now you."

Sean reached over and took the pad from Lindy. He wrote something on it, handed it back. It was an address.

"Drake and Darren lived in an apartment about half a block from the park. But Drake took off, left the place when his son got popped, and is now living here."

"You mind telling me how you found him?"

"Reveal a source? Lindy, you shock me."

"Fair enough." She slipped the pad into her briefcase and clasped it shut.

"You're free to stay the night," Sean said.

She felt her insides starting to heat up. "Sean, look, I'm serious. I'm giving up men for Lent."

"You're not Catholic."

"And I don't even know when Lent is. Don't get technical."

Suddenly he put his hand behind her neck, pulled her to him, and kissed her. She let him. For a long moment she lingered over flame, heard the crashing of oceans.

Then she pushed him away.

"Lindy—"

"Lent."

She made it to the door, and out.

FOUR

† † †

1.

When Leon Colby was two years old, his father, a Baptist minister in Cleveland, put a football in his hand. It was a toy football, a little rubber thing, but still pretty substantial for a toddler.

As the Reverend Calvert Colby liked to tell it, two-year-old Leon took one look at that ball and smiled, love at first sight. But what happened next, Reverend Colby always insisted without hesitation, was the most remarkable thing: young Leon reared back with the ball in his right hand and threw it, hard. Harder than anyone was ready for, most of all the reverend, because it hit him right in the forehead.

But even that, as legend had it, wasn't the most incredible thing. It was that Leon Colby, age two, had thrown a tight spiral at his daddy's head.

Leon never took the story all that seriously, with his daddy given to tall tales and storytelling. But one thing was sure—he never knew a day when he did not love football.

It was the competition he craved and loved and embraced. All the way through school and his illustrious UCLA career.

To Leon Colby, football was all about getting the *W*. Winning. There was nothing like a hard-earned victory to charge him up.

That's why, when he came into the DA's office, he always tried to get the tough cases. Even when he was doing misdemeanors—your .08 DUIs, your shopliftings—he loved going to court, even if his case was reed thin. Getting in front of a jury was like playing in front of a packed Rose Bowl. No feeling like it in the world.

But as he'd matured as a prosecutor, he came to see the value of a good disposition. You could dispo certain cases and get the same *W* on the score sheet, and save yourself for the big game days, the ones that had to go to trial.

He wasn't sure yet which would be best for the DiCinni case. Taking it to trial would mean plenty of good pub, but the kid's age was a wild card. Though the majority of good citizens were fed up with kids murdering other kids, you just never knew what could happen in the court of public opinion.

Lindy Field was a wild card too. The Marcel Lee case had taken something out of her. Her breakdown was not one of the better-kept secrets in the legal community of Los Angeles. But desperation did strange things to people.

Sometimes it made them stronger.

But you had to take things step by step, the same way you did when you learned the new playbook at training camp. And the step this morning was to interview the cop, Glenn, who would be his only LAPD wit at the prelim.

"So you remember what you wrote in your report?" Colby asked Glenn, a thirtyish officer who had come to Colby's office for the interview.

"Sure."

"You found the suspect how?"

"Three guys had him pinned to the ground, in the sandbox."

"Pinned to the sand then."

"Huh?"

"I like specificity, Officer Glenn, understood?"

The cop looked at him with unsure eyes, which is exactly what he wanted. Shake these young ones up early and they might make decent witnesses later on. Some, of course, were lousy through and through, like birches with tree rot. You couldn't do much but cut them off and try to minimize the damage in court.

Glenn cleared his throat. "I think I put it in my report that he was in the sandbox."

"Then that's what you testify to, right?"

"Yeah." Showing a little attitude.

"Now it says here, Officer Glenn"—Colby drew out the name the way a disappointed parent would—"that the suspect was 'belliger-ent.' You know what that word means?"

Glenn looked at him like he was nuts. "Of course."

"What then?"

"You know, belligerent. Yelling and stuff like that."

"Curse words?"

"Yeah, I think."

"You think?"

"Yeah, curse words."

Colby lifted the report to the officer's face. "Where exactly do you say that?"

Glenn looked at the pages. His attitude began to melt. As planned.

"It's not in there," Colby said, "and if you get on the stand and say anything like that, you're going to get hosed by the defense. You know who Lindy Field is?"

Glenn shook his head.

"Defense lawyer. She used to be good."

"Used to be?"

"She may be again. She has a thing against me."

"What thing?"

"Never mind. But I'm not gonna be on the stand, you are, and if you give her a hole she'll try to rip it into a door, through which she will stick her foot. You understand what I'm saying?"

"Stick to the report."

"Read it again. And again. I want you to know it cold."

"Sure."

There was something in Glenn's acquiescence Colby did not like. A smirk maybe, a little power play. Like he was doing Colby a favor just by showing up in the office. Like he had better things to do out on the street.

Hesitation started a gentle gnaw on the back of Colby's mind. Jaws of doubt quietly chewing, the sort of reaction he experienced from time to time with cops who played it fast and loose.

Usually he gave the cops the benefit of the doubt, just to stop the gnawing, but this time his instinct seemed hungrier than usual.

"One more thing, Glenn. You know there were several wits who gave statements to homicide."

"Of course."

"Including a couple of the guys who had DiCinni down in the sand."

"Yeah." He said it in a way that sounded like *So what?*

"Neither one of them came close to describing the kid as belligerent."

Wider eyes now on the cop. "So they didn't. You know civilians aren't trained."

"Yeah, but one of them, what's the guy's name"—he consulted his notes—"Crawford. Crawford said the kid had a stunned look in his eyes, sort of 'freaky' he said it was. Said the kid didn't say anything."

"Come on, Leon—"

"You can call me Mr. Colby."

"Sir, you cannot take those statements seriously. All sorts of things were happening. I know what I saw, what I reported, what other people said to me about seeing the kid firing the rifle. It's all there, that's all you need, isn't it?"

For once Colby agreed with Glenn. "Yeah, Glenn, from you that's all I need."

2.

Mona sat ramrod straight on the sofa, staring at the TV news and a video of the lawyer defending the killer. Walking into court for the arraignment.

Brad was eating his dinner—microwaved macaroni and cheese, which he made himself—on a TV tray in front of the recliner.

"Maybe we shouldn't watch the news anymore," he said.

"She said he isn't competent! How can they let her say that?"

"Lawyers represent their clients."

"It stinks. She needs to be stopped." Mona wasn't eating tonight. Skipping meals was getting habitual.

"Mona, let's just turn it off, huh?"

Maybe he wanted an answer this time. Mona gave him one. "And just crawl into a hole? No. Matthew needs us."

Brad winced and looked at the floor. His anguished look. Mona hated it. It was like an annoying screech entering her brain.

"I can't believe you're not outraged by this, Brad. What are you thinking?"

"Honey, I'm trying to keep myself sane. We can't let this thing get to us."

"Why not? Maybe a little anger is just what we need. We have to keep it or we'll lose."

"Anger will up and kill us if we don't watch out."

Now he was moving into his Dr. Phil mode, and she hated that even worse than the manipulative looks he could put on. "Anger at things that deserve it doesn't hurt anything. We need it. And she deserves it." Mona nodded at the TV, even though the news program had cut back to one of the talking heads in the studio.

"Lawyers have jobs to do. We'll need to get used to that."

"It's not her job to poison a jury by talking like that. I'm going to call Mr. Colby and—"

"Don't bother him, Mona. He knows what he's doing."

Brad had on his parent look now, his I-know-what's-best look. Mona turned away from it and looked at the TV. A Pepto-Bismol commercial had just started.

"No, Brad. This isn't just going to run its course. If you can't see that, I don't know what."

"If I don't see it? You think I'm clueless or something?"

"Maybe in denial." *Take that, Dr. Phil.*

"Me in denial? What about you?"

She whipped him another look. "That's a rotten thing to say. I'm the very opposite of denial."

"Mona—"

"No. Rotten." The thing inside took over—the junkyard fire, she had come to call it. Not a clean flame or a purifying blaze. No, this was the kind that burns garbage and sends toxins into the air. It was a poisonous flame, but it was no use trying to put it out. She didn't even want to. It made her feel alive.

She got up to leave the room, because walking away from Brad was the best thing when he got this way. Talking more would only make things worse. She wanted to crawl back in her space, the one with the walls that kept people out.

Besides, she had work to do—stopping this lawyer from trampling on Matthew's memory. And stop her she would.

3.

Cracks in the sidewalk pointed toward the dilapidated house. Made of forgotten clapboard and faded yellow paint, it tucked up against the San Gabriel Mountains in Sunland, about as far as you could get to the north of the San Fernando Valley without actually leaving. Sunland was like a desert community, where houses and trailers were divided by scrub brush and old fences, where the sun seemed to pound like a hammer before splashing into the cool Pacific an hour away.

Lindy knocked on the screen door, which rattled in its loose hinges. It reminded her of one of those doors on an old farmhouse. But this was Los Angeles County, not Dorothy's Kansas.

She heard movement behind the wooden door. The creaking of the floor straining under weight. Then the noise hesitated, as if the person on the other side of the door was waiting for Lindy to do something else. Like leave.

She knocked again, softly. No need to get anybody riled up.

"Who is it?" came a deep, scratchy voice, a woman's voice. From the hack that followed, Lindy guessed she was addressing an inveterate smoker.

"My name is Lindy Field. I'm here about Darren."

There was a long pause. "I got nothing to say."

"I want to talk to Drake."

The interior door opened a crack, and Lindy could barely make out a face peering through the screen. "Drake ain't here."

"I think he is."

"You a reporter?"

"I'm a lawyer."

"Don't believe you."

"You see any cameras on me? Any recording equipment? All I've got is what you see, and you can see it's just me. So what are you going to do?"

The woman opened the door a little wider. She wore a drab gray housedress. Her hair was streaked with gray and fell unkempt around a craggy face. Lindy could smell a mixture of tobacco smoke and burned food coming through the screen. She thought of rats.

The woman looked Lindy up and down. "You don't look like a lawyer."

"I went to law school and passed the bar and everything."

Another voice, a man's voice from within said, "Let her in, Alice."

The woman unlatched the screen door and pushed it open slightly. Lindy pulled it open the rest of the way herself.

She walked into a dark house where all the windows were closed up and curtained. A single lamp on a table provided the only illumination.

4.

"Mr. DiCinni, you can't hide forever."

They were sitting now in what would have been called the living room. But the place didn't look right for living. More like existing.

"Why not?" Drake DiCinni said. "Whoever wrote that down as some law?" DiCinni had a jutting forehead, was half bald, and wore what hair he had left close to the skin. He looked like he was wearing a rust-colored skull cap. His close-set eyes challenged her from above a small nose, which looked like it had been broken and not set properly.

The woman called Alice sat in a plastic chair near the kitchen. She had not bothered to introduce herself, nor had Drake DiCinni explained the relationship.

"The police will be looking for you," Lindy said.

"Why? I didn't shoot anybody."

"Your son did. They'll want to talk to you."

"Everybody's gonna want to talk to me. Isn't that the way it goes? Shouldn't I be on *Larry King* by now? Somebody gets shot in this country, somebody else gets to be a celebrity."

"Your son is facing multiple murder charges, Mr. DiCinni. He's going to need help. Your help."

"I can't help him."

"He can't help him," Alice said.

"Alice, I can handle this."

"My house."

"Just let me." He looked at Lindy, his eyes hollow. "I don't want to testify in court or anything."

"This is your son we're talking about, sir. His life."

"His life is over, don't you get that? I tried. His whole life I tried. After his mother ran out, I tried. After he got in trouble at every school he ever went to, I tried. But he's bad. He was born bad."

"I don't think that's true."

"You got any kids?"

Lindy shook her head.

"Then don't tell me. I got the blood of six people on my hands, 'cause I brought him into the world."

"You really should go," Alice said.

"No," Lindy said. "Not yet."

With a sigh, DiCinni looked at Alice. "Let me talk to her."

"Go ahead, if you want to."

"Alone."

Alice scowled at Lindy. "I don't like this."

Drake turned in his chair. Lindy saw a blue tattoo on the back of his neck. A spiderweb. "It'll be all right," Drake said.

"I'll be in the back," Alice said. "You need me, holler."

I'm not going to bite him, lady.

The woman in the white dress walked out of the room, dripping attitude.

"So what do you want?" DiCinni said.

Lindy took a legal pad out of her briefcase and clicked open a ballpoint pen. "Start by telling me about Darren, his mother, you, his birth. Start there."

DiCinni stared into space, his lips tightening. "His mother ran out. When he was barely a year old. What kind of a woman does that?"

"What was her name?"

"I don't want to talk about her."

"Just the name?"

"Look it up."

Was this going to be the drill? She'd ask a question and get a head butt in return? One of her old law professors, Everett Woodard, used to tell the class you shouldn't rep somebody unless you walked a mile in his moccasins. Tried to get in his head, understand his life situation. Same for key witnesses. Do that, Woodard used to say, and you'll be well ahead of the other guy.

She tried to put herself in Drake DiCinni's moccasins. The guy's son had just murdered six people. Something that bad happens to a man, he's going to be messed up.

"Mr. DiCinni, I don't want to make things hard on you," Lindy said. "I just want to get at the facts here, best I can. And then leave you alone."

He shook his head and looked at the floor. "Trudy," he said. "She was a hooker. I was working as a bartender. She used to come into my place all the time. I'd listen to her. She liked that. I saw something in her. Maybe it was just that she talked to me nice. Nobody did much of that when I was growing up."

"Where was this?" Lindy said. "Where you were a bartender?"

"Vegas."

"Okay."

"So I guess we sort of circled around each other then figured out we were maybe in love. You don't need to hear the whole thing. She got pregnant and wanted to get married. Funny, huh? Just like in the old days. The chick wants to get married. So we did. But I made her go into detox first, and she wanted to."

"What was she hooked on?"

"Meth."

Lindy jotted a note. *Brain damage? Mother on drugs.*

"Anyway," DiCinni said, "this and that, Darren is born and—"

"Was he okay? I mean, any details of the birth that you need to tell me about?"

"Nothing. He was a little small, I guess."

"How small?"

"I don't remember that stuff."

"Go on."

DiCinni heaved a deep breath. "Look, we didn't have much to live on, she couldn't get a job. I don't know, the pressure. You're in a one-room with a baby all the time. She couldn't take it, so she just leaves."

"Where is she now?"

"Dead."

"How?"

"She went back to the old life. Some cop calls me one night at three in the morning, says she's been found in an alley. Good riddance, I say."

Sentimental fellow. Lindy tried to imagine him testifying in court. What impression would he make? Would it help or hurt Darren?

"Let's talk about the gun," Lindy said. "How'd Darren get it?"

"I kept it locked up. The lock was broken. The cops must have figured that out."

"I don't know what the cops have figured out yet."

"Well, that's what happened. I used the thing for hunting. I actually hunt and eat what I bag."

"Not much hunting around here, is there?"

DiCinni shrugged. "I haven't done much lately."

"You show Darren how to shoot?"

"I took him a couple of times, sure. Out in the desert. But I taught him to respect the gun, what it could do, and never to use it when I wasn't around."

"Was Darren a problem the last few years? Around home?"

"Nothing that'd make you think he'd ever do something like this."

"Is there anything you can think of, anything at all, that can help me understand why Darren would ever do such a thing?"

Drake DiCinni's mind suddenly seemed to shift to a different place, the way an abrupt realization momentarily takes over the body. The air seemed to snap with static, with an electric charge that felt like the key to the whole case.

But just as suddenly Drake's face changed from comprehension to disregard. "What are you asking me that for?"

"Because," Lindy said, "you are in the best position to know."

Drake stood up. "Get out. I have nothing more to say to you."

"Mr. DiCinni—"

"I'm through talking."

"You have to help him."

"He can't be helped, don't you get that? You're just a little cog in a big machine. You think you're in control of anything on earth? You control nothing. Now get out of here and leave me alone."

5.

Riding to Roxy's, Lindy thought about the hatchet jobs some fathers did on their kids. She felt her own wound again, knowing she always would. There was no medicine for it, for what fathers did.

Roxy Raymond lived in an apartment on Sherman Way in Canoga Park. Not the best section of town, but a good place for getting back on your feet after visiting the abyss. Roxy had been an investigator with the PD's office when Lindy was there, but an addiction to Ecstasy ended that. Lindy helped Roxy through the detox.

Roxy opened her door holding a red can. "I'm hunting cockroaches. Come join the fun."

Roxy had some sort of Mediterranean blood in her, mixed strikingly with a large dollop of Scandinavian. Long black hair, dark skin, sky blue eyes. Lindy knew it was the kind of look that drove men mad, made them do crazy things in the night or conjure wild dreams in daylight.

"You don't have to do the cockroach thing," Roxy said. "But if you see one, yell, 'cause I'm in the mood to kill. These babies are big."

Her apartment was simple, eclectic. Roxy had her watercolors, unframed, attached to the walls, and some kind of unidentifiable fabric on the floor doing an imitation of a rug. The place smelled of incense and dishwater. R&B played softly in the background.

And on the coffee table, which had various scuffs, lay a big, black book.

"I'm glad you called," Roxy said. "Let's go do something. I'm feeling cramped in here."

Lindy eyed the black book as she sat on the sofa. "Since when are you reading the Bible?"

"Since a month." Roxy tossed herself on a beanbag chair that might have done duty in the Berkeley of the sixties.

"What's the occasion?"

"Met a guy."

"A Bible salesman?"

"An artist, wiseacre."

"He's got you reading the Bible?"

Roxy pointed at herself with both index fingers. "I took the plunge. Baptized and everything."

"Like in water?"

"Duh."

Lindy was amazed, but only somewhat. Roxy did have a spontaneous personality.

"Hey, come to church with us." Roxy sat up, like she'd just had the greatest idea in the world.

"Church?"

"Why not?"

"I haven't been in a church since . . ." Since her mother died.

"Come on. We have a great minister—"

"Who is this guy? Where'd you meet him?"

"At group."

"He's an addict?"

"Nah, he was there supporting a friend of his. We started talking, one thing led to another . . ."

"And *boom*, you're Mother Teresa."

"Hey now . . ."

"Sorry. I'm a little tense. You got anything to drink?"

"Like what?"

"I was thinking of the hard stuff. Dr Pepper."

"I've got diet."

"I said the *hard stuff*."

"Sorry, *chica*. You have to drive."

Roxy went into the kitchen and returned with a couple glasses of Diet Dr Pepper.

"You ready to go back to work?" Lindy asked.

"Yeah baby!"

"I might have a case for you to help me with."

"What kind?"

"Murder."

Roxy whistled.

"If I take it. It's the boy who shot those kids in the park."

Roxy froze midgulp. She lowered her glass silently.

Lindy told Roxy what she knew so far, up through the interview with Drake DiCinni.

"Guy sounds like a real loser," Roxy said.

"And that's what's sticking in my throat."

Lindy looked into her friend's Nordic eyes, which had a difference about them now. A knowingness. Roxy didn't look as confused or vulnerable as she had the last time Lindy saw her. Maybe it was her new boyfriend.

"Take the case," Roxy said, "and do what God meant you to do."

Lindy shook her head. "How'd God get into this?"

"He's into everything. That's something I found out."

"Oh yeah? Why didn't I get the memo?"

"It's all in here." Roxy picked up the Bible.

And that's when a little snap went off inside Lindy. She had always believed in something out there, even flirted with Christianity in high school. But that seemed a long time ago.

"Does it say in there how come God let this kid turn out the way he did? How come he let this father even have a kid?"

Roxy looked a little pained. "I know there's hard questions."

"Well, when you get an answer to any of 'em, let me know. And while you're at it, let me know why I got the father I got."

"What about your father?"

"Forget it."

"No, tell me."

"Why?"

"You come here and drink my Dr Pepper, you ask me to work for you. And you're my friend. You got me through a rough time. Maybe I can do something for you."

Lindy leaned back and looked at the ceiling. She'd never talked about it, not with anyone.

"So I had a lousy father," Lindy said. "It's not like I'm the only one."

"Come on."

"What's the big deal? He drank, he beat my mom up, he beat—" Lindy stopped suddenly, an unwelcome memory unfurling in her mind. She closed her eyes, fighting it back. "Forget it."

"Hey, girl, I'm sorry I—"

"Forget it, I said." Lindy, embarrassed, wiped the wetness in her eyes with the back of her hand.

A long, penetrating silence passed. In that silence, ideas fell and shifted inside Lindy's mind, a rearrangement of mental furniture. Her assumptions changed, and she regarded the changes and knew what she had to do.

"I'm taking the case," she said. "Let's get to work."

FIVE

✝ ✝ ✝

1.

"Please try to talk."

Mona shook her head. It felt empty, like her heart.

"I don't mean to push you," Brad said.

But he did, and Mona knew it. She also knew this was hurting him. She didn't want to hurt him. She loved him. They'd had one child, Matthew, born after two miscarriages.

She loved him but she was not ready to talk about *it*.

"We are going to get through this," Brad said. He reached across the table—the dining room table she had found at a garage sale early in their marriage and had restored herself, a table set with a banquet of fond memories. She did not reach halfway.

"Brad, I'm sorry. I just need more time."

"I know. We both do."

In the silence Mona heard the clock ticking on top of the refrigerator. She'd picked that up at the same garage sale. For fifty cents. Strange how clearly she could remember that.

"Let's just talk about something," Brad said. "Anything."

Mona took a sip of coffee. It was lukewarm.

Brad picked up the front page of the *Daily News*. "Did you see this? There's a group up in Santa Cruz, wants to bring a lawsuit on behalf of overweight pets. Going after owners, the pet food industry, even—"

Mona closed her eyes.

"—the pounds. Hey, that's kind of a joke, isn't it? Overweight. Pounds."

Mona rubbed her temples.

"You know who I think is behind it? The Atkins people. Wouldn't that be a great conspiracy theory?"

Nodding her head, Mona tried to smile for him. But she couldn't.

The mirror was not doing her any favors. She could hardly stand to look at herself. Where once her copper-colored eyes had reflected light, they now seemed muddy, like the streets of a southern town after a flood. Had she cried enough tears to wash the light from them?

And where once she had a face that people said looked younger than her thirty-eight years ("You could have been an actress or a model," Brad used to tell her), she now fought every wrinkle. The scar near the corner of her mouth was where a precancerous growth had been cut out by her HMO surgeon two years ago. The scar had always looked like a dimple to her, but that was when she was looking through eyes that could still see hope. Now they saw every flaw on her face and the gray strands showing up in her auburn hair.

She was able to go through the motions of humanity—to walk, to speak, to give the impression of rational thought. But behind the movement she wandered, dazed, lost in her own illusion, the inhabitant of permanent nightmare. And when she paused to reflect, she threatened to topple into a bottomless, empty pit.

And God would not save her from falling. He was not above; he was not present. If anything, he was below the pit and silent.

She remembered reading about some theologians' concept of God as being powerless to intervene in life. Things happened that were bad, and God grieved along with the rest of us.

At the time she'd shaken her head and even said something to Brad about how loony some people were, even people who taught at the university level. Maybe especially people who taught at the university level. And Brad had laughed, being a graduate of UC Berkeley and knowing full well that the hallowed halls of higher learning were rife with a brand of theism that birthed cancer in the soul. "I believe I had Satan for freshman biology," Brad used to say. "He used to grade us with a pitchfork."

Now she wasn't laughing. Maybe these theologians and academics had a point. Maybe this whole Christianity thing was an exercise in denial.

She didn't say so to Brad, of course. He'd worry and start yapping about getting some counseling, and she just couldn't handle that right now. She did not want his strength, rooted as it was in a doctrine she could not confirm. She did not know what she wanted.

She knew she didn't want to go to church that Sunday. It was too soon, and she didn't want everybody coming up to her with hugs and wishes and tears and offers of dinner and anything else they could do. She wanted to be alone with her grief.

But Brad insisted in his gentle but firm way that she go. And a very small part of her thought, *Okay, I'll give God a chance, but he better not blow it this time. He could have saved Matthew, and he didn't.*

2.

The church stood on a hillside north of the Valley, just off the 118 freeway. And from the looks of things, it was a pretty popular place.

Cars streamed into the parking lot. Lindy, holding her Starbucks in hand like it was a magic back-from-the-dead elixir, hoped Roxy would be able to find a spot without bending a fender. She was so excited about seeing her guy, she was giddy.

Lindy hadn't been sure what to wear and settled on her closing-argument suit, a dark blue pinstripe ensemble with skirt and coat, very conservative. She needed juries to believe there was a little conservatism inside her, especially by the end of her trials. The conservative image was usually a tough sell, but at least she could dress the part.

The auditorium was getting packed quickly. Roxy, wearing more makeup than usual and dressed in, of all things, a dress, gazed around the crowd like a meerkat.

"I don't see him."

Lindy smoothed her blouse. "No hurry."

"You seem a little anxious."

"Anxious? I look anxious?"

"Like a CEO on *60 Minutes*."

"I'm in foreign land here."

"We don't eat our young."

A nice-looking young man with wavy blond hair handed Lindy a program and showed a row of white teeth.

"Welcome," he said. He looked about twenty.

"Thanks," Lindy said.

The young man pointed to Lindy's Starbucks cup. "Want me to take that for you?"

"You try, I'll bite your arm off."

The smile disappeared.

"Kidding," Lindy said. "Here, I'll kill it for you." She downed the remainder and handed the guy the cup. He took it and hurried off, as if he couldn't wait to pass out programs in another part of the lobby.

"Friendly joint," Lindy said.

Roxy almost jumped in the air. "There he is!"

A lean man of around thirty, wearing a Hawaiian shirt, white slacks, and leather sandals, headed toward them. His smile, seen through a clipped brown goatee, seemed genuine enough.

"This is Travis Kellman," Roxy said.

He shook Lindy's hand. "Thanks for coming."

"Life is about risk," Lindy said.

They settled into some seats, Travis sitting on the other side of Roxy. A pretty good band played up on the stage. All right. Not so bad. And then everybody stood up and started singing the words displayed on a big screen.

Lindy stood up so as not to draw attention. She just listened. It was pretty weird, all this singing. People were really into it, clapping and swaying. Their enthusiasm was nothing like the singing in church she'd seen in the movies, with people holding hymnals and trying real hard to sound interested.

Then it was time for the preaching. The pastor's name, according to the bulletin, was Clark Bennett. And when he got up to speak he owned the place.

This guy could talk, and he looked good. Tall, slender. Midforties, Lindy guessed.

He would have made a good lawyer. A great lawyer, in fact. He spoke for forty minutes and Lindy wasn't bored once.

Afterward, Travis Kellman invited them to brunch, but Lindy wanted to go home. She wanted to get to the Sunday *Times*, back to the normal world, whatever that was.

She knew deep down it wasn't a normal world, not with kids like Darren in it. And part of her wished the church thing was real so it could help her out.

But Travis Kellman offered to pick up the tab, and so she acceded to brunch.

3.

"So what kind of artist are you?" Lindy asked Travis Kellman in her cross-examination voice.

Roxy kicked her under the table. They were at a little bistro called La Frite, a place with big windows and outdoor tables with yellow umbrellas. The buffet-style brunch came up salmon and capers and shrimp for Lindy. The other two had egg concoctions.

Lindy ignored Roxy's nudge and kept her eyes on the goateed fellow.

"Photo surrealism," Kellman said.

"You're a photographer?"

"No, a painter. But I paint to make my work look like a photo. When I succeed, that is."

"What's the surreal part?"

"I put in something that is not real. Like water rushing down a drain, and men in a rowboat going down with it."

"Bizarre."

"What's bizarre about it?" Roxy snapped.

"He just said it's surreal. Isn't that right, Travis?"

"Right."

"So where'd you pick up this bizarreness? Where are you from?"

Roxy said, "Lindy, will you stop?"

"It's okay," Kellman said. "I'm from San Diego, originally."

"Went to school down there?"

"Yeah. Till I dropped out and bummed around Europe."

"What about your family?"

"Normal. Mom's a receptionist. My dad was a cop."

"Was?"

"He died last year."

"Sorry."

Kellman nodded.

"He must have been one of the good ones," Lindy said.

Kellman looked at her oddly. "Good ones?"

Uh-oh. Just crossed some line with him. Get sensitive, stupid. "You know what I mean."

"I don't think I do," he said.

"Police. Cops. Some good, some bad."

"Mostly good, wouldn't you say?"

She sensed his question was pointed, inviting argument. "May I speak freely?"

"What have you been doing?" Roxy piped in.

Lindy shot her a glance then looked at Kellman. "I think cops in any big city are under a lot of pressure to lie in court. You get pressure from the DA, you get pressure from your own higher-ups, you get pressure from the citizens who want the streets cleaned up, and they don't care how it's done. And eventually that kind of stuff reaches critical mass, and the ACLU has to step in, or the feds, and order you to clean house."

Roxy poked at her sausage omelet with thin-lipped chagrin.

But Travis Kellman spoke evenly, "Hey, look, I'm not going to deny there have been abuses."

"Abuses? Remember Rampart?" The scandal involving the gang unit at the LAPD's Rampart Division had broken the city wide open several years ago. "Remember a kid named Franklin Jones?"

Kellman kept his eyes on her and put a forkful of egg in his mouth.

"They offered him a deal, the prosecutors did. Plead guilty to selling drugs he had not sold and serve eight years in prison. Or he could risk being convicted at trial and, as a three-time loser, be sentenced to life. In doing this the prosecutors and judges just accepted the word of cops that he was guilty. Turns out the evidence was planted. The cops were lying."

"But that's being dealt with."

"Is it?"

"Where haven't there been abuses? You saying defense lawyers never hide evidence? Never lie to the court? Never tell the court so-and-so wasn't on your witness list because you just found the guy, when all the time you had him in your back pocket? Let him who is without sin cast the first stone."

"But we're always fighting against the machine. The government has all the resources, and they never get spanked. We have a job to do too."

"And so do the cops. And let me tell you, the majority of them are good, honest people. Hard as that may be for you to believe."

"They just don't do enough to get rid of the bad ones, unless, by chance, somebody with a video camera catches one beating the heck out of some poor kid."

"Oh yeah, the video that doesn't show what led up to the whole thing. And then the politicians get involved. Let's throw this cop to the lions, give 'em some meat. A cop who was out there trying to protect everybody, and now he's told doing his job means he's a villain. Cops with wives and kids and families, putting it on the line every day out there. Get wise."

"So now I'm not wise?"

"Very few of us are wise. That's why I go to church."

"There's stuff that goes on in churches that isn't always so hot, either," Lindy said.

Roxy put her face in her hands.

"Let's see," Kellman said. "Cops. Christians. Is there a group you don't have problems with?"

"Aerosmith."

4.

This was not supposed to be the deal.

God either didn't care about her anymore, or he'd gone back on his promises for some reason. That reason could be good or bad. Mona knew the Bible said it had to be good no matter what, but how could going back on your word ever be good? Wasn't that the first thing she'd learned in the schoolyard, to keep her promises? So why shouldn't God have to keep his too? What was his secret?

And why did God keep secrets? Especially when she was dying inside?

As she moved through her childless house, loss continued to burn in Mona's chest. Unyielding heat, relentless.

She had tried several things in the last few days to douse the flames of bereavement, to silence the incessant voice that accused God. She had always believed God was love. Her parents had backed up what she'd learned in Sunday school.

But Matthew's death blasted that easy faith, leaving only a loveless crater behind.

Activity had always been her deliverance. No one could ever accuse her of slacking off on anything, once she made up her mind to take action. She could take any activity and make it completely her own. By force of will, she could impose perfection on disorder, pattern on chaos. By making something perfect she could douse the flames, fill the emptiness. She could get back to life without God's help. She didn't need it.

Mona began to cook. She would create a meal for Brad and herself that would make them both weep at the splendor of it.

For a few short hours, while Brad was out running errands, she managed to keep the flames around her heart on a slow burn, lapping at her but not consuming. She did not listen to music, as she used to when at work in the kitchen. Nor did she turn on the little TV over the sink.

She worked in silence, devoted to creating, to perfecting.

Brad's reaction to the presentation was initially, and predictably, delighted. Mona was a little annoyed at that, the fact that she knew what he'd do. His obviousness was grating. He was trying too hard now to be pleased by anything she did. His kid gloves were beginning to rub her raw.

Still, she put on the smile she knew he expected. She set the table with the wedding china, which she had not done in years, not since that Christmas when Brad's brother and his family came down from Redding, all six of them piled in a van. The silver was from the set she had indulged in after Matthew was born and the doctor said she could bear no more children. She could not make that part of her life perfect, so she would have to rely on distractions, like entertaining. But this sterling set in the redwood box had sat unused since, save for one formal dinner six years ago.

This incongruity sometimes bewildered even Mona. Why didn't the things she'd paid the most for ever satisfactorily serve their intended uses?

"This," Brad said, putting down a full plastic bag marked Home Depot, "is magnificent."

"You like?" She knew he did, and would make a fuss over it, but she wanted it all, every last drop of his approval, even if it annoyed her. Another incongruity she recognized but felt little reason to analyze.

"How could I not? Candles and everything."

"Yes," Mona said, "and you are going to be pampered."

He almost teared up then, and Mona wished she could feel the appreciation she knew he deserved.

"You didn't have to go to all this trouble." Brad came over to kiss her. She turned her head and let him kiss her cheek.

"Wash up and sit down. I want to serve."

"Can I change?"

"Just wash. Keep your tie on. It's more elegant."

He nodded. "For you, anything."

When he returned from the bathroom she had the salads out, Waldorfs with her own innovative twist. They'd chilled in the refrigerator precisely thirty-five minutes. She had sliced the apples into symmetrical wedges and shelled and chopped the walnuts herself. The bagged variety would have ruined the purity of it all. Mayonnaise, sugar, allspice, celery, lemon juice—each in its proper balance, meeting her approval.

"May I say the blessing?" Brad asked.

"Sure." Mona closed her eyes and bowed her head.

"Dear Lord, we thank you so much for your love for us—"

Mona opened her eyes just a bit, looked at her salad. Was the quantity of walnuts just right? She did not want to overpower the apples.

"—and for this food you have so graciously prepared—"

He *has prepared? What do you think I've been doing for the last six hours?*

"—we ask—"

You *ask.*

"—that you would bless it to our bodies. In Jesus' name—"

Walnuts.

"—amen."

Mona, without looking at Brad's face, delicately took up her salad fork. She heard the soft *chink* that Brad's fork made on his salad plate. Okay, it was the beginning of a perfect dinner. Right, right, right.

Until everything began to unravel.

5.

With Cardozo curled in her lap, Lindy hopped on the Internet to check her email. Her mind was still reeling with Drake DiCinni's intransigence. There was something abnormal there, a father giving up on his son like that. It didn't line up right, the pieces of this family puzzle.

But how could that puzzle be anything but deviant, with a thirteen-year-old mass killer in the family?

Not much email. Roxy on her "cute guy," and a plea to come to church again. "I feel like God is chasing after you, Lindy, I really do."

Just what I want to be. Stalked by God. That's a violation of California and federal laws.

But what if? What if God was really a player in all this? The possibility led to a host of questions she was not prepared to explore.

She shot through some spam, a few postings from a legal group she was a member of. She deleted everything, then went over to CNN.com to check the news.

The lead story was another about the senatorial campaigns of various talking robots in various states. When did politicians become such predictable bores? The only interesting ones were fringe candidates, the people with no chance of winning and no need to pull their rhetorical punches.

She found a link to an opinion piece on the "New Wave of Juvenile Violence." Naturally it led with the DiCinni case. The idiot who wrote it made some comment about "clever lawyers" who would try to "sway" juries into thinking these "monsters" were just "damaged children." He urged people not to be "fooled." Talk about trying to taint the national jury pool!

She groaned then moved over to Google, intending to do a search on juvenile justice and get a feel for the public's mood. There was no money for a jury consultant. She'd have to run with instinct and common sense.

Without thinking much about it, she typed in *Marcel Lee murder* on Google. She'd done this half a dozen times in the last year, hoping some newspaper would pick up the story. She'd certainly sent out enough press releases via email and fax. His appeal was pending. Maybe she was just hoping for some positive spin instead of the usual abuse heaped on defense lawyers.

She saw the usual hits. Stories from the *Los Angeles Times* and *Daily News*. About the trial, the appeal. Lindy went to the next page and saw some uninteresting squibs. One drew her attention. In particular, the word *conspiracy*.

Conspiracy? What was that all about?

Lindy clicked on the link.

A bold red banner on a black background appeared on her screen: *Hawkstar's Conspiracy Blog*. She read some of the text then saw a link labeled *LAPD*. She clicked on it and was taken to a page detailing some of the scandals, like Rampart, that had plagued the Los Angeles Police Department over the last several years. But then her interest spiked:

*There was a case a year or so ago, for murder. A guy named Marcel
Lee. Gang member. Shot another gang member. Remember that? And
there was a stink raised by his lawyer, Linda Fields, after the case, saying that the jury decided to believe the police officer.*

Linda Fields? This guy couldn't even get her name right and he
was writing about conspiracies? Oh, this was going to be rich.

She wasn't laughing, though. Seeing her name, even though mis-
spelled, on some guy's conspiracy page was a little freaky.

*That's a code phrase, folks. What she was saying without saying it
was that the cop lied. Now that's not very surprising, coming from a
defense lawyer. But I looked into the case myself and found out some
things that were disturbing.*

*You remember the Rampart scandal that hit the LAPD years ago?
They had this unit out there in gang territory that violated the law all the
time to get guys. One time they even framed a guy. And there was a code
of silence.*

Whenever you come across a code of silence, think conspiracy, fans!
Amazing.

This guy, probably without knowing it, had it right. The Marcel
Lee case did suffer under a code of silence written by the cops and
the DA's office as well, if turning a blind eye to obvious lies could be
called a "conspiracy."

She bookmarked the Web page and looked at some of the guy's
other theories.

Oswald did not act alone, of course. And there was an oil conspiracy that stretched to the White House, a steroid conspiracy that
had Major League Baseball in a vise, and some sort of cabal responsible for the rise of Britney Spears.

Great. A nut. Lindy decided not to note this Web site in any briefs
on behalf of Marcel. But it might be worth getting in touch with the
guy to find out if he had any truly useful info she could use.

When her search for an email link came up empty, she took a stab
and created an email to the Web site, addressing it to "info@." She
wrote this:

If you want to discuss conspiracies re: LAPD and the like, contact me.

6.

Mona hurled the bowl of au gratin potatoes at the wall. It shattered in a yellowish mess next to the rosewood hutch. As the pieces fell, she realized it was the serving dish given to them by Brad's mother and also, in the same instant, that she felt not one ounce of guilt.

The rage that filled Mona was so consuming she could almost step out of her body and observe it. She did not know when or how it would die, but she knew how it began. With a look.

The conversation between her and Brad had proceeded along a cold, routine pattern. He spoke of his day with a jauntiness overlaying the words like the too-sweet frosting on a Bundt cake. She tried to take interest in what he was saying. She could not.

Between accounts, he would linger over the food she had prepared so carefully, commenting constantly on how good it was. She couldn't tell if his sentiments were sincere or yet another clumsy attempt to salve her wounds. Of course, he had wounds himself. But in his way he did not let them show. Perhaps she would not have been so resentful if he had hurt with her, had been weak with her.

So when he grimaced after biting into a piece of garlic chicken, it burst on her emotional radar.

"What?" she said. "What is it?"

"Huh?" Brad's expression of confusion did not convince.

"What's the matter with the food?"

"Nothing. It's wonderful."

"Something's wrong. I saw you. You just bit into something and you didn't like it."

"No, honest."

"You're *not* being honest. I want you to be. What is wrong with the food? Let me make it right."

"You don't have to do anything. I didn't—"

"I saw you."

"Maybe you thought I—"

"Are you saying I'm seeing things? You think I'm hallucinating?"

"I didn't say that."

"You didn't have to. I want you to stop it."

Brad spread his hands, starting with the gestures now. "Stop what?"

"Stop telling me what I'm thinking. Stop trying to psychoanalyze me all the time."

"Mona, honest, I'm not trying to—"

"Just say you'll *stop* it. That's all I want to hear right now. And then I want you to tell me what is wrong with the food. Do you understand me?"

"Listen to me carefully," Brad said. "There is nothing wrong with your food."

"Stop it!" The mellow light of innocuous conversation flipped instantly to the harsh beam of accusation. Under its glare, Mona was unable to see anything except the potato dish, more imperfection, sitting there mocking her feeble attempts to bring order to her world. She threw it against the wall.

"Mona, don't." Brad got out of his chair and started around the table toward her.

Mona got up quickly and pushed her chair into his path. "Don't touch me. Don't do anything. Don't even think of cleaning this up. I'm going to clean it up. I am going to make it right."

"Let me help you. Please."

"Help yourself. Leave me alone. I'm sorry I ruined dinner." The whole ugly table laughed at her. She grabbed a corner of the table-cloth and, like the magicians used to do, pulled with all her might. But instead of leaving the contents undisturbed, everything came crashing to the floor.

Brad's expression of shock was more than she could bear.

"Get out! Get out! Get out!"

"Mona . . ."

She screamed so loudly her throat spasmed.

SIX

✝ ✝ ✝

1.

"How you doin', Pop? Lookin' good."

Leon sat on the arm of the sofa, knowing his father could not answer. The Reverend Calvert Colby, dressed in a white bathrobe, slowly looked up at his son and, just as slowly, nodded.

"Yeah, you're lookin' good," Leon lied. But it was a soft lie, a white lie, the kind you told when you wanted to encourage someone who was on the final lap.

Leon turned to Rosa Mendez, the live-in caregiver who had also been a longtime member of Reverend Colby's church. "How's he been?"

Rosa said, "He is getting along. Lots of people visit."

"That's good. You like that, Pop? You like the visits?"

His father nodded again. Leon's stomach clenched. What a practical joker life was. What a bad practical joker. The punch line wasn't funny, a permanent residence in a prison of sadness.

You take a man who once had a booming voice and animated features, who could bounce around a pulpit in a one-man assault on the gates of hell. You take a man who could sing with the gospel choir and fill any room with the sound of righteous conviction. You take a man who didn't know the meaning of nuance, who saw the world without shades of gray, you give him confidence in his calling and inject passion into his message. And then you watch life have its joke.

You watch as his wife of forty years wastes away with cancer. And then you watch this man, who covered his heartache with trembling utterances of scriptural hope, you watch him fall off the stage one night with a massive stroke. You watch as doctors come and go, and deliver news that is not good, that robs an anointed man of the very faculties that mean the most to him. You watch as he loses his ability to talk, let alone sing. You watch him waste away, a once ample-bellied man shrinking into a stick figure who can barely stand.

And when all that has happened, you come to the house weekly to check in because you can't talk to him on the phone. You come because you're the son and that's what you do.

"He eating okay?" Leon said to Rosa.

She pointed her finger at his father. "He need to eat better. He push around his food too much. I have to get mad."

Calvert looked blankly at Rosa.

"He get his Milky Way?" Calvert Colby had always liked Milky Ways. He used to say it was God's proof that he wanted men to be happy.

"I don't give unless he eats," Rosa said.

Leon nodded, took out his wallet, and gave Rosa a twenty-dollar bill. "Go easy on him. Let him have a Milky Way every now and then."

Rosa took the money.

"Now don't you worry about me, Pop," Leon said, giving voice to what he was sure occupied his father's feeble mind. Before his stroke, Calvert Colby had made plain his hope that Leon would come back to church. It was a source of sorrow for him that his son had chosen not to become a preacher, and worse, to give up on Christ.

Leon sometimes wondered if that sorrow was partially to blame for his father's stroke.

Now there was a thought that might drive him crazy. He buried it deep.

Leon patted his father's thin arm, then reached for his right hand. They always shook hands at the end, and his father, while severely weakened, still gave the grip his all.

2.

Judge Greene said, "Colby make you an offer?"

"Twenty-five to life," Lindy said. "Some offer."

They were sitting out on Greene's redwood deck, which had an incredible view of the ocean. The judge had done all right for himself. His wife, whom Lindy had never met, was out doing something social. Word was she had major bucks. This was not a world with which Lindy was familiar. She almost laughed thinking of her mobile home in the canyon, with its view of charred hills, big boulders, and a Los Angeles County reservoir. Even when she closed her eyes and thought real hard, she still couldn't imagine it was an ocean.

Greene thought a moment, his eyes looking out at the sea, darkening in the oncoming night. What he must have seen with those eyes over the years. What they all had seen in the criminal-justice system. Enough darkness for three lifetimes.

"Could be just the thing for your client," Greene said. "It's not life without parole. He could get out."

"To what? And what's prison going to do to a boy?"

"There have been cases," Greene said, "where lives have been turned around."

"Can you count them all on one hand?"

"Maybe both hands." He was trying to soften the blow of what might be inevitable, and she appreciated the effort. Unless she could get the insanity defense to fly, Darren DiCinni would spend most of the rest of his life in adult prison.

Nothing could soften a blow like that.

Lindy listened to the waves breaking on the shore. She normally welcomed this calming sound. Now, though, it reminded her of ships crashing into rocks.

"Can any good really come out of this?" Lindy said. She realized that was what she wanted from him. To know. Even if it was bad news, just knowing something for certain would help.

"We can't rule that out," Greene said. "I mean, look at that ocean. We can't comprehend its size. What's happening here, we can see a little of it. But what happens beyond the horizon? What's the water doing miles out to sea, or on the other side of the world? I think the world is like that. If I didn't, maybe I'd go a little bit nuts myself."

Lindy tensed.

"I'm sorry," Greene added quickly. "I didn't mean you."

"It's a fact, Judge. You deal in facts. I went nuts after Marcel Lee. I couldn't handle it. Why'd you bring me into this?"

Greene waited a long time before answering. "Can I tell you something, Lindy?"

"Of course."

"I'm a private man. I don't wear my heart on my sleeve. A judge has to be objective. But I'm also a religious man, Lindy, and that's what keeps me going."

She was not surprised at this, though she was surprised she had not thought of him as religious before. A judge with religion—that was not a creature she was anxious to embrace.

But Greene was a good man and a good judge.

"The Bible says that God's plans cannot be frustrated by man. And yet man has a part to play in the way things turn out. Maybe I thought getting you back into the game was the best way to help you."

"But this one, this case. It's so over-the-top compared to anything I've ever handled before."

"That's where God comes in."

"Oh, so he waits until now to intervene? The whole thing about evil messes with my mind. I don't see how he lets it happen."

"It's messed with a lot of minds over the centuries. One thing I know, as a judge: there is such a thing as evil, and that's the way some people are."

"So what about lives changing?"

Greene shook his head slowly. "Rare. It can get so deep in a person. That's why we have prisons. And the death penalty."

"I'm against the death penalty, you know that."

"Sure, but evil has to be dealt with. Bad people deserve punishment. Like Marcel Lee. I know you had a rough time with that case, but he is a bad man, Lindy. You did your part in the system, you represented him well, and now that's over for you."

"I don't know if it'll ever be over for me." She paused. The breeze had turned suddenly chilly. "I went to church."

Greene turned toward her. "Really?" He seemed more astonished than anything else.

"Quite a shock, huh?"

"Not at all. I would encourage you in that, Lindy."

"My mind is expanding a little too quickly at the moment. Like the universe."

"Step at a time. My advice: don't get personally involved with DiCinni. Stay professional. Whatever the outcome, know that you did your part."

For a long time they sat in silence, Lindy feeling the strength of this judge who had become her friend, who had selflessly reached out to her. She drew from his strength. She wished she had more of it herself.

3.

"They taking care of you?" Lindy asked.

Darren shrugged. Once again they were in the attorney-interview booth at county jail. And once again Lindy was trying to set her client at ease so he would open up at least a little bit.

"Anything you want to tell me about? I can rattle some cages if they're doing anything you don't like."

He shook his head.

"I came to tell you that a doctor's going to examine you."

That brought a frown to Darren's face. "I'm not sick."

"I mean a psychiatrist. You know, someone to go over what's going on inside you. Just talk, that's all. But it needs to happen."

Darren DiCinni's eyes flickered for a moment. "You think I'm crazy?"

Lindy wanted to shout *Yes! Don't you realize it? You're damaged goods, and there may be a way to heal you, but I don't know what it is.*

"Something's wrong, Darren. You don't kill people without something being wrong. You realize that, don't you?"

He frowned as if he did not understand.

"Darren, suppose you try something. Suppose you tell me why you killed those kids. You have to talk about it eventually. I'm your lawyer. It's best to start with me."

He looked at her with that blank stare again. "My life is really over, isn't it?"

"It doesn't have to be. You're only thirteen."

"I'll never get out of here, will I?"

Trying to stop his slide down a pole of despair, Lindy said, "That's an open question. Getting people out of here is what I do, Darren. And if you give me a little, I can help you more."

She waited for him to respond to the pleading in her voice. *Just come to me halfway.*

The young prisoner, lost in the orange jumpsuit that looked like an ill-fitting Halloween costume, slumped on his stool. "I've done what I need to do."

"Need to do?" Lindy said. "What do you mean, Darren?"

He shook his head.

"Darren, what did you mean by that? I want to know."

He waved the back of his shackled hand at her, looked at the dull green wall.

"Tell me," she said. "Please, trust me. What is it you needed to do?"

"Shut up," he said quietly.

No, she was not going to shut up. She had just seen a fissure in the mountain. A thin shaft of light shone out, but the mountain was threatening to close up again. If she didn't drive a wedge in now she might never get the chance.

A wedge. Something to shove into the tiny crack.

"You want to know about me?" she asked. "Want to know why I'm here?"

Darren was silent for a moment, then slowly nodded.

"I'll tell you, but you've got to make a deal with me. You've got to give me something back, okay? Deal?"

Nothing from him. Oh, well, she had to dive in anyway.

"I was pretty messed up as a kid," Lindy said. "A real troublemaker. My dad and I didn't get along too well. He didn't really like me. And then, I don't know, something snapped in me when I got to be a teenager. About your age I guess. I started doing things behind my father's back."

Darren's eyes moved a little, but he was looking right at her.

"Then he ran off. That was really hard on my mom. I tried to deal with it. I started drinking and stuff like that. Let school slide. There was a teacher at my school, though, wouldn't give up on me. Managed to get me into junior college. Long story short, I got through college and into a law-school program at night. I went on to do mostly juvenile work with the public defender's office. And then . . ."

She was about to tell him about Marcel Lee. She stopped herself. She was backtracking to some other part of her past when Darren spoke.

"Do you believe in God?" he asked.

That was unexpected. And the crack stayed open.

"Do you?" he pressed.

"What made you ask me that?"

"I just want to know."

In the split second between question and answer Lindy relived the bar exam—she felt all the anxiety, all the information jumbling around in her head, all the hope that when it came to crunch time something would make sense. Only that was just the bar exam. This was a kid's life.

"Sure," Lindy said.

"Why?" He was challenging her, a prosecutor cross-examining a defendant who tried to get by with shallow answers.

Lindy shrugged. "It's just one of those things you know. There has to be a God."

"Yeah, but what's he like? What do you think he's like?" He moved his hands around in the desk shackles and leaned forward. His default reticence was replaced suddenly by some odd curiosity.

"I think God knows everything. But what he does with that knowledge is beyond us."

"Oh yeah?"

"What are you trying to tell me, Darren?"

"I know God."

"Tell me about him."

He smiled then, like a kid who knew where the answers to the test were and had copied them down. But he did not say anything further.

"Darren, I really want to know."

"No, you don't. You don't really want to know."

"Why don't you believe me?"

"You're getting paid to do this, aren't you?"

"That doesn't mean I don't believe in this case, in you."

"You better believe in God," he said. "You better."

And then the fissure sealed shut, crushing Lindy with frustration.

This kid better be crazy, and she'd better find a good doctor to verify that.

4.

"I think it would be a good idea to be apart for a while."

Mona heard her own voice. It sounded clipped and precise and emotionless. It surprised her that she wasn't crying.

Not even Brad's look, his shocked and hurt face, brought tears to her eyes. She wondered if he'd cry. Every now and then Brad would tear up at an old movie. He would try to hide it, but Mona always knew. He'd pretend to scratch his head when he was really wiping his eye. Like when John Wayne looked at his gold watch in *She Wore a Yellow Ribbon*. Got him every time.

And she couldn't resist holding him when he did. She would tear up and grab him and hug him, even though he told her not to. He was embarrassed and tried to cover up. Usually she had the waterworks.

Now she was the desert as Brad's eyes misted ever so slightly.

"Do you mean . . ." he said, then started again. "What do you mean?"

"I mean apart for a while. I don't want to have a repeat of last night."

Brad waited a long time before responding, and Mona knew he'd picked up that there was more to her words than she'd let on.

"You don't actually think," he said, "our marriage is in trouble?"

Can't you see it? Where have you been?

"I'm not saying anything," Mona answered, "except I think we need some time apart."

"I don't think that's a good idea. Not a good idea at all."

"I think it is a good idea."

"So that settles it?"

"Yes."

Brad normally sat during upsetting discussions. It was Mona's observation that this was his way of anchoring himself to something. He did not like emotional upheaval. And his chair in the family room, a brown recliner, was his favorite. Mona, who was standing with arms folded, expected he would remain there as the discussion drew to a close.

But he did not. And Mona knew that meant trouble.

SEVEN

† † †

1.

Lindy went over to check on Mr. Klinger. He was in his favorite soft chair, circa 1958, watching a sitcom.

"Ah, Lindy! Come and watch how bad this is."

She looked at a couple of actors pretending to be flummoxed.

"Not funny," Klinger said, waving his arms. "Now Sid Caesar, he was funny. Funny this is not."

"Why don't you turn it off, Mr. Klinger? Might be better for your blood pressure."

"What about you?"

"Me?"

"You with that crazy kid."

Lindy sighed and sat on his modern sofa, circa 1965. "You've been watching the news."

Klinger wiggled his bushy white eyebrows. "I don't want you should get in too deep."

"Impossible in a murder case."

"Murder! That was a massacre. Kid like that." Klinger shook his head sadly as canned laughter filled the room. "Why, Lindy? Why did he do that terrible thing?"

"I can't really talk about it yet, Mr. Klinger."

"God told him to do it, is what he says?"

That much was public information. Lindy nodded.

"Ah, God maybe isn't dead," Klinger murmured, "but he's out getting a second opinion."

"Do you believe in God, Mr. Klinger?" Suddenly, she wanted to know very much what he thought. Maybe because of his age. Maybe eighty-some years on the planet had filled him with burnished insight.

Klinger turned thoughtful. A burst of laughter and applause came from the sitcom. He flicked it off with the remote.

"My father was a rabbi, did you know that?"

"No, I didn't."

"He used to say God created the world in six days. On the seventh day, he rested. On the eighth day, he started getting complaints. And it hasn't stopped since. I got complaints too, Lindy. There's so much pain in this world."

He paused, looked at the floor.

"But then I think, we laugh. A God who can make laughter, he can't be all bad. So why don't we laugh all the time? This is the question. You know the story of Job?"

"A little. God took everything away from him."

"Ah, you got one little detail wrong. It was Satan who took everything. God just let him do it."

"Doesn't that amount to the same thing?"

"Only to a smarty-pants lawyer! I had a dream a long time ago. Satan was the producer of a TV show. That's very close to the truth, by the way. And he wanted me to tell some jokes he wrote. But the jokes weren't funny. I said to him, 'You're not a Jew. Only Jews are funny.' He said, 'I am the producer and you will say what I write.' I told him, 'No,' and he fired me. And I never worked again."

"Not a very happy dream."

Klinger leaned toward her with a glint in his eye. "But there's more. I went out to the street and started telling my own jokes. I got a million of 'em. And people started laughing. All over the street. And soon there was thousands of people, all laughing at my jokes. And Satan looks out the window of the fancy office building and tells us all to shut up. But I kept telling my jokes, and people kept laughing. And he screamed until he lost his voice."

He paused. "So I figure our job here is to make people laugh when we can. Make life easier for the guy next to you. That's our job. And when we do that, Satan loses his voice."

Lindy got up and kissed Emil Klinger on the forehead. "I think God made you just right, Mr. Klinger."

He looked at her wide-eyed. "My blood pressure just went from almost dead to *whoopee.*"

Lindy picked up his pill dispenser, sitting on a small table, and opened it. "Don't forget the blue one before bed. Good night."

She kept thinking about God as she spooned out Cardozo's food and waited for Roxy to show up to discuss the case. Something was eating at her, like a little ferret gnawing at the wires in her brain.

Maybe it had to do with the way Darren looked at her when he talked about God. Like he had some sort of special knowledge about things divine that she didn't. Like he was some kind of thirteen-year-old prophet with a hidden message from on high.

Of course that was absurd. How much can a thirteen-year-old know about anything?

But then, how much did she know? She told him she believed in God, but what did that really mean? She did have a back-of-the-mind belief, a nonthreatening corner of her mind where she could park God, leave him there to fiddle on his own.

Then there was Roxy, who was so into the God thing now. When she arrived, and the two of them settled down with Diet Dr Peppers, Lindy brought the subject up first.

They sat in the front of the trailer, looking at the lights of the Valley. The hot and dry night air blew down from the Santa Susanna Mountains, reminding Angelinos to be thankful for water.

"Did you go to church on Sunday?" Lindy asked.

"Yeah, of course." She seemed fascinated that Lindy would even ask. "You want to come with me again?"

"I don't know."

"Are you thinking about it?"

"Here's what I'm thinking about." Lindy turned slightly on her lawn chair, facing Roxy directly. "What makes Christianity any better or worse than any other religion?"

"Well, Jesus, for one thing. The main thing."

"You think he really happened? Like in the Mel Gibson movie?"

"Oh yeah."

"But the part about rising from the dead. That's kind of hard to buy."

"But without that, there really isn't any difference. I mean, otherwise Jesus is just a guy who died."

"Maybe just being good to people is what God cares about, you know?"

"Jesus was God. Is God."

"That's kind of outlandish."

"That's what it says in the Bible."

"The Bible is just one book."

"It's the revelation of God."

"What kind of revelation? People hear God all the time in different ways. It's—"

"What? What were you going to say?"

Lindy paused. "Darren says God told him to shoot those kids."

"So?"

"So there you go," Lindy said. "Maybe sometimes God makes you crazy."

"You think I'm crazy?"

"I didn't say that. I said sometimes, in this case, maybe Darren."

"You're going to use a God-made-him-crazy defense?"

"What else have I got? He's got to be crazy, or he's going to be fish fried in prison. What do you suggest I do?"

"You don't know what you're talking about."

"Hey—"

"What are you putting me down for?"

"I'm not, Rox—"

"God is real to me."

Lindy put her hand on Roxy's arm. "I'm a jerk. Sorry. I'll go to church with you again."

"Really?"

"Let's talk about the case now, huh?"

Roxy poured a long shot of Dr Pepper down her throat then picked up a pad and pencil. "What do you want me to do, chief?"

"First, I want to get a written statement from Darren's father. Colby is not going to call him as a witness. Wouldn't do his case any good and could possibly hurt it."

"Hurt it how?"

"Maybe the jury sympathizes with Drake, doesn't want to punish him by sending Darren to prison for life. Or maybe the jury hates him, puts the blame on him, so it doesn't want to punish Darren for having a loser for a dad. Either way, it's a risk for Colby. Question is, do we call him?"

"Why would we?"

"Well, he could help us the same way he could hurt Colby. But he could also say things that would make the jury think he did what he could with Darren, but the kid was just uncontrollable. That's the problem. Thing is, though, the jury is going to want to hear from him. They'll think it's pretty odd if he doesn't take the stand, and when things get odd in court the jury usually holds it against the defendant. But I have no idea how his father'll come off. I'm sure Colby's looking for him. If he finds Drake, he could nail down a statement that'll haunt us. Let's see if we can get a statement first. You game?"

"Game." Roxy jotted a note.

"Darren said his dad is religious, taught him about God. I want to follow up on that."

"Check. Should I do anything on the parents of the kids who got killed?"

"No reason. Nothing they did or didn't do has any bearing on the shooting. In fact, I'm going to try to keep them off the stand."

"How can you possibly do that?"

"First of all, we're going to stipulate to the fact of the shooting. We're going to take that off the table as an issue. Cut the legs off Colby. Everybody knows Darren did it, everybody in the world who watched the evening news. So the only reason Colby would put parents on the stand is to generate sympathy for the victims and increase the jury's hate for Darren. Which makes the evidence prejudicial. I will make a 352 motion, argue that the prejudice outweighs the probative value, and if the judge denies me, take that issue up on appeal."

"Is Darren going to take the stand?"

"No way. This is going to be an insanity defense. Has to be. That's the only way to keep him out of prison. You know what'll happen to him in there, don't you?"

Roxy nodded. There was no need for either of them to say more.

"See what you can find about what went down in Vegas with Drake and his wife."

"On it."

"We're going to need a good expert," Lindy said. "Get on the horn and ask around. I don't want any county guys. Let's go private."

"Will the court pay for that?"

"Probably not. I've got some money socked away."

Roxy shook her head. "Why would you do that, Lindy?"

A sigh came out of Lindy's deep place, the place where she dumped the pain of loss. All defense lawyers had such a place. "He'll die in prison. If he's not killed they'll take his soul."

"Hey, Lindy," Roxy said, "you said *soul*."

2.

"I can't let you do this." Brad was on his feet, facing Mona, his face twisted with fear and uncertainty and a bit of the lost little boy she had seen in the early days of their marriage. As a child, he didn't have much of a home life. No doubt he thought he was losing another home now.

Mona didn't care. She couldn't. There was only so much room in her for caring now, and it was filled up with death.

"I'm not asking you to let me, Brad. Listen to me for once. This is the way it *is*."

"No."

He took a step toward her, a threatening step, unlike any movement she'd ever seen him make. Or was it just her imagination, her interpretive frame, which was all messed up now, twisted and grief-streaked?

She took a step back.

Brad's face hardened before her eyes. Into what? Resolve? Anger? They were in uncharted waters, and Mona mentally thrashed about, trying to find something to keep her afloat.

"Brad, stop it," Mona said. "Stop trying to control me."

"What about you?" He took another step.

She started breathing faster. "Brad, stop where you are."

"What are you talking about?"

"I don't want you to touch me."

"I'm your husband. What kind of talk is this?"

This time he took two steps and Mona stumbled backward into the kitchen. It was like falling into a cave. She thought she might lose her balance and hit the floor.

She reached for the countertop with her left hand, found it, steadied herself.

"You're not well," Brad said.

"I am not crazy!"

"I didn't say that." He put his hands out.

"Just go away, Brad."

"I can't let you stay like this."

"I don't want to see you right now."

"You are my wife—"

"Stop it."

She felt something in her hand and thought, *Please stay where you are, Brad.*

Brad's face had turned into a chiseled rock. The soft light she'd always seen in his eyes was gone, replaced by something that resembled desperation. And she had no idea what a desperate Brad would do.

Lock her up? Send her to a hospital to get checked out, sedated, probed?

No way could she go there, do that. Matthew needed her.

When Brad made his move, hands coming to her shoulders, the thing in Mona's hand—a hard thing—seemed to move on its own. Her hand was just along for the ride.

The hard thing hit Brad square in the face.

3.

"Dr. O'Connor, my name is Lindy Field."

"Yes?" The doctor's tone over the phone was hesitant. Par for the course with these psychological types. Lindy had gotten his name from an old prosecution witness list and tracked him to County-USC Medical Center.

She readied her pen over the legal pad on her kitchen table. "I wonder if I might ask you a couple of questions about mental competence in a minor. I just have—"

"Ms. Fields, I—"

"Field."

"—can't simply give out such information over the phone."

"I'm not asking you for expert testimony here, doctor. I merely want to get some guidance. I didn't have anyone to turn to, and I'm sure that this could lead to your paid testimony." A thought struck her. "You have not been contacted by the district attorney's office in the matter of Darren DiCinni, have you?"

"No."

"Then if you could just point me in the right direction? I'm sure you've read about the case."

"Yes. Terrible."

"I need to get into my client's head. Of course, until you and I have an agreement I cannot reveal very much. But hypothetically we can talk about the possibilities."

"That is very difficult to do, Ms. Fields."

Lindy ignored the error this time. "Can you at least tell me about some of the danger signs and potentially troubling mental situations for young teenagers?"

"That will take us into an entire field of study, you know."

"Sure."

"Without foundation as to the facts, it's very hard to speculate."

"Let me ask you this: Is it possible for adolescent boys to be subject to powerful delusions, hearing voices and the like?"

"Of course that's possible. The delusions and the manner of false auditory suggestion are subject to the maturity level of the individual minor. That takes into account all of his background and so on."

"Of course. But for a kid of thirteen to do something like this, what's the likelihood he *isn't* legally incompetent or insane?"

"Those are legal definitions—"

"Just as a preliminary opinion, based on experience."

There was a long pause. "It's not likely."

"What are the percentages—"

"Ms. Fields, I'm afraid I need to get back to my rounds."

"Just a few more quick questions."

"Why don't you schedule a consultation with me?"

"To be honest, I have to be very careful about doling out the bucks on this one. Can we agree to meet just to see if it's possible that you would be interested in taking on this case?"

"I don't think I'm going to be taking on any expert testimony for a while."

"Is there anyone you can recommend?"

"To be quite honest, Ms. Fields, this is a very explosive case. I don't feel comfortable making recommendations right off the top of my head. Tell you what, I'll ask around, and if anyone bites I'll give you a call."

"That would be—"

He hung up without asking for her number.

4.

"Mr. DiCinni, you've been a bad little boy."

Leon Colby folded his arms and sat on the corner of his desk, giving himself the advantage over Drake DiCinni, who slumped in the spare, county-issue chair. It was the way he liked to talk to reluctant witnesses. Gave an immediate sense of who was in control.

Only Darren's father, sitting there like a caged squirrel, said with his body he wasn't buying the power game. Which only made Colby all the more determined to see him squirm.

"You can't hold me here," DiCinni said. Colby noticed that the cop who had escorted DiCinni to this interview wore a half smile as he leaned against the open door.

"That'll be it for now, Officer," Colby said. "I'll let you know when Mr. DiCinni is finished talking to me."

"That'd be now," DiCinni said. But he didn't get out of his chair.

Leon Colby leaned forward. "Where have you been, sir?"

"I don't have to answer that. You're buying yourself a lawsuit here. The county—"

"You're not going to sue the county or anybody else, Mr. DiCinni. You want to sit in front of a jury, with your record, and try to convince them you've been wronged?"

"My record isn't so bad."

"Not so good, either."

"No felonies."

"I see you've been charged with felony assault."

"They dropped the charge."

"You're Mr. Clean, I suppose."

"I don't make trouble."

"You've got trouble right now, don't you?"

The squirrel shifted in his chair, swinging his knees around from one wall, where Colby had his calendar, to the other, where a framed picture of his mom and dad hung.

"My kid? You think I had something to do with that?"

"You want to tell me why he did it?"

"How am I supposed to know? He's a freaky kid, always has been. Probably got a drug bath in the womb from his good-for-nothing mother."

"You don't sound like you're very concerned about Darren."

"What do you want me to say? That I'm all broken up about it? You want to know what? I'm relieved. I couldn't do anything with him. Maybe the state can get him the help he needs."

"You saying he's crazy?"

"What do you think?"

"What I think doesn't matter. I'm interested in what a jury's going to think. Maybe they'll think Darren is a very bad kid."

"What do you want from me? To help you out? You want me to testify against my own kid?"

Colby studied the squirrel's pointy face. The nose and chin looked like they'd been put in some sharpener. "I just want to know the truth about what happened. I want to know about your relationship with Darren."

"What for?"

"To satisfy my curiosity, let's just say."

"Forget it." DiCinni stood up.

"Sit down, Mr. DiCinni."

"I don't think I will. You want to arrest me, try. We'll see what your boss has to say about that."

"Don't go too far away from town, Mr. DiCinni."

"You got no authority over me. Don't pull that."

Now Colby stood up. He looked down at the squirrel. "You want to press it? You want to try me?"

For a brief moment DiCinni trembled. Then he gathered himself up and said, "I'm leaving now."

"There's the door," Colby said.

"Yeah, and I'm going through it. Watch me."

Colby did watch as DiCinni steamed out of his office, and he felt the old urge to tackle his opponent and lay him out flat, like the time he caught that Trojan receiver, a hot prospect, from behind. He wouldn't take down DiCinni physically, of course, but the urges in the old football sinews never quite went away.

He sat down at his desk and studied the age-stained walls. The case was a little like these—not clean. It wasn't the kid. If at the age of thirteen you can snuff the lives of children, your life is over. It deserved to be over. This kid couldn't be rehabilitated, and he wasn't mentally ill.

So what held back that certainty he cherished when he prosecuted a case? He wanted that big-game feeling, that no-holds-barred championship zeal.

Maybe he was just tired. Yeah, he was getting a little older. He still chugged up and down the court with the office basketball team, mainly banging under the boards. Yeah, maybe he just needed to conserve his energy a little better these days.

Certainly it couldn't be Lindy Field that was bothering him.

5.

Books were preferable to men.

The thought hit Lindy as she lay in bed, getting ready to read. A book did not demand sex. It did not try to talk her out of her better judgments, though a good novel could seduce her. But that was a proper kind of seduction, one that didn't leave her head full of regret and remonstrance in the morning. And in the morning, she didn't have to figure out a nice way to kick the book out.

Lindy's luck with men had not been good. The one guy she thought she might actually marry, another public defender, Maxwell O'Neill, had, in the end, turned out to be the quintessential loser. She should have seen it all along but was blinded by hope. She did want to marry someone, but the singles' scene in L.A. stunk, restricted as it was to clubs and bars, where overdressed and over-stressed men tried too hard to look suave.

But under their surface was just . . . more surface. They didn't read newspapers; they watched Larry King. They thought Sean Penn was God and tried to brood like him. They looked more like unhappy puppies.

Once she met a man at Oasis who seemed to have it all—brains, talent, looks. And he wasn't an actor (*oh, thank you*, no self-absorbed narcissist with perfect teeth who went on casting calls). His name was Raymong ("not Ray-*mond* and please not Ray," he said) and he was dark and handsome. He worked as a tutor for poor kids while running his own graphic-arts business. And he knew who John Cheever was.

So it was promising and stimulating, this conversation with Raymong in the meat plant that was Oasis. So his eventual invitation to visit his home was, in her mind, the most promising development in her love life since the dumping of Max O'Neill.

Upon entering Raymong's apartment, he revealed that he was gay. And that he had need of a lawyer to do some work, *pro bono*, for his graphics business, and would Lindy be interested in exchange for more "good conversation"?

She had to laugh. The one good man she'd managed to meet in three years of club hopping and, natch, he turned out to be gay. Another L.A. story.

Then Sean McIntyre came along. He seemed to have it all—looks, intelligence. Sure, he was a little too sold on himself. But he read books. He could talk about a wide range of subjects. And he was straight.

Their early dates had been wonderful, but now they'd arrived at the inevitable: the pressure to hop in the sack. Why did that always have to be the way? Why did a relationship always come down to that choice?

Tonight the only choice she wanted was which book to read. She read history and philosophy as well as Lisa Scottoline and Dave Barry. She had no criteria other than the book had to capture her by the end of the first chapter, or she was unlikely to go on.

What should she read tonight? It was her habit to read something light the night before going to court.

Maybe the new Scottoline.

She thumbed it open.

Cardozo dashed into the room in a cat-fright way.

"Hey, what's up?"

He jumped on the bed and relaxed.

"Mouse chasing you or something?"

She heard a faint sound, like the twisting of sheet metal. Was it windy outside? Something brushing up against the trailer?

And then the trailer moved. Almost imperceptibly, but it moved. The way it would when heavy feet walked its floor, sending ripples of motion outward.

Skin tingling, Lindy threw off the covers and fairly leaped off the bed. She wore an extra-large T-shirt that flapped around her like an ungainly tent.

The gun. She had a revolver in a drawer. This was Box Canyon, which for some residents was the last outpost of the Wild West. A man took care of business himself here, and so did women who lived alone. The gun had been a gift from one of her Harley-riding friends.

Now she wondered if she'd actually have to use it. The gun had never been fired.

Was it even loaded?

The floor squeaked.

The kitchenette.

Cardozo mewed. Lindy almost shushed him but stopped herself.

She was bathed in light. If she shut it off, though, the intruder would know she was aware of his presence.

Hide. The closet. She was small enough to fit comfortably and could watch for the intruder.

Or would she just be setting herself up in a little prison awaiting execution?

No sense calling 911. It would be all over before they got here.

Kill the light and rush him? No, that was the movie way, the Uma Thurman way, and she was no Uma.

It was at this moment Cardozo chose to leave the bedroom.

"No," Lindy whispered.

Too late. His tail disappeared past the partition.

The intruder would see Cardozo. She was sure of it. She had no choice.

Uma.

She switched off her light and jumped through the darkened doorway.

6.

Dear God, what had she done?

Hit her husband.

Unforgivable.

Mona sat in her empty house in shock, the new constant in her life. It stretched across the rooms, an invisible but perpetual companion.

She'd hit him in the face with a cookbook. His nose bled. And then he left. Just like she wanted.

Maybe she *was* crazy. Maybe Brad was better off without her.

No time to think of that now.

Matthew needed her. Brad would have to understand that.

Her son needed balance restored to the universe. God wasn't interested.

She would have to do it.

She would.

The dull ache that had been with her since Matthew's death began to cover her like a second skin, and she welcomed it. She did not want to be comfortable ever again. Comfort led only to complacency.

Pain would keep her purpose alive, and the ache would motivate, push, keep her aware.

Matthew's killer would have to die. He was only thirteen, but he would have to die. They had told her that he would not get the death penalty, but prison. And in prison he would surely die.

Balance would be restored.

And if anyone tried to keep him out of prison, well, she would have to find a way around that.

7.

Lindy knelt at the far end of her long, tin box, gun pointed at darkness. She had made the move and whoever was in her trailer knew he wasn't alone.

But nothing happened. No quick movement in the shadows.

Am I losing my mind? Had she conjured up this whole thing? Was her mind reaching for mental tricks to deal with the stress?

Or was he still here, as quiet as she?

She would wait him out, then, gun ready.

No sound. No movement.

Except the humming motor of Cardozo, purring against her leg.

Lindy stayed put, oblivious to time. She might have stayed there for ten minutes or an hour.

Finally convinced she was alone, she made a tentative move.

She half-expected someone to jump out at her now, like in some bad horror movie. A screeching owl or a hand from the grave.

It didn't come. Lindy made it to the kitchenette and turned on the light.

She was alone. Cardozo padded in to observe her foolishness. "Oh man."

She got Cardozo a salmon treat, checked her doors and windows. All secure.

Talk about being on edge. On the day before she was to appear in court on the 1368, she had conjured up an elaborate fantasy. What did that tell her?

You really are in bad shape, Lindy. You are faking your way through this case. You better get it together or you won't be doing Darren or any other client a bit of good.

But she found it difficult to sleep, and she read until 2:00 a.m. Even then, she never entirely shook the feeling that someone had actually been inside her home.

EIGHT

† † †

1.

Friday, Lindy dropped into the ninth circle of hell known as Department 11.

In California, it was up to a criminal-court judge to declare whether a defendant's mental competence was in doubt. If such doubt existed, the criminal matter stopped in its tracks, and the judge kicked the case over to civil court for a full trial on the competency issue.

To get to that stage, Lindy would have to provide substantial evidence that Darren's competence was questionable. This would not be easy, because bizarre behavior or statements were not enough. California courts consistently held the defense to a high bar of proof, but Lindy was determined to jump it.

Unfortunately, the hearing landed in the courtroom of Judge Varner Foster, an ancient jurist who seemed to have been on the bench since the kidnapping of the Lindbergh baby. Foster delighted in making defense attorneys crawl in abject obeisance to his authority, and Lindy had tussled with him before. His bushy white eyebrows suggested sedated lab rats, stirring only to scorn certain defense motions.

Foster would be bad enough. The other obstacle in her way was a former linebacker who loved nothing better than cutting off defense lawyers' legal legs.

Leon Colby sported an icy look, his "game face." That was okay. Lindy had one of her own. And today, she imagined her face boasted of winning this motion despite the odds, because she had Dr. Ben Kitteridge on her side.

Lindy had moved the court for the appointment of an independent expert to examine Darren, and Dr. Kitteridge's name came up first on the available list. He had served Lindy as a witness a few times in her public-defender days. He made a good impression on judges and juries, with his avuncular demeanor and gentle command of the facts. People trusted him.

Further, Kitteridge's report had been superb. Now all he would have to do was testify to objective facts indicating Darren's inability to participate meaningfully in his own defense.

The judge called the hearing to order at two in the afternoon— what lawyers called the dead zone. After lunch, both jurors and judges were prone to dozing unless the lawyers kept things hopping. Lindy was ready. She did not want Foster snoozing on this one.

Lindy called Kitteridge to the stand. After stating his qualifications for the record, Lindy began her examination. "Did you have occasion to interview the accused, Darren DiCinni?"

"Yes," the doctor said. "I completed my interview and examination two days ago. I have a copy of my written report in front of me."

"How was this examination conducted, Dr. Kitteridge?"

"I asked a standard battery of questions which apply to this profile," the witness said. "First were basic cognition queries, followed by questions of increasing complexity relating to the matter of mental competence."

"Tell the court first, please, how Darren responded to the initial questioning."

Kitteridge put on glasses and referred to his report. "He was nonresponsive for the most part. His demeanor was vacant. He had trouble focusing. His span of attention was extremely limited."

"Do you have a scale of assessment for attention span?"

"We do. There is a standardized scale from one to ten, ten being the highest level of focus. Darren, in my opinion, rates no higher than three."

Lindy paused, took a quick glance at the judge. He was looking vacant himself, pulling at one of his eyebrows and blinking toward the back wall.

"Moving on," Lindy said a little louder than normal, "what did your specified examination determine?"

Kitteridge glanced again at his report. "Darren is confused about his incarceration and does not appear to understand what is at stake. Further, when I asked whether he understood the basic difference between right and wrong, he did not respond with requisite specificity. My conclusion is that he would not be able to meaningfully participate in his own defense."

Clear, concise, to the point. Dr. Kitteridge sounded better than ever.

Lindy finished off by having Kitteridge tell the court how many times he had testified in similar matters and how often his opinions had been upheld in subsequent court proceedings.

Then it was time for Leon Colby to cross-examine.

Lindy watched him closely, part of her giving in to a certain awe. The man commanded an audience, no doubt about it. He moved across the floor smoothly, confidently. He held no notes, only the copy of Kitteridge's report Lindy had provided him.

"Dr. Kitteridge," Colby said with a nod of greeting.

"Good afternoon, sir," Kitteridge said.

"You interviewed Darren DiCinni at Men's Central Jail, is that correct?"

"Yes."

"And you spent approximately an hour and a half with him?"

"That's right."

"That's a pretty long time to spend with someone who can't focus." Colby's tone possessed the coolness of an assassin. Lindy thought of that guy who played the big-cheese terrorist in *Die Hard*. Smooth as Arabian silk, but everyone knew he'd shoot anybody in his way.

Ben Kitteridge shifted only slightly in the witness chair. "Time spent with a subject is not an indicator of focus in and of itself. What the subject does during that time is what counts."

"And you asked him a number of questions."

"I did, yes, sir."

"And he answered them?"

"Not in the way that would indicate—"

"Excuse me, doctor, and focus on my question. Darren *answered* your questions, did he not?"

"Some, yes, but the answers were not—"

"Thank you."

Lindy stood up. "Objection, Your Honor. The witness should be allowed to answer—"

"Overruled," Foster barked. "He's an experienced witness, he knows the drill. Answer what the lawyer asks. Go ahead, Mr. Colby."

Lindy sat down, her pulse up-tempo. Better not object too much. Foster was extra cranky today and she needed all his goodwill. What there was of it, anyway.

Colby looked at the witness. "I am particularly interested in your assertion that Darren DiCinni cannot understand the nature of the charges against him. You see that in your report?"

"Yes," Kitteridge answered.

"You based that on a few yes-or-no questions, is that right?"

"Questions that have been tested time and time—"

"Doctor, please. My question can also be answered yes or no. These are yes/no questions you asked Darren DiCinni, right?"

"Yes," Kitteridge said, beginning to look a little flustered. *Hang in there*, Lindy thought. *You're doing fine.*

"And one of your conclusions is that Darren really does not appreciate the difference between right and wrong, isn't that true?"

"That's true, yes."

"Then let me ask you a hypothetical question."

Once more Lindy got to her feet. "I'll object to that as going beyond the scope of direct, Your Honor. Dr. Kitteridge is here to testify about his findings. I did not go beyond the four corners of his written report."

Foster did not immediately rule, which Lindy counted as a partial victory. "Mr. Colby?" he said.

Leon Colby did not hesitate for a second. "I would cite to the court the *Tamayose* case, which held there should be a *wide* latitude allowed in the cross-examination of expert witnesses. The court specifically stated that hypothetical questions which are *fair* in scope and *fairly relate* to the state of the evidence are not only permissible, but desirable."

"Ms. Field?" said the judge.

"*Tamayose* does not hold that hypotheticals can be used as a back door into areas not covered on direct."

"I remember the case," Foster said. "And I believe the judge is given great discretion in this area. Mr. Colby, go ahead and ask your question."

"Doctor," Colby said, "assuming that Darren was not under the influence of any drug or medication or alcoholic beverage, and assuming further he set out to kill several innocent people, wouldn't it—"

"Hold it!" Lindy said. "Your Honor, this is ridiculous. Mr. Colby is asking a question based upon the very facts at issue in this case. Whether Darren set out to do anything assumes the mental element in question, here and at trial."

Colby said, "Your Honor, if Ms. Field would regroup for a second, she would understand that assuming facts is what *hypothetical* means. And if Your Honor is not satisfied that the question does its job, I know you will disregard it."

Foster nodded. "Objection overruled."

Colby repeated the first part of his hypothetical, then added, "Assuming all of that, Doctor, if the subject were to drop his weapon and raise his hands in the air, would that affect your conclusion as to his understanding of right and wrong?"

Boom. Lindy could only watch as Kitteridge thought this over.

"It might," Kitteridge said.

"Nothing further," Colby said.

2.

"Prosecution calls Dr. David O'Connor," Leon Colby said.

O'Connor? The doctor Lindy had talked to by phone at County-USC. Colby didn't have him on the notice list. She could object now or wait to hear a little of his testimony. She might find a foothold for some solid cross-examination. She decided to wait.

O'Connor's face made Lindy want to look up the word *smarmy* just to see if his picture was there. He was dressed in a slate gray, Italian-cut suit. Not bad for a county physician.

After eliciting a litany of qualifications, Colby asked, "How long have you been acquainted with the accused, Darren DiCinni?"

"I was assigned by the Department of Social Services to do an assessment on the subject, for the first time, two years ago."

Two years ago?

"Your Honor, may we approach the bench?" Lindy said between clenched teeth.

"Without the reporter," the judge said.

"No," Lindy said. "I want the reporter. I want this down." She looked at the good doctor sitting there on the witness stand. He averted his eyes.

"Come on up then," the judge instructed, and then motioned to the reporter to join them.

"Your Honor," Lindy said, giving a sideward glance at Colby, "Mr. Colby seems to have overlooked a couple of things. First of all, this witness is not on his list. Second, that this doctor previously examined my client is something the prosecutor's office should have shared with me, don't you think?"

Judge Foster looked at Colby. "Your response?"

"Your Honor," Colby said, "we will have all of the paperwork ready for Ms. Field to look at. But we were not aware of this witness or his previous examination of the defendant until last night."

"Have you ever heard of a telephone?" Lindy said.

"I will remind my learned colleague and Your Honor that this is a mental-competence hearing, and that the defense has had every opportunity to conduct its own discovery and consult with its own expert witnesses."

"Discovery does not include the outright lying of prosecution stooges. This O'Connor is a . . ."

"All right," the judge said. "That will be enough. Ms. Field, Mr. Colby has a point about your own efforts."

"But I'm trying to tell you there is something unethical going on here."

"Come on, Lindy," Colby said.

"Ms. Field, I'm not going to engage in a test of ethics here. If you have a complaint to make, you may do it in writing in the proper order of things. I will allow you to vigorously cross-examine this witness. If I find that there is some unfinished business, I will grant a continuance for you to do more research and preparation. But if I find that any delay will not be of further assistance to this court, I will be prepared to rule. Let's go back to work."

Colby returned to the witness and asked, "What was the occasion for your assignment to examine Darren DiCinni?"

"The subject had been taken in after a violent confrontation at school."

Colby said, "What was the nature of that confrontation?"

"The subject attacked another student with an aluminum bat."

"What happened to the student who was attacked?"

"He was hospitalized."

"Was the defendant aware of his actions?"

"Objection," Lindy said. "Speculation."

"I'll sustain the objection," Judge Foster said. "Needs a foundation."

Colby was unconcerned. "You examined Darren DiCinni shortly after that?"

"Two days," said Dr. O'Connor.

"And what, if anything, did he say to you?"

O'Connor almost smiled when he answered. "That he was a bad little boy."

Lindy exploded to her feet. "Objection! I have no written report, Your Honor. No notice from Mr. Colby and no reason to buy this story. This is rank hearsay."

"Ms. Field!" Foster's lab mice were dancing on his face now. "Get control of yourself."

"Your Honor, if I may—"

"Sit down," the judge ordered. "Your objection is noted, and I will say this for the record. We have a witness under oath and you are going, I assume, to cross-examine. That's the way the system works and you know that, Ms. Field. I'm perfectly capable of determining credibility here. That's my job. Now let us move on."

Smarmy O'Connor testified to similar "facts" from his examination of "the subject." It was his opinion that Darren was not only aware of right and wrong but could easily participate in his own defense.

Then Colby quietly turned the doctor over to Lindy.

"We've talked before, haven't we, Doctor?" she asked.

Without so much as a blink, O'Connor said, "I believe so."

"You recall my calling you at County-USC?"

"I believe so." And he smiled.

"Do you believe it or know it, or don't you know the difference between the two?"

"Ms. Field!" The judge snapped.

"Withdraw the question," Lindy said. "Do you recall the conversation we had at that time?"

O'Connor frowned in a way that looked theatrical. "I really wouldn't call it a conversation, Ms. Field. I think you were a little upset."

"Oh really?" Lindy said, feeling the scorn dripping out of her like acid. She told herself to keep it from pouring over. "Might that have been because you wanted to stonewall me?"

"Your Honor," Leon Colby said wearily, "must we have this?"

Foster was quick to respond. "Ms. Field, that is an absolutely improper—"

"It is not improper," Lindy snapped, not caring that she interrupted the judge.

"I rule that it is," Judge Foster said. "There will be no more—"

"The man is a liar," Lindy said.

Varner Foster looked as if he'd been slapped. "You can be held in contempt for accusing a witness in open court—"

"I do so accuse," Lindy said.

A stillness overtook the courtroom, one of those pregnant movie moments. Lindy felt like camera one was giving her a close-up. Varner Foster flinched once, as if he could not believe what he'd just heard. Then, quietly, he said, "I will therefore hold you in contempt of court."

Lindy froze in place, like a ruined statue stuck in a warehouse. "You what?" She could not believe he'd actually done it.

But Foster's eyes narrowed with unyielding resolution. "You heard me, Ms. Field. I suggest you get yourself a lawyer."

3.

Outside the courthouse, Lindy faced a bank of microphones and a rippling sea of reporters' faces. They looked rabid and grotesque, like she imagined the crowd in *A Tale of Two Cities*, gawking and cheering at the thrill of the guillotine.

And there, right in the middle, smiling at her, was Sean McIntyre. Of course.

"I have a statement," Lindy said. She didn't really but figured as long as the pack was here she'd throw them some bait. Maybe a few would chew sufficiently to realize that what was happening in the justice system was actually worse than the guillotine. At least the blade gave you a quick death. What they did with juveniles was slice a piece at a time from their flesh, making the torture last for years.

The reporters quieted, readied pads and pencils. Camera eyes turned toward her. Human eyes opened wide with anticipatory glee. A story was about to break. A defense lawyer in the biggest case of the season was ready to spout. She almost laughed at their predictability.

"This hearing was a sham," Lindy said evenly, formulating the headline she wanted the media outlets to grab. "The DA wants to make this one of his tough-on-crime cases. We have an election coming up, don't we? Ambition always takes away good judgment. It removes the desire to do what's right and replaces it with a *just win, baby* mentality."

She swallowed, hard, and hoped the cameras wouldn't pick that up. But she had just opened her mouth wide and either stuffed it full of shoe, or thrown a gauntlet down on the desk of the Los Angeles County district attorney. Or both. Either way, it was not going to get any more pleasant for her after this.

So what?

"Somebody should explain to Mr. Colby that this isn't football. We had a doctor in there, O'Connor, who testified for the prosecution on competency. We might as well have had a parrot on the stand, a parrot from Mr. Colby's living room."

Most of the reporters laughed at that, scribbling wildly. Oh, tomorrow was going to be rich.

"My client is a thirteen-year-old boy. *Boy*. He's sick. He is not competent to stand trial. Are we crazy in this country? When did we decide to get rid of sick kids as fast as we can without trying to help them?"

"When they start killing people?" some clown called out, causing a few guffaws.

Lindy threw a couple of eyeball lightning bolts his way. "You find something funny about this? I don't. I don't find it funny to have lying witnesses on the stand. If you think this is funny, why don't you go back and look at the transcript of the Marcel Lee case? And why don't you ask Mr. Colby what size blinders he wears?"

Sanctions she heard in her mind. She was going to get slapped by a judge for certain. Who cared? The judges needed to hear this too. Except Greene. And she wondered what he'd have to say.

"You saying your client's not guilty?" a woman with a Channel 7 logo on her blazer shouted.

Lindy held her ground. "You have to be responsible to be guilty, and if your mental state is messed up, you're not responsible. My client is messed up. Why is that so hard for people to understand?"

"Maybe because he shot five kids and one adult." That was Sean.

Lindy's face went geothermal. She wanted to brush his teeth with a microphone, preferably hot-wired. "If you were any more ignorant of the legal system you'd be a danger to society."

Hoots from some of the reporters, good natured catcalls thrown Sean's way, then back at her.

"Listen to me," Lindy said. "If we decide to throw kids away, let's just close up shop as a society. Let's sit back and forget about doing anything for anybody, except the ones who were lucky enough to be born with money or privilege or whatever else. Let's just sweep them all away so we won't have to look at them anymore. Because when we do we're going to see ourselves reflected in their faces, and it ain't pretty, is it?"

"You accusing the DA of an ethical breach?" someone finally said, an older guy she didn't know.

"I wouldn't blink on this one. You might miss something."

4.

After faking out the reporters by pretending to leave, Lindy slipped into the parking lot behind the courthouse. She played a grown-up version of hide-and-seek, a game at which she had excelled in elementary school. Hiding seemed to be one of the best things a person could do. It was like being invisible.

And Lindy often wanted to be invisible.

What things would she be able to see if she herself could not be seen? She could slip into police stations and listen to the cops talk about cases. She could pick up when prosecutors were not playing straight with the facts. She could become the justice crusader, a new comic-book hero, rooting out evil in the hearts of men.

She could, in other words, make a difference. She could do some good. She could save the people who needed saving.

But so long as she was in a body, she'd have to walk around like every other poor slob and fight the battles as they came, face to face, nose to nose.

Alone.

At least for the moment the reporters did not see her. Being "vertically challenged" was a plus in this case, as she could easily lean against an SUV and have the perfect cover.

She waited in hopes that he would come out soon, the good doctor, who would most likely have taken one of the witness spaces in the parking lot. She had seen him in conversation with Colby in the hallway before her off-the-cuff press conference. Maybe she'd be able to catch him.

And do what? Something, anything. Get a look on his face. Find out what was going on. Because whatever it was, it stunk.

Ten minutes. Fifteen. She kept looking into her shoulder bag, pretending to rummage, whenever someone walked by. Pretty soon she'd have to make a move, or a security guard would start asking questions.

Twenty minutes. And then out he came.

He even walked arrogantly, this O'Connor. He stopped when he saw her, and his whole body seemed to clench.

"Business done for the day?" Lindy said.

O'Connor reached into his pocket. "What are you doing out here?"

"What did you think you were doing in there?"

"You mean testifying?"

"That's what you call it?"

"Excuse me, but I—"

"You lied to me."

His face tightened as he pulled out his car keys. "I did nothing of the kind."

"You told me you didn't know anything about my client. But two years ago—"

"As I recall our conversation, Ms. Fields, you did not ask me if I had examined your client."

"Don't you think that little bit of information was important?"

"I don't volunteer that kind of information. You should know that would be improper."

"Then you said you weren't going to give expert testimony."

"I was contacted by Mr. Colby after you called. I changed my mind."

"Why? Money?"

"I don't have to—"

"And you told me Darren was not mentally sound."

O'Connor's eyes hardened. "You have selective memory, Ms. Fields. As I recall, we talked about likelihoods."

"But now you're sure?"

"In my opinion Darren DiCinni is competent. That's my opinion now."

"What about sane?"

"Ms. Fields, I—"

"Field. The name is Field, no *s*."

O'Connor jangled his keys. "I really can't talk to you anymore."

"Did you ever ask Darren about God?"

The doctor singled out a key then looked at Lindy. "Off the record, Ms. *Field*, you're not going to get anywhere with that angle. Not these days."

"But what if it's true?"

"It won't fly." He made a move toward his car.

"Why'd you put me off, Doctor? Just answer me that."

He did not answer. He unlocked his Jaguar, got in. Just before pulling out he lowered the window. "Do not contact me again," he said.

5.

They were demons, and Darren knew it.

They had him back in his cage now, his keepers. They would try to get him to dis God, but he would ignore them, wait them out. Beat them. They pretended to be jail guards, and sometimes they faked like they were on his side.

They would talk to him sometimes.

He wouldn't answer. You don't talk to demons, you stare them down.

And that's what he did.

No way he was going to be fooled.

So he stared. And he blocked out voices.

He would beat them, and God would approve.

6.

Everett Woodard had been Lindy's favorite law professor at Southwestern. He taught criminal law and she could still recite the flash cards created to help her study for his legendary exams. Like the M'Naughten rule for the insanity defense: *Mental disease or defect of reason + did not know nature and quality of act—or if did know, did not know it was wrong.*

Today, she wanted to talk to him about this rule. Darren's case was all about the insanity defense, and Woodard knew it backward and forward.

Woodard greeted her warmly in his cramped office. He had sounded a bit tired over the phone, most likely due to his prodigious work habits. At fifty-two, Woodard still logged long hours doing appellate work, mostly for indigent clients. He'd grown up in poverty in Inglewood and was kept out of gang life by a strong mother. He earned his success and could have made a high six-figure salary at any of a number of large law firms. But he chose instead to train new lawyers and work on behalf of those who could not afford legal representation.

"So here's the walking news story," Woodard said.

"Don't believe everything you read."

"In your case, I think I will. Who else would give the DA a public tongue-lashing like that? My my."

"Was I out of line?"

Woodard flashed a smile that made him look like a little boy on a holiday. "Not in my book. You might've gone too easy. But I'm not the judge."

"Oh yeah. That. I guess I need a lawyer. Think you can—"

"Consider it done. And get a good apology ready."

"Apology!"

"Lindy," he said like a scolding parent.

"Oh, all right."

Woodard's office was crammed with books of all sorts, from law to sociology to criminology to literature.

"But if I'm going to do that," Lindy said, "I want you to testify for me."

"Testify? About what?"

"Mental state. *Mens rea.*"

"I'm not a mental-health expert."

"Mental-health experts aren't worth the paper their lousy degrees are written on."

"Sounds like you had yourself a bad experience."

"The yahoo who testified is sleaze on ice. My guy couldn't get Darren to talk at all. Foster's not going to rule for me with dueling experts, so I need your testimony on what the law *means*. In class we talked about the M'Naughten rule, and we came up on the whole issue of what *know* means."

"And what do you remember?"

"Still the professor, eh?"

"It never ends."

"All right, then I will prove to you that getting the top grade in your class was no fluke."

"I'm all ears."

"At issue is the meaning of the word *know*. It can mean either being intellectually aware or having a moral appreciation."

"Explain."

"Well, I may know that it is wrong to kill someone, in the sense that I can articulate those words and therefore have some concept of what wrong means. But in order to be sane I must also have the capacity to appreciate the wrongfulness of my actions. Most jurisdictions leave it to the jury to hash it out."

"Well done. You get an *A* on this part of the exam."

"Now I'll ask you a question: If you were convinced that God told you to do something, you would think that was good, right?"

Woodard nodded. "That's called *command hallucination*, a very tough mental nut to crack."

"But what if a person really believes it's God talking?"

"The problem is proving that. All you have is the subject saying that's what was going on in his mind."

"But here's my angle: What if you're a kid? You don't have the background, the experience of life yet. Your brain is still forming. You're more susceptible."

"But the judge and then a jury; that's what you've got to worry about. The God-told-me-to defense, or the devil-made-me defense, these don't fly anymore. People are just too cynical, even when it comes to kids."

"Can I give it a try? Can I make an argument to you?"

Woodard smiled. He had always loved interplay, often vigorous, with his students. "Be my guest. But I warn you, I'll fire back."

"I wouldn't have it any other way."

Lindy paced in front of Woodard, as she might in front of a jury. "To be guilty of a crime means not just that you commit an act, but that you also have *mens rea*, a guilty mind."

Woodard folded his arms across his chest. "Continue."

"Because in this country, we only punish people who are *responsible*. That's the basic premise of the criminal law."

"You're making a speech. Make your argument."

"You can't punish someone who is insane, because he doesn't have a guilty mind."

"That's circular. Tell me *why* we can't punish him."

"Because it is immoral to punish someone without cause, and none of the justifications for punishment exist in the case of the insane person."

"Explain."

"Let's take a hypothetical. A two-year-old knows how to fire a gun. He's seen it on TV. He finds his daddy's gun and fires it at his daddy, killing him. Is he guilty of murder?"

"I concede that he is not."

"Well, what if a baby in a thirteen-year-old body kills? We would say that a thirteen-year-old with a baby's mind does not have criminal responsibility, wouldn't we?"

"The line is very fine."

"But there is a line. If there is no line, law loses meaning. We don't punish people who are not responsible for their actions."

"Tell me why not."

"Because punishment without responsibility doesn't fit with any theory of justice. Take retribution, the revenge theory. Someone must suffer for the purposeful harm they have done to others. But it is immoral to make someone suffer who does not deserve to suffer. Only a guilty mind justifies such suffering. Otherwise, punishment is merely torture."

"What about other theories?"

"How about deterrence? We punish wrongdoers to send a message to potential wrongdoers. But those who are insane cannot process the message. Deterrence simply doesn't apply to those who cannot be rational."

Woodard nodded but kept his skeptical air. "There are still other theories."

Lindy thrilled at being in the thick of an argument, just like when she'd been in his class, speaking with all her energy because the law *mattered.*

"Education. The punishment of criminals educates the public about what we consider good and evil. But if we punish the insane, are we not educating the public that inflicting pain on the mentally weak is good?"

"Any more?"

"Rehabilitation. Here, punishment is supposed to help the offender return to society. This theory has fallen on hard times, and no one buys it much anymore. But in the case of the insane, it fits perfectly. Because we *treat* insane people in the hope that they can get better."

"And what if they don't?"

"They remain in a facility. But that facility is not a prison."

"What about those who say the insanity defense should be abolished? It's been abused."

"Oh, really? When it works less than 1 percent of the time? How can you possibly call that abuse?"

"Because it's the rich-man's defense, effective only for the ones who can afford to hire top lawyers and experts."

"That's no reason to deny it to those who deserve it."

"Deserve?"

"Yes!" Lindy was heated now, her argumentative furnace set on full. She was in the grip of something and let it have its way. "They deserve compassion, don't they, if they're mentally ill through no fault of their own? That's what gets me about the mob mentality. Somebody kills; everybody wants to string him up! How is this different from the lynch mobs of a hundred years ago?"

Woodard, still playing the devil's advocate, answered with commensurate heat. "People are sick and tired of criminals getting away with murder."

"It's not murder if they're insane!"

"You're arguing in circles again. These people are dangerous and shouldn't be allowed on the street. If they go into a hospital they can get out, maybe kill again."

"I'm not . . ." Breath left her, like she'd been punched. "Don't you see what I'm saying? . . . I can't lose him! I can't . . . Wayne . . ."

"Lose him? You're a lawyer not a—"

Lindy put her hand on her throat.

"What is it, Lindy?"

She couldn't speak. She sat heavily in a chair, her mind swirling. The name. She'd said the name.

"Lindy, what's wrong?"

She didn't answer.

"Let me get you a glass of water."

"No."

"Who's Wayne?"

"My brother," she said.

"I didn't know you had a brother."

Lindy looked at her professor. "I lost him, see? I lost him."

Woodard pulled up a chair near her and sat, silent, waiting for her to talk if she chose to.

She closed her eyes for a long moment.

7.

"It was when my father's drinking got bad," Lindy said. "He was a 'Nam vet and came back changed. Was he a bad man? I don't know. All I know is he got drunk all the time, and by the time I was fourteen he was beating up my mom, he would hit me, and sometimes he would hit my little brother."

"Wayne," Woodard said.

"Yes. When dad would come home, screaming drunk, I used to take Wayne and hide in the closet with him. We protected each other there. I'd say to him, 'We'll stay together, you and me.' And he'd say it back. 'Together, you and me.'"

She paused, letting the black memory out. Maybe in doing so, it would finally leave her alone.

"This one night, there was a storm, and we heard him yelling up the walk. Mom told us to get to our rooms. I took Wayne to the closet with me. But then I heard my mom scream in pain, and I couldn't take it. I ran out. I saw him slapping her. I don't know. I forgot everything and ran at him as fast as I could. I threw myself at him. We went down. I was on top of him. I smelled the whisky on him. I'll never forget that smell."

It came back to her, turning her stomach again.

"He was strong. Even with his beer belly and war wounds, he had iron hands. He grabbed me by the throat. He lifted me off him like I was a pillow. He got on his knees, holding me. I couldn't breathe. He slapped my face with his other hand. My mother screamed and tried to pry his hand off my neck. I was sure I was dead."

Lindy spoke with a distant voice now, almost as if she were hearing this account for the first time.

"He didn't let go, and I was starting to fade. And then, suddenly, his hand left me. I fell on the floor. And then he fell next to me. And I saw blood on the floor. I thought it was mine. But it wasn't. It was my father's. I looked up and saw Wayne standing there. He was ten years old. He had this look on his face . . ."

Lindy felt tears coming and bit her lip. She had to finish.

"He was scared. And I saw what he'd done. He'd taken a kitchen knife and stabbed my father in the side."

The blackness in her mind deepened. "My father made an animal sound, an awful animal scream, and he got up and hit Wayne in the face. He hit so hard . . . it was like hitting a soft melon. The sound of it . . . Wayne went down. He went down . . ." Lindy slumped in her chair.

Woodard touched her arm. "You don't have to say more."

"Wait." She straightened up, her vision blurred by tears. "My father saw what he'd done and he ran out of the house. Wayne was on the floor. He wasn't moving. I went to him and my mom was screaming and crying. I called 911. I was aware enough to do that. They found my father in his car, dead. He ran into a telephone pole across from my elementary school. They said it was drunk driving, pure and simple, but I wonder if he ran into it on purpose. I think he wanted to kill himself for a long time."

She took a moment to gather herself for the hardest part.

"Wayne never came out of it. He hung on in a coma for a week. But he never came out of it. I lost him, see? I was the one who was supposed to protect him, and I lost him . . ." She was starting to choke on words, sobs coming up like irregular beats of her heart.

"When they buried him I didn't go . . . I couldn't take it . . . I didn't go. I stayed in the closet . . ."

"Lindy—"

She buried her face in his shoulder and he held her, the way her father never had.

NINE

† † †

1.

Sunday, Lindy turned to Roxy just outside the church doors. "I have this terrible feeling I don't belong here."

Lindy's stomach actually roiled, the way Dorothy's must have when she stepped out of the farmhouse into the land of Oz. Last time she'd been to church with Roxy, Lindy came as a one-time visitor. This time, she was here not just because Roxy wanted her to be, but also because some restless need beckoned her. God ideas had been klunking around in her head. The DiCinni defense had something to do with it, but even apart from that, she realized she wanted to *know*.

After talking about Wayne to Everett Woodard, her need to know had grown into an insatiable hunger.

Even so, she felt like an imposter.

"This is church." Roxy took Lindy's arm as they joined the crowd entering the front doors. "Everybody belongs here."

"You sound like an advertisement."

"You going to be a poop about this or what?"

"Much better."

Roxy punched her in the shoulder.

Inside the auditorium, the worship team was pounding out a song, the congregation standing and clapping. The atmosphere was sort of fun, which was a shock to Lindy's system. Church, fun? Well, why not?

At least she could relax a little. Recharge. Let her brain rest. This was Sunday, the big day of rest, right? Relax and forget, for just a little while, about the case everyone was talking about. And no cameras. She could be anonymous in a crowd for a change.

They found seats on the outer edge of the human sea, which was fine with Lindy. Travis Kellman joined them.

There was more upbeat music, some announcements, a soloist—a girl of about eighteen who could really belt out a song—then the featured attraction. That's the way Lindy thought of it, anyway.

The big preacher. The sermonator.

Pastor Clark (as Roxy called him) still had the stage presence that had previously impressed her. This morning, though, he didn't have that glint in his eye, or the energy. He looked serious, which made Lindy all the more interested in what he was going to say.

"As we all know, for over a month this community has been reflecting on a terrible tragedy," he said. "Six innocent people, five of them children, gunned down in an act of senseless violence."

An electric jolt shot through Lindy.

"When such things happen, right in our own backyard, we can't help but be affected. Here in our own congregation, one family was affected directly. And as the church, we must be ready to be there for them."

Heat filled Lindy's head.

Pastor Clark said. "I can't help but ask, Where was God? I know many of you ask the same question. It's human. It's understandable."

"You all right?" Roxy whispered.

Lindy rubbed her temples. "No."

2.

Seated in the far left corner, Mona thought, *Yeah. Where? You got an answer for me? It better be good.*

She tried to ignore the heads that turned her way. Friends, mostly. Well-intentioned people. But she did not want their looks right now. Why hadn't Pastor Clark cleared this with her first if he was so concerned about her?

And then it hit her, the reason Brad insisted she come to church this morning. Pastor Clark had called Brad. She was sure of it. And Brad hadn't told her. So it was a conspiracy.

She almost walked out then, but Brad deserved at least this much time. He sat silently next to her, his nose still red from her right cross with the cookbook.

"A prophet in the Bible raised that very same question. His name was Jeremiah, and he was the prophet in Judah when the Babylonian army brought it to ruin."

Her mind tuned him out. She didn't want to hear about prophets or Babylon or anything else for that matter.

All she wanted to hear was Matthew's voice.

If you want to do something, God, do that.

3.

"Come on," Travis Kellman said. "I want you to meet our pastor."

"No, thanks," Lindy said.

"He'd love to meet you," Roxy said.

The three of them were moving slowly toward the exit with the rest of the crowd. Lindy couldn't help but notice most of them were well dressed. There was some money here.

"I don't want to meet your pastor," Lindy insisted. "He seems like a very nice guy but I—"

"Come on." Travis was already moving ahead, like a point man in some military operation.

"I don't want to," Lindy said.

"Don't be so shy," Roxy said.

"I'm not shy. I'm annoyed. I want to go home."

"Real quick. Do it for me."

"You playing that card again?"

"What card?"

"The do-it-for-me card."

"That's a terrible thing—"

Lindy sighed. "You're right. I'm sorry. Okay. I'll say hi to the guy. Then can we go home?"

"Sure. Come on." Roxy started to make her way through the crowd.

Lindy followed reluctantly. What was she going to say to this pastor anyway?

Make it an experiment, Lindy told herself. *See what happens. Maybe you'll get a sign from God! Wouldn't that be a kick in the head? Maybe God would deliver a little good news about how to handle the DiCinni case.*

The crowd thinned out a bit in the foyer. A relief. Travis was waving to them from the far end, where a smaller crowd had gathered. No doubt that's where the pastor was, like some human magnet attracting the shards of humanity.

With a sigh, Lindy followed Roxy.

They came to the outskirts of the pack, and indeed Lindy saw Pastor Clark shaking hands and smiling in the midst. And there was something magnetic about him. Lindy likened him to some of the highly successful trial lawyers she'd seen in action.

And then, behind her, she heard a scream.

4.

"Get her out of here!" Mona cried out. She could not believe the killer's lawyer was here, in her church.

When the lawyer turned, Mona noted with perverse satisfaction that the look on the woman's face was as wide-eyed as Mona's soul.

When no answer came—the small assemblage seeming stunned at Mona's outburst—she looked at Lindy Field directly and screamed again, "Get out!"

Mona was vaguely aware of Brad coming up behind her. She could almost feel the voice coming out of him. *How is poor Mona snapping this time?*

Or maybe Brad had given up on her.

The killer's lawyer stood shaking her head, like a person looking at a horrible accident from the sidewalk, speechless. Had this been any other woman, Mona probably would have felt sorry for her, maybe even rushed up to her and put an arm around her shoulder and told her everything would be all right.

No, everything would not be all right. It would never be all right. And it would never be all right as long as she was in Mona's church.

And then, as if the knot of people suddenly came to collective awareness, various people rushed into the breach and started trying to bring order to the situation.

At which point Mona lost all control. "No no no no no." She repeated the word over and over, like a mantra. It suddenly felt like her only link to sanity. Get rid of the woman and she would be safe. Matthew would be safe. The church was stained now, stained by this lawyer.

She had been right about Brad. He was there with his arms suddenly around her, squeezing her as if to strangle her with calmness. She struggled against his arms and broke free.

"Get her out of here!" Mona looked at the killer's lawyer. For a long moment their eyes locked. Then Mona was led away by some arms around her shoulders.

5.

Sunday afternoon.

They let him have his half hour on the roof. The caged roof. What they called the exercise yard. He and the other K–10s, in the little cages within the cage.

The deputy unshackled him and in he went, into the iron closet. He knew about closets. Closed spaces didn't scare him. He'd been in enough of them, locked in darkness. What was outside the closed spaces is what scared him.

They had a thing you could use to do pull-ups or leg raises. He'd seen the others do it, guys with big biceps covered with tattoos.

The ones who talked to him at night.

Smoked all them kids, dawg? Think that make you somethin'? I'll make you somethin'. You look me up when you out.

Would he get out?

Yes, the answer came. Yes. God told him so. He didn't even have to do a thing.

The deputy locked the cage.

He wondered what his lawyer was doing. What was her thing any-way? The way she looked at him. Like she was interested.

He was interested in her and he didn't know why. Maybe because he never had a mom or sister.

He sat down in the corner. He wondered why he never cried. He wondered why he wasn't normal.

Part of him wished he could be normal, but the other part, the stronger part, always overcame that. Because he heard the voice of God. *You're not normal. You're all powerful. You will defeat them all.*

He let the voice go on and on, saying familiar things, things he'd heard his whole life. Because he had never been without the voice of God. Never. Ever since he could remember hearing things, he heard the voice.

Leaning against the bars of the cage, the voice had its way.

And then, suddenly, a new thought. A brand-new one. It came into his head as clear as a guard's voice telling him it was shower time.

Clear and new and full of power.

Join me, God said.

TEN

✝ ✝ ✝

1.

Lindy woke up Monday morning with a spiritual hangover.

That's what she thought of it, anyway. Too much religion, too much thinking of otherworldly stuff.

The incident at the church was still an open wound. By now she had calmed down from the anger and the hurt. Roxy told her who the woman was, the mother of one of the kids Darren shot. Lindy guessed she was entitled to freak. But at a church? What kind of religion did they teach there?

She tried to forget about it with coffee and KNX Newsradio. The morning report hit on political intrigue down at city hall, where the mayor was trying to explain to the Latino community why he hadn't appointed a Hispanic as police chief. Just another contribution to L.A. politicians' usual political flummery. There was some sports news, but thankfully nothing about the DiCinni case.

That's because they were in the purgatory between a ruling on Darren's competency and a preliminary hearing. And Lindy had her work cut out for her, not to mention a contempt citation hanging over her head.

The hearing was scheduled to resume at eleven o'clock. That gave Lindy time to fire up her laptop and look at the *L.A. Times* online. Before that she made a quick check of her email. When she did, she saw a message waiting for her with the subject line *Your inquiry re: police.*

She opened it.

You inquired about information re: conspiracies. What do you know?

And that was it. No name. She looked at the email address, a cryptic mix of letters and numbers from some server she didn't know, and certainly not from the conspiracy Web address. That didn't necessarily mean anything. Web sites often forwarded emails to other addresses. But it was a little curious.

Now the author was asking her for information. She would have to tread carefully, or risk committing thoughts to email that could be distributed anywhere.

She replied: *Who are you? How'd you get started in all this?* and sent it off.

Probably a dead end, but at this point she would take anything.

She clicked her bookmark for the conspiracy blog site. No updates since her last visit.

She surfed a little more, scanning some legal sites, then her cell phone chimed "Dream On," the Aerosmith tune that was Roxy's ring.

"What's up?" Lindy said.

"Meet me at Starbucks. I've got stuff for you."

"Like what?"

"I've been earning my keep."

"Anything good?"

"Just get here."

Their usual meeting place, for any reason, was the Starbucks on Platt in West Hills. In good weather they had a favorite table outside. Lindy pulled up her Harley and saw Roxy waiting.

Lindy ordered a triple-venti white-chocolate mocha and sat down. "I've got half an hour, then it's back to court. So what've you got?"

"It's what I don't have that bothers me." Roxy pulled a pen-scratched piece of yellow legal paper from a manila folder. "Your client's father, Drake DiCinni?"

"Yeah."

"I can't trace him. He doesn't have a backward trail."

"What's that tell you?"

"Maybe the guy's real name isn't Drake DiCinni. Maybe he changed it."

"Which would bring up the question of why."

"Sure."

"What else?"

"Maybe he's covering his own trail. Maybe he's gotten rid of some records."

"Can he do that?"

"Some can. I'll keep looking. But there's also the chance somebody *else* tinkered with his records."

"Who?"

"That's the question. It's all speculation right now. I'm just throwing things out. In any case, it looks like there's something majorly off in this guy's background."

"But that might not have anything to do with Darren. He might have other reasons for covering his tracks."

Roxy nodded. "And you don't believe that for a minute, do you?"

Lindy smiled. "Maybe I'll just go pay Mr. DiCinni another visit this afternoon. You want to come?"

"I'm meeting Travis. We're going to the Getty."

"Tough life—" Lindy looked up and almost fell out of her chair.

"Hello, Pastor Clark," Roxy said. "Lindy, you remember our pastor."

Up close, he looked down-to-earth. He wore jeans and a burgundy T-shirt with his church's logo on it.

Lindy looked at Roxy. "What a coincidence."

"All right, I set it up, okay? Clark asked me what the best way to talk to you was."

"You're not going to yell at me, are you?" Lindy said.

"No, no yelling," he said. "I wanted to apologize for what happened at church on Sunday."

"No problemo, Reverend."

"May I?" Clark indicated a chair. Lindy nodded, and he sat. "Mrs. Romney, the woman who screamed at you, she was clearly out of line, even though you might understand why."

"Of course I do. She lost a son. I'm defending the accused."

"And I wanted you to know that I'm very sorry it happened, and I hope you might give us another try sometime."

Lindy grimaced. "I'm not so sure that's a good idea. You want a notorious defense lawyer in your midst?"

"Believe me, we have others."

"Notorious?"

"Maybe not notorious."

"I wouldn't want to cause a disturbance. This woman probably would rather I didn't show up."

"You're welcome any time."

"Thanks. Really. And for what it's worth, you preach a . . . you do a really good job preaching." She looked at her watch. "And speaking of apologies . . ."

2.

"It's George Mahoney."

Mona opened the door.

"Is this a good time?" he said. "Brad said it might be."

"What's this about?" Mona couldn't decide how to respond, knowing George Mahoney from church, in a passing way, and knowing he had once been a policeman. He was now active in the community in some fashion.

"If I could just have a few minutes."

"I'm sorry," Mona said. "It's just that I—"

"Sure. I know." His voice was soft and understanding. She could imagine him making all kinds of people feel comfortable.

"Come in, please."

He accepted her offer of coffee and she brewed a fresh pot, cleaning the filter twice before brewing, measuring the coffee carefully.

He was looking at the family photo on the piano in the living room when she came in with the coffee.

"He was a fine-looking boy," he said.

"You take anything in your coffee?"

"Black."

They sat. A simmering discomfort bubbled just below the surface of Mona's chest.

George Mahoney was a few years older than she. His reddish-brown hair was thick and perfect.

"I talked to Brad on the phone this morning," George said.

"He called you?"

"I called him. I wanted to see how you all were doing."

"That was nice."

"I mean, this thing has hit the whole church."

"I don't want that."

"No, that's the way it's supposed to be." George leaned forward in his chair, his elbows on his knees, his face earnest. "We're all part of the same body, it says in Corinthians."

Mona nodded.

"I heard about the incident," George said. "You know, with the lawyer."

"I guess everybody's heard. There was even a thing about it in the *Daily News.*"

"I didn't see that."

"Yeah." Mona sighed. "It was buried inside a story about the trial."

"That had to be a shock, seeing her."

"Something came over me. I just couldn't handle her being there. It seemed like . . ."

"A violation?"

"Yes."

George took a sip of coffee, the way he must have done countless times when interviewing witnesses. "What I did see was her little press conference on TV the other day, the one where she ranted against the justice system."

"That was awful."

"It sure was. It was obvious what she was doing, trying to poison the jury pool. I don't think it's going to work, but I hated to see it nonetheless."

"Couldn't someone put a gag order on her or something?"

"Maybe. But that's up to a judge." He paused and Mona realized she was feeling something she hadn't in a long time—*safe.* She was in the presence of a police detective, an honest one, a Christian. She could trust him.

"Let me tell you why I'm here," George said. "I haven't come to see you before this because I thought you needed some time for healing, and I know you still do. But maybe I can help a little."

"Thank you."

"After being on the streets for a long time, and seeing what happens to real people when the justice system is perverted, I saw a need to form a little support group. We don't have a name or anything. We're just a little group of people who have been victims of crime, or whose loved ones have been victimized. And we get together and figure out ways to support each other."

"That sounds nice."

"It really is. And we're active. You know how much good MADD has done."

"Sure."

"They show up in court to support the prosecution of drunk drivers, and they have made a real difference. We want to do the same in other parts of the criminal justice system. We'd like to offer you our support."

"Support?"

"Coming to court with you. Speaking out when this crazy lawyer speaks out. Showing the judge there are real people out here with real justice issues. No need to make any decisions now. But I'll give you my card." He removed one from his wallet. "And if you'd like to come to a meeting, just to see what we're about, that'd be great."

She took his card with its official LAPD design. It felt good in her hand. Like a lifeline of sorts.

3.

"Your Honor," Everett Woodard said, "my client would like to make a statement."

Oh, this was going to be fun. Lindy stood in front of Judge Varner Foster, Leon Colby, the media, and all those family members, imagining the TV images being broadcast around the world. There were probably a billion Chinese watching her eat crow.

"Go ahead, Ms. Field," Judge Foster said.

"I would like to apologize to the court," Lindy said. "And to Mr. Colby, and to the witness, Dr. O'Connor. I was out of line. I lost it, and I shouldn't have. I extend to the court my assurance that it won't happen again."

The judge took his time responding. *This is what it must be like to turn on a spit.*

Finally, he said, "Ms. Field, we all understand this is an unusual case . . ."

We? Everyone in the world but her? One billion Chinese people?

" . . . and it will continue to be so. That makes the imperative of professional ethics and conduct even more critical than usual. When I was a young lawyer—"

Oh no . . .

"—I was known as something of a hothead myself—"

Great! I'm an official hothead now.

"—but I learned through many a trial that the best way to make an impression on judge or jury is to operate with restraint, and poise, and decorum—"

All the things I don't have, right?

"—and that lesson was perhaps the most valuable I ever learned. I would like to pass that lesson on to you, Ms. Field."

Thank you, Judge. And now let's—

"And like my father, I believe the best lessons are those that hurt a little. So I'll impose a fine of eight hundred dollars, and we will consider the matter closed."

Eight hundred? Did he say eight hundred?

"Eminently fair, Your Honor," Everett Woodard said. "Thank you."

Lindy echoed, "Thank you." *Yes, and thanks to all the people of the world watching on television. I am also for world peace . . .*

"Then we are ready to proceed," Judge Foster said. "Dr. O'Connor, will you please retake the stand?"

With a jaundiced eye directed toward Lindy, the doctor came forward and sat in the witness chair.

"Continue your cross, Ms. Field."

Softly, softly.

"Just a few more questions," she said. "Doctor, if a boy the age of Darren DiCinni truly believed that God told him to do something, ordered him to do it, would it be reasonable to conclude that the boy might think it the right thing to do?"

"In this case," the doctor said quickly, "I don't think so."

"How about in *any* case?"

He waved his hand. "Oh, I'm sure anyone can concoct a set of facts that would fit your desired conclusion, but that's not what I see here."

"Your answer then is *yes*?"

"That's not what I said, Ms. Field."

"Your answer is *no*?"

"Please, not what I said either."

"Is it *maybe*? What is it, Doctor?"

"It is what I said, that's all."

Lindy sat down.

"Do you have any more witnesses, Mr. Colby?"

The prosecutor said, "No, Your Honor."

"Ms. Field?"

"I would like to call Professor Everett Woodard to the stand."

"Object as to relevance," Leon Colby said.

"Your Honor," Lindy said, "Professor Woodard is one of the most eminent legal minds in Los Angeles, and his specialty is criminal law. His testimony is relevant on the issue of the legal meaning of *mental competence* for standing trial."

"And while I'm sure Your Honor appreciates the offer," Colby said, "it is quite clear that the judge is the sole interpreter of the law, and if you desire each side to submit briefs, that is your prerogative. But as Professor Woodard's testimony is not of a fact-finding nature, it is therefore irrelevant to this proceeding."

"Yes," Judge Foster said. "I quite agree. While I respect the professor's legal mind, his testimony is not required. Will there be anything else?"

"I would like to ask the court's indulgence," Lindy said. "I want to ask one more mental-health professional to interview my client. It will be done this week, I assure you."

"Denied," Foster said. "Anything else?"

"I will submit the matter to Your Honor," Leon Colby said.

Lindy sighed. "I would argue that the prosecutor has not carried his burden of proof."

"And I would remind the defense," said the judge, "that the burden in a 1368 is on you. And I find that you have not met the burden. I hold the defendant competent to stand trial."

4.

"We are not going to let you go through this alone," George Mahoney told Mona. "You are part of us."

The group called itself Victims of Injustice and Crime, or VOICe, and tonight twenty members gathered in the home of the founder, Benni Roberts. She had welcomed Mona with a hug and words of welcome and support.

The woman had energy and good looks. Around forty, she emanated success, dressed as she was in a St. John suit that looked impervious to wrinkles. She had a pin in her left lapel, all gold and diamonds.

Benni's home, a spacious colonial in the hills of Encino, looked down on the San Fernando Valley. Members filled the living room, most of them wearing large, round VOICe buttons. Each button had a different photograph in the center. It didn't take long for Mona to figure out that these were the pictures of loved ones who had died due to some criminal act.

"Each one of us is concerned with justice, because we've all been touched by crime, and sometimes, by the way the system is set up against victims," Benni explained. "In my own case, three years ago, my son was killed by gang members in a random drive-by. They just pulled up to him on the street, right down here at the corner, and asked him where he was from. Josh didn't know that was a gang challenge. So he said he wasn't from anywhere. One of the gang members pulled out a gun and shot Josh in the face."

Mona listened with a sense of dread and instantly shared grief. This strong woman had been through exactly what Mona was going through. And she had come out on the other side, done something with her grief.

"Josh was only sixteen. The police managed to find two suspects, twin brothers it turned out, who a witness could identify. The police got a search warrant for the mother's house, where the twins lived. They went in and found a gun that matched the description of the gun the witness saw in the hand of the shooter. Ballistics matched the bullet that killed Josh to the gun."

Benni paused, and Mona realized everyone in the room was hanging on her words, as if hearing them for the first time.

"But it turns out the police didn't follow the exact rule for serving the warrant," Benni continued.

George Mahoney added, "It's called the knock-notice rule. It requires police to knock on a door, announce their presence, and wait for a response. Well, they knocked, announced, waited twenty seconds, and went in. A judge ruled that twenty seconds wasn't a long enough wait. Result: the gun could not be used as evidence."

One of the other women in the room said, "Can you believe it?"

Benni said, "I nearly lost my mind. And that's when George, who was one of the police officers, came to me and said we need to do something about this judge. That's all I needed to hear. I started VOICe, and the first thing I did was talk to the press and name that judge. I called him a disgrace. Meantime, his ruling was being appealed. People started making contributions to VOICe, and I was able to hire a great appellate lawyer. That's where the power comes from."

"We got the decision reversed," George said. "Last year we went to trial again."

Mona sighed. "So justice was finally served."

Benni's face hardened. "Oh no. The new judge let the defense lawyer run all over the witness. You see, the witness was also a gang member. A rival gang. The defense lawyer tied him up in knots and the judge let him get away with it."

"What happened?" Mona asked.

"The jury came back with a not-guilty verdict."

"And that's that," George said. "The two scum who did this are walking the streets right now, because they can't be tried again for the crime. Double jeopardy. And all because of two judges who perverted justice."

"But they won't be able to do it for long," Benni said. "We have so many people ready to target them in the next election, they won't be on the bench. That's the power of VOICe."

Power. That's what Mona wanted. Needed. The power to do something. The power to make a difference. The power to help Matthew.

She almost cried out with gratitude. She was home. This was her church.

5.

Lindy knew the crummy little house in Sunland was deserted, even before she reached the door. The lifelessness about the property made it seem suitable for ghosts.

So when she knocked, she didn't expect anyone to answer. Her expectations were borne out.

She decided, since she'd come all this way, to try the back door.

The side yard was a strip of brown grass and dirt patches lining a profusely cracked cinder block wall. Probably the result of earthquakes and neglect. Dust and spatters of dry mud coated the house. An ancient gas meter stuck out from the wall like an old man's chin.

She felt the crush of weeds and dirt clods under her motorcycle boots. She'd never make it as a cat burglar. Especially not with the dog on the other side of the wall barking its fool head off.

The bark sounded mean. Pit-bull mean. There were a lot of them out this way, with owners just as mean, who didn't really care if little Bluto bit off the leg of a postal worker. Some didn't even care when a toddler got chewed to death, which had happened more than once.

The backyard looked like a fading postcard from the fifties. Clothesline posts with drooping wires leaned at odd angles. A cracked cement walkway led from the porch to the unattached garage, a miniature of the house, with windows covered in grime and oily rags.

A fruitless apricot tree twisted out from the center of what had once been a lawn, its spindly limbs pointing in several directions at once.

Lindy stepped up on the concrete slab that was the back porch. A rusted screen separated her from the door. The upper left corner of the screen flapped over, leaving a triangular hole.

Her rattling knock went unanswered.

The pit bull kept barking. He sounded hungry.

She knocked again, then tried the screen door. It creaked open. She tried the inner door, and found it was unlocked.

She opened that door now, stuck her head in. "Hello? Anybody home?"

Nothing.

Maybe they just weren't home. Maybe they were hoping to avoid her. Maybe they were dead in the bathroom.

But she had come all the way out here and wasn't going to just ride away into the sunset. She could wait.

"Turn around," said a voice, the male equivalent of the pit bull's bark. And for that reason alone Lindy was afraid to turn.

"Turn around now."

Her slow rotation brought her face to face with the largest hand-gun she'd ever laid eyes on. And it was held by one of the largest hands she'd ever seen, connected to a tree-trunk arm covered in dark blue tattoos.

At the end of it all was a gray bearded, mean-eyed dude who surely just returned from Hells Angels central casting.

"You're bothering my dog," he said.

6.

Leon Colby examined the list of possible witnesses for the prelimi-nary hearing. His chief investigator, Lorenzo "Larry" Lopez, had con-ducted the initial interviews.

"Like choosing which candy, huh?" Lopez said. He was a pretty good investigator, one Colby had worked with before. Around forty, hard worker, knew the streets. He was dressed in a brown suit and wore his shirt without a tie. Here in Colby's office, with one leg over the arm of a chair, he looked entirely too relaxed.

"I'm not much of a candy eater." Colby scratched his trial goatee, his one superstition. Shave the goatee after a trial. Grow it back for the next one.

"What do you like?"

"Meat. You saw these people face to face. Which ones seemed most credible?"

Lopez shrugged. "They're all pretty good. Some maybe come across better than others, just because that's people, you know?"

"You practicing psychology now?"

"Hey, my brains, your good looks, we got this in the bag."

Colby shook his head. "There's always a weakness in a case. Even one like this."

"I don't see it," Lopez said.

"Look harder."

The investigator pulled his leg off the arm of the chair. "You serious?"

"Yeah, and I expect you to be too."

"Hey, Leon, chill a little."

Colby kept his irritation in check. This wasn't the time for a major face-off, but the man needed to know this case was not a walk in the park. Colby would have to win this thing, and in swift and unambiguous terms, if he was going to make a run at DA. In fact, avoiding a trial altogether would be best of all. A strong showing in the prelim might just convince Lindy Field to hang it up and take a deal, on his terms.

"You going to answer my question?"

"All right, man," Lopez said. His normally jovial face was suddenly all business, business he'd been dragged into. "I think the Kean woman would be good. She had a son out there who didn't get shot, and remembers a lot of details. Also Mrs. Glover."

Colby returned his gaze to the list of names and the chart he'd drawn up earlier in the day.

Victim	Age	Parents
Nick Marosi	11	Viv Marosi (present at game) Jack Marosi (not present); Divorced
James Glover	10	Marian Glover (present) Rick Glover (present)
Matthew Romney	11	Mona Romney (present) Brad Romney (present)
Bobby Landis	11	Robert Landis (present); mother deceased.
Cody Thompson	12	Janelle Thompson (present) Edward Thompson (present); Divorced
Joel Dorai	40	

"Any family for Dorai?" Colby asked.

"Not out here. Some friends."

"How many is some?"

"Two."

"That's not some. That's two. Come on, Larry. Who are these friends?"

Lopez looked at the small spiral notebook in his hand. "A teacher, who he worked with, Kim Fambry. And some guy named Stalboerger."

"Who is?"

"I think he's a computer guy."

"You think?"

"Come on, how deep do you need to go?"

Colby shook his head and scanned the list again. "How about Mrs. Romney? She seemed to have a strong appearance when I met her."

"I don't know," Lopez said. "She seemed to have something going on."

"What's that mean?"

"Like she's ready to blow. I'd wait until trial for her, when the jury's watching."

"We handle this right, maybe we don't need a jury."

Lopez flashed his teeth. "Maybe we need a nomination party, huh?"

"Just what are you saying, Larry?"

"I'm behind you all the way, Leon. You'll make a great DA."

7.

"You mind putting that cannon down?"

The bearded guy held the gun steady and eyed Lindy like she was some sort of bottle for target practice.

"You tell me what you're doing around this house," the guy said.

"I'm a lawyer. I came to interview a witness."

"Lawyer?" The guy looked her up and down. "You look about as much like a lawyer as I do."

"Want me to show you my bar card?"

"Wanna know what I really hate?"

"It wouldn't be a lawyer, would it?"

"Public defender got me ten years once. Did most of it in Soledad. Wanna know why I got it?"

Lindy didn't say anything. She knew she was going to be told.

"Because my guy didn't lift two fingers to do any work. I tried my own appeal, ineffective assistance of counsel, got squat. Eight hard in Soledad. Thank you, Mr. Lawyer."

The unforgiving eye of the barrel of the gun stared, unblinking, at Lindy's nose. Cold snakes of disquiet squirmed in her stomach. This section of the Valley was known for its denizens of the crystal-meth trade, guys who shouldn't be crossed. Most of them had done hard time and had very little to lose if they ever wanted to snuff out inquisitive and unwanted pests.

"I'm looking for Drake DiCinni," Lindy said. She thought the direct approach, and the truthful one, was best under the circumstances.

The bearded man squinted. "Don't know him."

"Does he live here?"

"Just told you, I don't know the dude."

"Do you know the people who live here?"

"This a deposition?"

"No, it's assault with a deadly weapon. Now why don't you quit messing around and lower that stupid gun?"

I'm dead.

But then the guy smiled. His teeth were like pylons coated with ocean grime. He lowered the gun. "Not even loaded."

"Not loaded!"

"You think I want to shoot somebody? I ain't going back to the slam."

Lindy realized her heart rate was dangerously high. "Are you crazy?"

"Just a good neighbor. Alice don't like no snoops."

"Listen, I am representing a kid accused of murder, okay? I'm not snooping. I really need to talk to the kid's father. But you say you don't know him."

"I don't know anything about his kid."

"Then you do know the guy who lives here."

"Yeah, a guy lives here. Friend of Alice. But his name ain't whatever you said it was."

"DiCinni."

"Not it."

"You mean that's not the name he gave you."

The big guy crossed his arms, tucking the gun below one of his massive biceps. "You're not by any chance a cop, are you?"

"I'm telling you, I'm just a lawyer trying to do what your lawyer didn't do. Some work."

The man nodded. "I believe you. It's a good thing too. 'Cause if you were a cop I might forget myself and blow your head off."

"I thought you said your gun wasn't loaded."

"Did I say that?" He pointed his gun at the apricot tree and fired. The explosion scattered a huge chunk of tree all over the yard.

"My mistake," he said.

8.

Why can't I pray?

For a long time Mona sat on the edge of her bed, asking herself the question. Was it because she had done something terribly wrong?

Was it because she had chased Brad away, refusing even to talk to him?

Why couldn't she pray about that?

The quiet house, haunted by the memories of Matthew's voice—she tried to will it back, the sound of his calling. From the bathtub when he was four and cried, "I'm overfloating!" Or when he accidentally dropped an army figure into the toilet and ran through the house shouting, "Man overboard!"

Mona put her head in her hands. *Why can't I pray?*

This time an answer came, a voice in her head at least as real as the remembered voice of her son.

Because there is work yet unfinished.

Work? What work?

Mona did not need a voice to tell her. She knew. The killer's lawyer had to be stopped.

And Mona was filled with fire.

9.

The closest Lindy had ever come to dying was the time one of her client's brothers mistook her for a narc and fired a shot close to her head. It seemed an intentional miss, a warning. But later Lindy discovered the guy was jacked up on PCP and had really tried to shoot her.

And now she had this crazy man firing guns and playing with her head. The gun he had just fired into a tree had been pointed at her face, and what if that had accidentally gone off?

Was her luck running out?

"Now you better be moving along," the man said.

Lindy didn't need to be invited twice. She stepped down off the porch and started for the side of the house.

"I'll just walk you," the man said, coming alongside like a prom date.

Great.

"Name's Wolf," the big man said, his smile halfway between amused and homicidal. "What's yours?"

"You don't mind, let's just leave it at this."

"That's not very sociable. After all we been through."

When they got to the front, Wolf put his hand on Lindy's arm, stopping her. "That your ride?" He was looking at her Harley.

"Yeah."

"Sweet." He went to it, ran his hand along the seat, bent over and looked at the engine. "Very sweet. Can you keep 'er on the butt?"

"Of course." Now, suddenly, they were pals.

"Little thing like you?" He loped his leg over the seat and settled onto the bike. He kept his gun in one hand and stroked the Harley with the other.

"You seem like a farm fresh," he said.

Lindy blinked.

"Good egg. That's what my pappy always said."

Pappy?

"So what's your handle?"

"Lindy Field."

"You're doing a capital case?"

"Not death penalty. A juvenile."

A light went on in his eyes. "You repping that kid who shot up the baseball field?"

Lindy nodded.

"Oh man, you are gonna need help. And I might be able to give you some."

"How—"

A horn blared as a dusty red pickup rolled by on the street. Wolf waved at the driver. A woman. He continued to watch as the truck pulled into the house next door, the house he had presumably come from, with the yard and the upset pit bull.

"My woman," Wolf said. "Been married twenty-two years December."

"Oh?"

"She stuck with me, all the time I was inside. You don't just find those kind of women walking around the mall."

"Right." All this talk of married bliss from an ex-felon, sitting on her motorcycle with a gun, was too absurd, even for L.A.

"So whattaya want to know?" he said.

A lot of things. "The man who lives here, with Alice. You know him well?"

Wolf shook his head. "Not too. Been over here a couple times to break bread."

"What's his name?"

"Michael something."

"What's he look like?"

Wolf described someone very much like the Drake DiCinni she'd interviewed, but when he mentioned the spiderweb tattoo on the back of his neck, that nailed it.

"And you're sure he called himself Michael?"

"Yeah. That's all I know about the dude. You saying he's the kid's father?"

"What I'm saying."

"Makes sense."

"Why?"

"He talked about his kid, but didn't say much. Got the feeling he was jacked about something. Wouldn't say. But if that's his kid, it seems to me a good reason to change your name. Around here people do it all the time."

"Do you have any idea where he is, or might be?"

Wolf shook his head. "Maybe to see his old lady. She's gotta be going through hell too."

Lindy cocked her head. "Drake . . . Michael, he has an old lady?"

"The kid's mother, yeah. He said they split up."

"He said he has an ex-wife who is alive?"

"I don't know if he said 'wife,' but they were together and now they're not. Kinda like a country song, huh?"

"Have you got any idea where this woman might be? The name of any city or anything like that?"

"Nope." Wolf slid off the motorcycle. "I gotta go tend to my own wife. She'll be wantin' me to fire up the barbecue."

"Wait!" Lindy fished in her back pocket and brought out a wrinkled business card. "Will you call me when they come back?"

Wolf took the card and gave it a glance. "I dunno . . ."

"At least tell this Michael to call me. Tell him I need to talk to him. About his son."

"I'll keep this." Wolf put the card in the pocket of his shirt. "You never know. I may get busted, may need a lawyer. You look better'n most."

10.

Lindy took the 118 freeway home, so she could roar. She could
always go faster on the 118, even though she had to keep a watch
for the Chippies. The highway patrol loved to park on the shoulders
of on-ramps. It was practically entrapment.

As she roared along, she mulled over her odd encounter with the
domesticated biker named Wolf. Was he just messing with her? The
whole episode with the gun was weird. Besides which, she'd had
biker clients before, and few of them were well versed in the truth-
telling department.

And where was Drake DiCinni?

She blasted down the 118 to Topanga, then dropped down into
the Valley. On clear days, she could see all the way across the Valley
from here, but lately it had been hazy. She hated that. She liked to
see where she lived and worked. It gave her a sense of belonging,
even hope.

Well, not today. She headed for Box Canyon. When she reached
the reservoir she started to feel like she was home, a comfortable feeling. She could talk things over with Cardozo. He would not pull a
gun on her. He might exercise his claws a little, but that was as bad
as it got.

When she walked in, Cardozo mewed and rubbed the side of her
leg.

"How you doin, huh? Been watching the homestead for meanies?"

She was about to turn on the TV news when she saw the blinking message light on her machine. Her cell phone was still hooked
up to the charger in the kitchen. The message light on the cell was
also flashing.

Lindy chose the machine first. It was Roxy. "Where are you? Why
don't you have your cell? Call me immediately."

The message on her cell phone was also from Roxy. Lindy held
down the 1 key, Roxy's speed dial.

She picked up after the second ring.

"Hey girl," Lindy said. "What's the big—"

"I've been trying to reach you—"

"I know and now—"

"Haven't you heard?" Roxy's voice was rising.

"Heard what?"

"Darren . . ."

"What's wrong?"

Roxy took a deep breath, almost a gasp. "He hanged himself."

11.

Mona carefully cut around the lawyer's head. As she did so she looked into the eyes of the image staring out at her from the newspaper. What was behind those eyes? How could this woman defend guilty people?

How could the system of justice, so called, allow lawyers to make such a mockery of the truth? If only they could be cut down before they did more harm.

Mona finished removing the head from the body and placed it on one side of the large piece of butcher paper she had laid out on the table. The collage was coming together, a permanent reminder of what was at stake. A tribute to Matthew and his teammates.

It was beginning to look a little like those Mafia charts she'd seen on TV shows. At the last VOICe meeting, she suggested that copies of pictures be swapped among the victims' families so all of them would have reminders of the dead. It seemed like a good idea to the majority, a way of sharing the grief.

For Mona, it was a way to get the pictures she needed to complete the chart. The only picture she did not want was the picture of the killer. She would not dignify him by placing his face on the same page with those who had died at his hand. She would, however, put on his lawyer. She needed an object to absorb her hate.

The Bible said to hate what was evil.

The aesthetics of sticking the pictures to the page did not concern Mona. She used double-stick tape. But she carefully calculated where to place each one. She supposed this was some form of therapy, and then promptly forgot all about such trivial things. This was deadly business.

The phone rang, startling her. For some reason she picked up this time. Something told her it was one of the VOICe members.

It was Brad.

"I had to check on you," he said.

Yes, she supposed he had to.

"I'm doing fine," she said.

"Have you heard the news?"

"What news?"

"Oh, Mona. I wish I could be there with you. Can I come over?"

"What news are you talking about?"

"The defendant, he tried to kill himself."

Mona felt a cold knife pass through her. "Tried?"

"They saved him, apparently."

"Why?"

"Excuse me?"

"I appreciate your calling."

"Mona, you sound so formal. It's killing me what's going on between us."

"I'm sorry, Brad."

"When can I see you?"

"I'll let you know."

After hanging up, Mona sat in front of the faces again. She was glad she couldn't see the killer. Suicide? That would have been one way to finish the story.

I wonder if it was a ploy to gain sympathy.

12.

The Los Angeles County–USC Medical Center was a jutting, monstrous organism of a structure east of downtown. With wings seeming to sprout from other wings, it had a Hydra-like quality about it, as if it would always be growing some nasty new appendage.

In truth, it needed to grow, though it had more square feet than the Pentagon. Already it treated about 800,000 patients a year, mostly poor, mostly emergencies—people shot, stabbed, beaten, or broken up in accidents of one kind or another. And inmates from county jail in life-or-death emergencies.

After checking at the desk, Lindy located Darren's room on the fourth floor. A cop stood at the closed door.

"I'm Darren DiCinni's lawyer," Lindy said.

"And?" the cop said, his expression unflinching.

"I'm going to see him."

"Not now."

"I said I'm his lawyer. I want to see him."

"How do I know?"

"Know what?"

"You're a lawyer."

"Oh, please." She fished out her bar card and showed it to him.

"I don't really care," the cop said. "I have my duty."

"Your duty does not include separating people from their constitutional rights."

He folded his arms but didn't move.

"Let her in," a voice said. Lindy turned and saw Larry Lopez.

"How you doing, Lindy?" He smiled.

"Larry. Long time." She didn't smile back at the prosecution's chief investigator in the Marcel Lee case. Lindy's blistering cross-examination of him almost got her thrown in jail for contempt.

"Missed you," he said.

"You want to tell me what happened to my client?"

Lopez shrugged. "He used a strip of blanket around the neck, twisted it into a knot himself. Pretty bad attempt. He passed out but didn't cash his chips."

"He wasn't on suicide watch?"

"Somebody must've blinked."

"I'll bet."

Lopez indicated the cop. "Don't be too hard on my guy, huh? Just doing his job."

"Aren't you all," Lindy said.

"You got the right to talk to him. I'll give you ten, how's that?"

"More if I need it."

Lopez nodded.

Inside, curtains separated three beds. An old man snored in the second bed, which helped dull the beeping of a monitor. The smell of sanitized death permeated the place.

Darren was in restraints in the third bed. Leather anklets held him to the rails. Lindy could see a jagged burn around his neck, reddish fading to purple. Darren turned his head slowly to see her.

"Hello, Darren."

He looked at her a moment then let his head roll back to the side.

Lindy took a chair and sat by the bed. Darren looked like a little boy, sick, staying home from school.

"Tell me what happened. Can you?"

He did not look inclined to talk.

"Anything we can talk about?"

Darren didn't move.

"If you don't talk, I'll have to sit here and do all the yapping. That's not a very pleasant sound, so they tell me."

Nothing from Darren. At least he did not tell her to go away.

"Well, I guess you want to listen to me for a while. That's your choice. You know we are having a preliminary hearing soon. People are going to get up on the stand and talk about what you did. The judge is going to listen and decide whether to make you stand trial. There will be a trial, no doubt about it. I'm going to fight for you no matter what. I just want you to know that."

The old man in the middle bed snorted loudly, as if commenting on her assertion.

"Hey, you remember last time we talked? You asked me about God. I just wanted you to know I went to church and I've been thinking about God lately. You know what I think? I think that church isn't the place to find God."

This got Darren's attention. He looked at her and seemed curious.

And suddenly images filled Lindy's head, memories, and they led her to something that needed saying.

"Funny," she said. "When I was a little girl, maybe about six, I remember getting lost at Disneyland. Can you imagine a better place to get lost? But I got really scared. I was there with my mom and dad and little brother. And we were walking down that Main Street they have there and we stopped for a minute to look in a shop. It was pretty crowded. I looked out the window and saw Snow White walking by outside the shop. Now you have to understand that Snow White was my favorite character of all time. I wanted to be Snow White. I wanted to dress like Snow White and sing like her. The only thing I didn't want to do was eat a poison apple and live with dwarfs in the woods."

Memories of Snow White? Why now? But Darren seemed to be listening, so she went forward.

"I ran out of the shop and my parents probably missed it. I ran outside to get a look at Snow White. She had a dwarf with her. I think it was Grumpy. He was skipping alongside her and they seemed to be in a hurry. I didn't think. I just ran, and I called out her name. She looked at me and gave me a smile and wave. It was amazing. Snow White! The real deal!"

Lindy laughed a little. And she thought she saw the corner of Darren's mouth move a little upward.

"Yeah, it was the biggest thrill of my life. I ran back into the shop. But I guess it was the wrong shop. It didn't look familiar, and I didn't see my mom or dad or brother. I did see this man with a very sour expression on his face. I'll never forget it. This guy was Grumpy times four, the ugliest, scariest face I'd ever seen. And suddenly I was very, very scared. I was lost, and Disneyland had become a scary place. I called out—Mommy! Daddy!—and I spun around looking for them.

"The man with the scary face came over to me and said, 'Can't find your mommy or daddy?' That scared me more than anything else. I ran out of the shop with my heart stuck in my throat, crying, and as soon as I got out the door I was swept up by my mother into her arms. She was right outside the door waiting for me."

She paused, the feelings coming back to her, the incredible relief that was so deep she burst into tears on her mother's shoulder. Mom held her close, patted her back, told her not to worry. *I would never let you get lost,* she said.

"So I think God must be like that," Lindy said. "We're down here and we're scared and we get lost. God's not going to let us stay lost."

She stopped, looked at Darren's furrowed brow. For a minute he stayed like that. What was he thinking? Lindy didn't press him.

Finally he said, "I went to Disneyland once."

Lindy almost slid off her chair. Light shone through the fissure again.

She put her hand on his arm. "Tell me about it."

ELEVEN

† † †

1.

The preliminary hearing in the case of the People of the State of California against Darren DiCinni began in the courtroom of Judge Doreen Weyer. Lindy had been in front of her before, and considered her fair. Weyer was a deputy DA for fifteen years before her appointment to the bench. At least she was not the sort of ex-DA who took pleasure in making defense lawyers jump through flaming hoops.

Of course the place was jammed with reporters. Lindy expected this but wasn't quite ready for the reality of reporters sniffing blood—hers. Leon Colby was taking a hard line. She was the nasty defense lawyer who would pull any trick to get Darren through some legal loophole. For the scribes, that was a formula for good press.

Most disconcerting, though, was the group of VOICe activists who managed to get seats in the courtroom. Wearing their red and white VOICe badges, they dominated a corner of the medium-sized courtroom, occupying twelve seats or so. A couple of them made eye contact with Lindy as she walked toward the counsel table. It was a good thing flame throwers were not allowed in court.

Roxy gave Lindy a playful nudge on the shoulder as they sat at counsel table. "I prayed for you this morning," she said.

"Good idea. I talked to Darren yesterday, about God and Disneyland."

"Interesting combination."

"The point is, I think I made a connection. A little one. So keep on praying, okay? I'm going to need all the help I can get."

161

Leon Colby walked into the courtroom. He ambled down the center aisle with a palpable swagger. It sent a vibrating blade through Lindy's middle, a feeling she got whenever she knew a prosecutor held all the cards. And Leon Colby displayed his hand with glee.

He smiled at Lindy and gave her a nod. Then he motioned that he wanted to talk. Lindy stepped to the prosecutor's table.

"Take a twenty-five to life, Lindy," Colby said. "He'll have a chance to get out."

"He needs treatment, not incarceration."

"No."

"You know he does."

"I don't know anything of the kind. You heard the expert."

"Some expert."

"Take the deal, Lindy. Let's get out of here and get on with our lives."

Lindy glanced behind her, then back at Colby. "Those red-and-white badges wouldn't have anything to do with this case now, would they?"

Stiffening, Colby said, "That's not gonna help you."

"They turn out the vote."

"I guess this conference is over."

He started to turn. Lindy put a hand on his arm. "Leon, there's stuff here that smells, and you know it. You've been around too long not to know it."

"I got a good sense of smell, and I'm not picking anything up."

"Why don't I believe that?"

"Maybe because you're just wired to smell your own imagination. Maybe it's because you're still fighting old battles. I don't know. But the kid's gonna end up doing life without parole, and if you're so all-fired concerned about him, you better think about a deal."

From the side door, Darren DiCinni shuffled in between two sheriff's deputies. He still looked like the vacant, lost teenager who had tried to kill himself. But Lindy knew there was something more inside him. After they'd met on the field of Disneyland memories, she felt at least he was starting to trust her a little. To listen.

He even gave her a half smile.

2.

Mona watched the killer, tried to see into his eyes. Vacant, remorseless. Wicked. What was he smiling about? Did he think he was going to beat this thing? He and his tricky lawyer?

Didn't the Bible talk about an eye for an eye? If God was just, then this killer would get what he deserved.

Janelle Thompson sat beside Mona. She was the mother of Cody Thompson, one of the murdered boys. Mona liked her, one of the more voluble VOICe members. She had a way of empowering victims with her words, making them feel important.

Brad was not going to come. He called yesterday and left a message. Mona was home but didn't pick up. She didn't want to have a long, drawn-out thing, especially not with the preliminary coming up.

She hoped he was getting along. She really did. Maybe after the trial they could—

"Nervous?" Janelle whispered.

"A little, I guess."

"Mr. Colby's going all the way on this one. He's the right man for the job."

"I sure hope so."

"I heard the judge is good too."

"This is only a preliminary. The trial's another thing."

"Don't worry," Janelle said. "We'll be out in force for that too. Any judge will see he can't get away with anything."

Mona nodded, trying to feel confident.

"And Mr. Mahoney," Janelle said. "He's going to help take care of things for us."

"I didn't know he was working on the case."

"He's not."

Mona shook her head.

"He's a former police officer, remember?" Janelle said. "He's got connections."

"I'm still not sure—"

"Just trust him. He knows what he's doing. Which is good for us."

After a long sigh, Mona said, "I'll take anything at this point." And just then the killer's lawyer turned and scanned the gallery, making eye contact with Mona.

An icy hand grabbed her heart. This woman profaned God's house by coming in to worship with people who cared about justice. This woman was trying to pervert justice. If only God would intervene and get this thing over with.

Mona did not avert her eyes. The lawyer did.

3.

I'll have to get used to her being here, Lindy thought. That woman who had reamed her at the church, along with all her cohorts and the red-and-white badges. Here to intimidate this judge and any other judge who sat on the case. And a jury.

Lindy would make a motion before trial to exclude these people from the courtroom. At least get a ruling to make them take off those badges. They were a veritable lynch mob.

The press sat on the other side of the gallery. Including Sean McIntyre. He smiled and winked at Lindy.

At 9:05 the judge entered. Everyone stood as Doreen Weyer took the bench. Weyer had allowed one pool camera in court. The proceedings would show up on the evening news, locally and nationally. Lindy had moved for exclusion and lost. Leon Colby did not seem upset in the slightest. What a great TV commercial it would make when he officially threw his hat in the DA ring.

Judge Weyer called the case. "Before we get to the first witness," she said, "I want to make sure we all understand that this is a preliminary hearing with an intense amount of interest. We have a camera in court, and many parties here who have a stake in the proceedings. And I mean from the defendant to family members to those who talk about the social significance of all things criminal. I want to say at the outset that I will not tolerate anything done for the benefit of the camera or publicity. I don't want any outbursts from the public or untoward actions by the press. And I trust that the two lawyers will conduct themselves with the utmost professionalism."

When Weyer said *professionalism,* she looked at Lindy. What was that supposed to mean?

"Mr. Colby," said the judge, "you may call your first witness."

Colby stood up. "The People call Marjorie Kean to the stand."

Lindy glanced to the gallery, where a woman of about thirty-five stood and came forward. She was dressed in a dignified suit and had short, stylish brown hair.

She was sworn and took the witness chair, then per the clerk's instruction stated her name for the record.

Leon Colby addressed her from the podium.

"Good morning, Mrs. Kean."

"Good morning." She seemed a little nervous, but only a little.

"You are a resident of West Hills?"

"Yes."

"How long have you lived there?"

"About seven years now."

Colby's manner was warm and friendly. "And what sort of work do you do, Mrs. Kean?"

"At home. I am a stay-at-home mother."

"How many children do you have?"

"Three. Jonathan is twelve, Megan is ten, and Hannah is seven."

"And is Jonathan on a park-league baseball team?"

"Yes. The Royals."

"What is your husband's name, Mrs. Kean?"

"Jerry."

"And is Jerry one of the coaches of the Royals?"

"He's an assistant coach, yes."

"Turning your attention to the morning of June 26, were you at the park with your family?"

"Yes. All of us were there for Jonathan's game."

"What time was the game supposed to start?"

"Nine."

"And what time did you arrive?"

"About half an hour before."

Colby put a white poster board on an easel. It had a diagram on it. "Mrs. Kean, I am going to ask you to look at a diagram, marked People's One for identification, and ask if this is a correct representation of Capistrano Park."

The witness gave the diagram a glance. "Yes."

"Will you indicate for the judge which diamond was being used for Jonathan's game that morning?"

Mrs. Kean pointed at the chart. "The upper right."

"Let the record show that the witness has identified the northeast baseball diamond on People's Exhibit One."

"The record will so reflect," the judge said.

"Did the baseball game start pretty much on time?"

"Yes. Around nine o'clock or so."

"Thank you. Now around nine fifteen, did something happen that—"

"Objection," Lindy said. "Leading as to time."

"Sustained."

Colby nodded, all professionalism and cool efficiency. "During the course of the baseball game, Mrs. Kean, did something out of the ordinary happen?"

"Oh my, yes."

"About what time did this event take place?"

"It was about nine fifteen."

"How do you know that?"

"That's what it felt like to me. I also saw stories in the paper that said what the time was."

"All right. May the witness approach the exhibit, Your Honor?"

"She may."

"Now, Mrs. Kean, if you would please approach the chart. I am going to hand you a red marker and ask you to indicate with a letter K where you were standing at approximately nine fifteen."

Mrs. Kean took the marker and put a red K near the home-plate symbol.

"Let the record reflect that the witness has put a K along what would be the first-base line."

"So noted."

"You may resume the stand, Mrs. Kean.".

She did.

"Where you indicated, Mrs. Kean, is that where the people watching the game sit?"

"Yes. Those are the stands."

"I see. And were there other people in the stands?"

"Yes."

"Do you know approximately how many?"

"I'd say about twenty or so. Mainly the parents of the kids."

"Please describe for the court what took place at approximately nine fifteen on the morning of Saturday, June 26."

Mrs. Kean took a long, labored breath. "I was watching our team hit. Jonathan was on deck. I think there was one out. All of a sudden I heard a gunshot."

"Did you know it was a gunshot?"

"Not then. It was a loud cracking sound, and everybody looked over. And that's when I saw him shooting."

"Is the one you saw shooting seated in the courtroom today?"

Mrs. Kean looked directly at Darren DiCinni. "Yes."

"Will you point to him, please?"

"Right there." Mrs. Kean pointed.

The judge said, "Record will show the witness has identified the defendant."

"You say you saw the defendant shooting. What was the weapon?"

"A rifle."

"And when you saw the defendant, where was he in relation to where you were sitting?"

"He was coming toward first base."

Colby pointed to the diagram. "That would be about here, Mrs. Kean?"

"Yes."

"I am going to indicate with a black *D* on the exhibit the spot where the witness first saw the defendant." Colby marked it. "So you had to look to the right to see the defendant?"

"Yes."

"What else did you see at that time?"

"I saw that Ollie Jones was screaming something. He was looking down. And that's when I saw one of the kids from the other team, facedown by first base. I saw red on his shirt. It was horrible." A sob choked her voice.

Everyone in the courtroom seemed to freeze in a legal tableau; no one willing to be the one to disturb it.

"I'm sorry," Mrs. Kean said.

"Can I get you a glass of water?" Colby said.

Mrs. Kean shook her head. "I'll be all right."

"Can you tell us what you saw next?"

"Next. There was all sorts of screaming and shooting and people running around. It was total chaos. I looked for my husband and Jonathan. Jerry had Jonathan in his arms. Jonathan wasn't hurt. I ran to them and saw kids falling. Most of them were just scared, and they fell to protect themselves."

"What else did you observe, if you can recall?"

"I saw a couple of grown-ups trying to pull Mr. Dorai from third base. I could see the red on his shirt. I could see . . ." Once more her voice trailed off.

"Just one more question, Mrs. Kean. Did you see the defendant after the shooting stopped?"

She nodded. "He was running, toward the sandbox area, where there's swings and things. Two men chased him, and they caught up to him and tackled him."

"Thank you, Mrs. Kean."

"Cross-examine," Judge Weyer said to Lindy.

Lindy did not know what to ask the witness. All the judge wanted was some basis to establish the minimum level of cause to bind over Darren for trial. Mrs. Kean was no doubt only one of several witnesses Colby had lined up. All would say essentially the same thing.

Normally, if identity was in question, Lindy would be able to focus on that issue. But everyone knew Darren DiCinni was the shooter, so challenging that fact would be pointless.

Still, something about the account bothered Lindy. She wasn't sure what it was. But she could ask a few questions and maybe figure it out as she went along.

"Good morning, Mrs. Kean."

The witness did not answer, but gave a curt nod.

"I'd like to ask you just a few questions. I know this has been difficult. When you heard the first shot, which you described as a crack, were you looking at the field, at the game?"

"Yes."

"And the sound of the shot caused you to look to the right?"

"Yes."

"Which is when you saw my client with a rifle?"

"That's right."

"Was he aiming the rifle? Was it in shooting position?"

Mrs. Kean thought a moment. "Yes, it was."

"Could you tell where he was aiming?"

"Toward the field."

"Can you remember a direction?"

"I'm not sure I know what you mean."

"I'm trying to determine if you got the impression that my client was shooting randomly."

"Oh yes."

"You stated he was near one of the adults, a Mr. . . ." Lindy looked at her notes.

"Jones," Mrs. Kean said. "Ollie Jones, one of our coaches."

"Did Mr. Jones try to apprehend Darren?"

A momentary look of confusion came to Mrs. Kean's face, then she said, "I don't remember. I was looking for Jonathan."

"I see. Did you get a look at my client's face?"

"Briefly."

"A profile view?"

"Yes."

"And you said he was aiming the rifle."

"I said it was in a shooting position."

"All right. Which means his face was along the butt of the rifle."

"I guess so."

"Don't guess, Mrs. Kean, if you can—"

"He was shooting children! You expect me to be clear about anything that was happening?"

Lindy paused and could almost detect Leon Colby's head pop behind her. The witness had inadvertently called into question the accuracy of all her observations. Lindy let the answer linger in the air over the judge's head.

Finally, Lindy said, "Is it fair to say, then, that you did not get a full look at Darren's face?"

"Whatever," Mrs. Kean said with a note of disgust.

"Please answer yes or no," Lindy said.

The witness looked at the judge, as if to plea for relief. "Please answer the question in that fashion, Mrs. Kean."

"All right," she snapped. "No."

"So you could not tell what his expression was, whether he looked crazed or out of it or—"

"Objection." Colby's voice rang out. "That's an argumentative question, loaded with buzzwords for the court."

"Thank you, Mr. Colby. The court can sort out words that buzz. Sustain the objection."

"I have no further questions," Lindy said.

4.

"Please state your name for the record," the clerk said.

"Oliver Monroe Jones."

Leon Colby stood at the podium. "Good morning, Mr. Jones."

"Good morning, sir."

Oliver Jones looked like a man you could trust. He was one of those witnesses, Lindy thought immediately, that a jury would warm to. A straight shooter with no ax to grind. No wonder Colby picked him as a witness. He was showing her just how strong his case would be in front of a jury.

"What do you do for a living, Mr. Jones?"

"I'm an electrician."

"And you live and work in West Hills?"

"Yes, sir."

"Mr. Jones, you have a son, is that correct?"

"Yes. Jeremiah. He's eleven."

"And he is on a park-league baseball team?"

"Yes, sir."

"You are a coach for the team?"

"I help the coach, Mr. Young."

"Directing your attention to the morning of June 26, were you and your son at a baseball game at Capistrano Park?"

"Yes."

"The name of the team?"

"We're the Royals."

"What time did you arrive at the park?"

"About eight. I helped Ed set up the field."

"Ed is?"

"Edward Young, the coach."

"And what time did the game begin?"

"Close to nine o'clock, I believe, sir."

"All right. What was your assignment with the team?"

"First-base coach."

"I am going to ask you to approach People's Exhibit One, and place a letter *J* with a marker at the position you were in as first-base coach during the game."

Jones got up and went to Colby's diagram and wrote a *J* on it near the first-base line. He sat in the witness chair again.

"Now, Mr. Jones, please describe the events that took place during the early portion of the game."

Jones's warm expression dropped several degrees. His eyes narrowed a bit as he looked into a bad memory.

"I was coaching first base. We had a boy on first, Nick Marosi. I was looking at home plate, getting ready for the next batter. Then I heard something like a loud . . . *crack*. It scared me. I turned around and saw this kid with a big rifle. And he was aiming it. I couldn't believe it."

"The boy with the rifle, do you see him in court today?"

Jones pointed to Darren. "He is right there at that table."

"Record will reflect the witness has identified the defendant," Judge Weyer said.

"What happened next?" Colby asked.

"It was like everything stopped for a second. No sounds or movement or anything like that. And then the kid, the defendant, he fires another shot. And then turns and fires another one, only this one is right past . . ."

The witness stopped, his mouth open. He seemed to fight for a breath. And then his eyes filled with tears.

The judge motioned for Colby, who went to the bench. She handed him a box of tissues. Colby handed them to Jones, saying, "Take your time, Mr. Jones. If we need to take a break, we will."

Jones shook his head, dabbed his eyes with the tissue. "I'm sorry. I don't need to stop."

"Just take a moment, sir, and then continue."

Jones regained his composure, then said, "I turned around to the field, because everybody was screaming. And then I saw Nicky. He . . . he . . . there was blood. He was on the ground and crying and . . ."

Oliver M. Jones was not able to continue. He put his face in his hands and cried. The judge called for a fifteen-minute recess.

Lindy went cold. Jones's tears were a more powerful testimony than any words to the horror he witnessed. She turned to Darren. He was staring forward like a zombie.

Lindy put her hand on his arm. It startled him, like he had been suddenly awakened.

A deputy came to take Darren to the lockup for the duration of the recess.

5.

"Mrs. Romney?"

Mona turned around in the court hallway. "Yes?"

"My name is Sean McIntyre."

"Yes, I recognize you from TV."

"Not too much of a disappointment, I hope." He smiled. A handsome man with energy pouring out of him.

"Not at all." Mona felt at ease with him, yet cautious. He was a reporter after all.

"I was wondering . . ." McIntyre said, "I know this is all terribly difficult for you. But I was wondering if I might get a reaction from you after the hearing today. Just some of your thoughts, whatever they are."

"For TV?"

"Maybe. If you like the way it turns out. I don't want to push anything on you."

"I appreciate that, Mr. McIntyre."

"Sean. Please."

6.

"Good afternoon, Mr. Jones."

The witness only slightly nodded his head at Lindy. He looked tired and slightly afraid. Lindy wanted to tell him she wouldn't bite. But he probably wouldn't have believed her.

"I know how difficult this has been for you," Lindy said. "But I—"

"You don't know," Oliver Jones said. "You weren't there. You can't possibly know how—"

"Mr. Jones," Judge Weyer said softly, "I am going to have to ask you to allow Ms. Field to ask you questions, and you answer them. Nothing more. I'll make sure Ms. Field follows proper procedure. All right?"

"Yes, ma'am," Jones said. "I'm sorry."

"That's all right. This is a tense time. Go on, Ms. Field."

Lindy swallowed. This was going to be tougher than she thought. "Mr. Jones, you testified that you were near first base when you first heard the sound that you later determined came from a rifle, is that correct?"

"Yes."

"And you made a mark, a letter *J*, on the exhibit Mr. Colby provided?"

"Yes, I did."

"I would like to ask you to make another mark on it, with Her Honor's permission."

Judge Weyer looked at Leon Colby. "Any objection?"

"As long as we can make sense of it when she's through," Colby said. This brought chuckles from the gallery.

"Go ahead, Ms. Field," said the judge.

"Mr. Jones, please step to the chart here and with a black marker place an *X* where my client was when you first saw him."

Jones got up and went to the board. He looked at it a moment, then placed an *X* on the chart near the first-base line. He started to return to the witness chair.

"Please stay here for a moment, Mr. Jones."

He looked surprised.

"Mr. Jones, when you turned around at the sound of the rifle, did you turn to your right or your left?"

He thought a moment. "My right, I believe."

"And you say you saw my client, with the rifle in a shooting position?"

"Yes."

"But not aimed at you."

"Past me. Toward the field."

"As best you can, Mr. Jones, will you please indicate with an arrow the direction in which you perceived my client was aiming the rifle?"

"Your Honor," Colby said, "is all of this really necessary for purposes of this preliminary hearing?"

"Is there an objection?" Lindy snapped. "I missed that."

"That's enough," Judge Weyer said. "Mr. Colby, do you have a specific objection?"

"Relevance."

"Overruled. Anything else?"

"No, Your Honor." Colby sat down.

Just serving notice, Lindy thought. *He's going to be in my face every step of the way.*

"Now, Mr. Jones," Lindy said. "If you will please draw an arrow from the X in the direction that you say my client was aiming."

"I'll try," Jones said.

"That's all I'm asking."

Tentatively, Jones drew a small arrow.

"You testified that after you turned around and looked at my client, he proceeded to take another shot?"

"Yes."

"In the same direction?"

"Yes."

"And then he turned the rifle toward you?"

"Yes."

"And fired again?"

"Yes."

"Will you please, with an arrow, show the direction of that third shot?"

"It's the one that hit . . . Nicky."

"If you can, draw the arrow for us."

Jones's hand shook slightly as he drew another arrow.

"Thank you, sir," Lindy said. "You may resume your seat."

When Oliver Jones was seated again, Lindy said, "So you were the person closest to my client as he was shooting the rifle, is that right?"

"Yes, I guess."

"After that third shot, what did you do?"

"I . . ." He stopped again, and Lindy wondered if he'd have another breakdown. The emotion in the air was as thick as summer haze.

"Take your time, Mr. Jones."

"I don't . . . I'm okay this time. Don't worry. I'm sorry. Can you please repeat the question?"

"Sure. After the third shot that you testified went past you, what exactly did you do? What was your reaction?"

"I turned back, like I said earlier, and saw . . . Nicky."

"Yes. And he was on the ground, with blood on his shirt?"

Jones nodded slowly.

"Mr. Jones," Judge Weyer said, "we need to have an oral response for the record."

"I'm sorry. Yes. He was down, with blood."

"And what did you do next?"

"I went to Nicky. I went to him but I . . ." Jones's breathing quickened.

Leon Colby said, "Your Honor, I wonder if at this time we might allow the witness to step down?"

"Your Honor," Lindy said, "I would like Mr. Jones to finish his answer. He was about to say something and I'd like to hear what it is."

"I don't see the purpose," Colby said.

"The purpose is my right to cross-examine," Lindy said.

Colby shook his head and looked to the judge.

"Ms. Field," said Judge Weyer, "can you wrap things up?"

"Yes, just a few more questions."

"Please."

Oliver Jones looked like he'd recovered a little. "You were about to say something," Lindy said. "You said that you went to the boy, *but*. Do you recall what you were going to say?"

Jones nodded.

"Please," Lindy reminded him, "out loud for the record."

"Yes." His voice was barely audible.

"What were you about to say?"

"I was about . . . in all the commotion . . . oh dear God, I could've stopped it." Jones looked up, tears beginning to slide down his face. And his voice rang out like a rifle shot. "I should have tried to stop him! I should have gone at *him*! I could have saved the others! I could have . . ."

He began to wail. That was the end of the questioning of Oliver M. Jones.

7.

Leon Colby's next witness was police officer Kirby Glenn. He looked a little nervous to Lindy, but all business.

"Officer Glenn, how long have you been with the Los Angeles Police Department?"

"Four years."

"Your current assignment is?"

"West Valley Division."

"Turning your attention now to the morning of June 26, did you get a call about a possible shooting?"

"Yes."

"You were in a cruiser with a partner?"

"Curtiss."

"And you responded to the call?"

"Yes, sir."

"What happened when you got to the park?"

"Officer Curtiss and myself, we got out of our vehicle and proceeded to the baseball diamond, where we were met with several people in an agitated state. Some of them pointed toward an area where there was sand and swings and such. I heard one of them say that they had the shooter under control."

"What did you do then?"

"We proceeded to the sand area and saw several male adults holding down the suspect."

"Is the suspect present in court?"

"Yes, sir, seated at the counsel table."

"The witness has identified the defendant," Judge Weyer said.

"Did you see a weapon?" Colby asked.

"One of the men handed me a rifle and said he had taken it from the suspect."

Colby walked to his counsel table and picked up the rifle. "Showing you what is marked People's Two for identification, is this the rifle you were given?"

The witness looked at the rifle and the tag that dangled from it. "Yes."

"Are those your initials on the tag?"

"Yes."

"Did you proceed to take the suspect into custody?"

"I did."

"How would you describe the suspect's demeanor?"

"He didn't offer any resistance."

"He was cooperative?"

"Objection, leading," Lindy said.

"Sustained."

"Please expand on your answer that the defendant did not offer resistance," Colby asked.

"He was cooperative," said Officer Glenn.

"Did you advise the suspect of his Miranda rights?"

"Yes."

"Did he say that he understood his rights?"

"He chose not to say anything."

"Did you question the suspect further?"

"No. We put him in the squad car and waited for RHD."

"That's Robbery Homicide Division?"

"Yes."

"Thank you. No further questions."

Lindy replaced Colby at the podium. "Officer Glenn, you characterized Darren as cooperative, after Mr. Colby suggested that word to you, is that right?"

"Objection," Colby said. "Argumentative."

"Sustained."

"Let me ask you, just what it was that leads you to suggest Darren was cooperative?"

"Like I said, he offered no resistance."

"But you also testified he didn't talk to you, correct?"

"Yes."

"That doesn't suggest cooperation, does it?"

"Not in that sense."

"You also said Darren chose not to answer your Miranda advisement. You used the word *chose*, did you not?"

"I may have."

"Shall I have the court reporter read your answer?"

"No, I remember saying that."

"Did you read Darren's mind?"

"Objection," said Colby.

"Overruled. The witness may answer."

Officer Glenn said, "Of course not."

"So how do you know he chose not to answer?"

"Are you kidding?"

"This is not a joke, sir. Answer the question."

With a disgusted shake of the head, the witness said, "It's obvious to me, and I think it would be to anybody who wasn't a lawyer."

"I move to strike that as nonresponsive and argumentative and unprofessional," Lindy said.

"I don't believe *unprofessional* is in the evidence code," Colby snapped.

Lindy whirled to face him. "Professionalism is not expected of our police? Is that the DA's position?"

"That's enough," Judge Weyer said. "What's going on between you two is not professional either. Let's cool it. There is a motion to strike the witness's last answer. I'm going to grant the motion. And

I will remind the witness to answer only the question he is asked, understood?"

"Yes, Your Honor," Glenn said.

"Officer Glenn, you do not have a degree in psychology, do you?" Lindy asked.

"No."

"Never practiced psychology, have you?"

"Only on the street every day."

"Sir, you have never received any specialized academic training in the field of psychology, have you, sir?"

"No."

"You advised my client of his rights, asked him for a waiver, and he did not give it to you. You did not ask him any more questions, did you?"

"No."

"Nothing to determine his psychological state."

"Of course not."

"In short, Officer Glenn, you have no way of knowing what my client was thinking at the time he was taken into custody by you, isn't that correct, sir?"

"I know people. I see them—"

"The question can be answered yes or no, sir."

"Objection," Colby said. "The witness should be allowed—"

"Overruled. Let's move on."

Lindy repeated the question.

"I had an indication what he was thinking, but that's just my opinion," Officer Glenn said.

"I think we've heard enough opinions," Lindy said. "No more questions."

8.

The local news droned on in the background as Lindy went over notes with Roxy. Cardozo perched at the window, looking out at the Valley evening. The day in court had drained Lindy. She'd run a marathon once and knew what it was to hit the wall. Her brain was fast approaching it.

"There's something bothering me about Jones's testimony," Lindy said.

Roxy nodded. "He was pretty emotional."

"It's not that."

"What then?"

"I don't know. I believe him, don't you?"

"Sure."

"But how sure of anything can someone be under that kind of stress? He and Mrs. Kean were together on the big picture, but not necessarily on the details."

"But what does any of this matter? Everybody knows what happened. Darren shot the kids. Everybody saw it."

Lindy shook her head. "Something's off. What is it?"

"You got me."

"Go over the names."

"Again?"

"You want to get paid?"

"I haven't been. You thinking of doing something new?"

"Funny. Give them to me."

Roxy rolled her eyes and picked up the list, one of several she had made of the names of Darren's victims. "You ready?"

"Let's go."

"Okay. We have Nick Marosi, age eleven. He was standing on first base. And then we have Bobby Landis, eleven, playing third base. Matthew Romney, eleven, was standing on third base for the other team. Cody Thompson was the second baseman for the White Sox. He was twelve. James Glover, right field, ten. And then there was Joel Dorai, one of the coaches."

"Like Mr. Jones, only at third base."

"I guess. I'm not much of a baseball fan."

"There's no pattern, is there?"

"Random. Wits say he seemed to be shooting at random, and everybody was scattering. What difference does it make?"

"I don't know. But something better make a difference, and soon. You want another Dr Pepper?"

"Sure. Might as well be up all night with you."

Lindy got two more cold cans from the fridge, handed one to Roxy. "So how are things with the boyfriend?"

Roxy sighed. "Don't ask, don't tell."

Lindy's eyebrows went up. "Explain that to me, will you?"

"It means that I haven't asked and I don't know how to tell. He's been quiet lately—"

"Uh-oh."

"He's been under some pressure. I can understand."

"Or so he says."

"He means it! He's a good man."

"How do you know? How does anybody really know anybody else?"

"You're a fine one to talk."

"What's that mean?"

Roxy's mouth opened but no words came out. She was looking over Lindy's shoulder. Then she pointed to the TV.

Lindy was on. Entering the courthouse.

"Oh, great." Lindy sat and watched the highlights of the hearing. The reporter's voice-over—Sean's voice—said, "It didn't take long for defense lawyer Lindy Field to heat things up in what was an emotionally charged courtroom."

Lindy watched her video-self confront Officer Glenn. *This is not a joke, sir. Answer the question.*

And the answer. *It's obvious to me, and I think it would be to anybody who wasn't a lawyer.*

The story cut away to a clip of Darren being led from the courtroom by a deputy sheriff. Sean's narrative continued.

"He didn't show the rest!" Lindy said. "I won a motion to strike!"

" . . . had an effect on the family members of the victims," Sean was saying. "I spoke to one after the hearing."

Lindy recognized the woman, the one from the church, the one who sat glaring at her in court, wearing the VOICe button. The caption identified her as Mona Romney. Her eyes looked tired, but her voice was strong.

"I don't see how they can allow it. The defense lawyer is only interested in badgering the witnesses, trying to get them upset. What she did to Mr. Jones was horrible, putting him through all that. And then trying to make a police officer look bad. It's so disturbing to have to sit there and watch that."

Lindy watched silently now, her mouth open, as Sean addressed the camera.

"All indications are, however, that defense lawyer Lindy Field has no intention of going soft on any witness. This trial is going to be a fight over every detail and every word. Relief for the families of the children gunned down is still a long way off. This is Sean McIntyre downtown. Back to the studio."

"Wow," Roxy said. "That Sean."

"I'll strangle him."

"It's like he's out to get you. What's up with that?"

"I don't know. But I'm going to find out."

9.

A soft but persistent knock rapped on the door. Mona looked out the peephole. She should have expected this.

She opened the door.

"I hope you don't mind my just dropping by," Pastor Clark said.

Pastor Clark wore his sincere face tonight. It was probably unfair to think of him as putting on a face, but she didn't care to revise her feelings. She would accept his presence as the good gesture of a good man who would come and go, leaving her precisely where she was before he came.

Mona, stoic, settled him in the living room. She did not offer anything to drink. He placed his Bible on the table as he sat down. Mona looked at it as if it were a weapon he might pick up and point at her. "I just wanted to come by and let you know that I, the church, all the resources we have, are here to help you."

"Resources?"

"Yes."

"Like psychological counseling?"

"If you want that, then we have some people who—"

"I don't want it. I'm fine." She was not fine. She knew it. But would not bend the cold steel of her resolve. To weaken now would hurt Matthew.

"I know in times like this it's very difficult to think things through, and if—"

"Have you ever lost a child, pastor?"

He shook his head.

"Then you have no idea what you're talking about."

He took the hit without the slightest frown. "I'm not going to argue that point. I will not pretend to know what you're going through. But maybe you can hear me out on one thing? And then I'll go."

"Fair enough."

"I've been to many homes, Mona, and I've sat with people going through all sorts of things. And even though I have not experienced everything they've experienced, I do believe I've been called by God to minister to people, and to do it through the Word."

He paused. Mona waited for him to get it over with.

Pastor Clark picked up his Bible and placed it on his lap. "The Word says something that's very hard, but is, I think, the key to the whole thing. It says to forgive those who have sinned against us, and I believe when we do that, God takes hold of us and brings us out of the depths."

His words came into her head and died there. She nodded, wishing he would go.

"You know as well as I do the emphasis Jesus placed on forgiveness."

Mona nodded, meaning nothing by it.

"If you can forgive the boy who did this, Mona, I know God will work in you. And in your family."

"Isn't that why you're really here? Because Brad asked you to come?"

"Brad's your husband, and I know he loves you deeply."

"Did he ask you to come see me?"

Clark swallowed and said, "I would have come anyway, Mona. I hope you believe that."

"It doesn't matter."

"May I have a word of prayer with you?"

"I'd rather not."

"Just a short—"

"Thank you for coming."

TWELVE

† † †

1.

Sean lived in a secure building, which meant that Lindy had to wait for someone to come out. She smiled at a young man as she caught the door. He seemed oblivious. A perfect urban role model.

Lindy took the elevator to the sixth floor. At Sean's door she gave a friendly knock then covered the peephole with her hand.

After a moment Sean's voice from inside said, "Who is it?"

"Domino's," Lindy said.

"What?"

"You ordered a pizza."

"I didn't—" The door opened. "I thought that was you," he said.

Lindy pushed past Sean, who was shirtless, wearing only a pair of jeans. "We're talking."

"You saw my report, I take it." He followed her into the living room. "I'm flattered."

"Don't be. And don't start with your little-boy routine."

"You know, you could get in trouble breaking into this building."

"I want you to lay off."

Sean smiled and ran one hand over his abs, which were, truth be told, rock solid. Why did men in L.A. who were halfway hot have to be jerks? "Let me get you something to drink, and we'll talk about this civilized."

"Sean, I don't want to be civilized with you. I want to know why you're out to make me look like a dummy. I want to know who's grinding your ax."

He shook his head.

"You're taking sides in this," she said. "Why? You used to be a pretty objective reporter. You have somebody you're trying to please? Your boss? The DA's office?"

"I'm no shill, Lindy."

"You didn't used to be. Why don't you get back on track and be a real reporter? Why don't you—"

"Where do you get off coming over here and telling me how to do my job? What have you ever given me?"

"I don't owe you anything."

"Yeah, the great Lindy Field, tough broad. Why don't you drop the pose for once, huh?"

She wanted to slug him. She bit her cheek instead. "Don't talk to me about posing. What was that whole setup, interviewing that witch who slammed me?"

"That 'witch' is a woman whose kid was shot in cold blood by your client. You don't have the right to question anything that poor woman has to say."

Lindy opened her mouth but no words came out. She fell back on a chair, wanting to disappear into it. She didn't care if she vanished here at Sean McIntyre's place or somewhere else. Place had no meaning. No place was a refuge.

The one thing she didn't want was to cry in front of him.

Sean heaved a sigh. He sat on the arm of another chair. "I'm sorry. I didn't mean to say all that."

Lindy looked at the window.

"No, I really did mean to say those things. I meant to hurt you, Lindy. I guess I wanted to get back at you."

She was barely able to say, "What?"

"Yeah. You hate me for some reason. You don't want to do anything for me. Sure, I've been a bonehead at times. I admit it. But never because I didn't respect you."

Lindy shook her head. It was hard to believe anything coming out of Sean McIntyre's mouth.

"Maybe what I'm trying to say, in my own inimitable way, is that you need to let other people into your life a little, and then give a little. You can't do any of this alone."

"You pretty well made that case."

"Would you be willing to try something?"

She looked at him.

"Try treating me like a human being again? A professional?"

"Professional what?"

"Writer. Lindy, I want the exclusive inside on this kid, and you can give that to me. And in return, I can give you something."

"What can you give me?"

He stood up. "Come here and I'll show you."

2.

What Lindy saw on Sean's computer monitor almost knocked her over.

It was the image of Darren DiCinni, in the park, rifle aimed.

"How did you get this?" Lindy said.

"I can't reveal my sources."

"But this . . . who took this?"

"My source."

"Yes, but how—"

"I can't go into it."

"Sean, this is crucial, this—"

"Sit down, Lindy."

Sean snatched a black T-shirt from the back of his desk chair and put it on. "If I let you look at this, I want you to give me the exclusive rights to your story and your client's. This is going to be a major book, and I want it. That's the professional part. And I'll want a deal on paper."

"We talked about this. I can't reveal confidences."

"You can reveal yourself. You can talk to me about your thinking on the case. I want to walk through it with you. And you can tell me what you can about your client, whatever you're allowed. I won't do anything with it until after the trial is over."

"What you have on your computer is evidence in a murder trial. I can have it subpoenaed."

"You try that, and I hand it over to Colby."

"You've really thought this through, haven't you?"

Sean shrugged. "I figured I'd talk to you about it first. I just didn't figure it would be tonight. But thanks for coming over."

"There might not be anything here that really helps me," Lindy said.

"Maybe not. But you'll never know, will you?"

"I don't know whether to spit in your face or thank you."

"Thank me. Do we have a deal?"

"You can't use anything I say until after the trial."

"Agreed. Deal?"

"Sure, now let me see—"

"No. A deal. Signed and sealed."

"I can't do that now."

"If you give me your word you'll do a written agreement, we'll go ahead with this."

Feeling like she was on the edge of a cliff, feet slipping, Lindy made the decision. "All right. Deal."

Sean smiled. "Welcome back to the world, Lindy. I can't help feeling this is going to be good for all concerned, especially us."

"There is no *us*, Sean."

"Give me time. All right. Sit down." He turned the desk chair for her.

Lindy sat.

"What you have here is not a photo," Sean said. "It's a digital image from a video."

"Somebody took a video of the shootings?"

Sean nodded.

"How did you—"

"Get it? Lindy, when I tell you I'm the best reporter in the entire free world, I'm not just blowing smoke. I have instincts. A sixth sense, if you will, only I don't see dead people with it. I see people who have something to tell me."

Lindy was starting to believe it. There on his computer screen was the act, the crime.

Unbelievable.

"Let's watch," he said and hit a computer key.

Interpreting the video was an exercise in frustration. With no close-up of Darren's face, Lindy could not detect any sign of possible mental defect—vacant eyes, frenzied expressions.

On its own, it was just a record of her client shooting people.

Shooting with increasingly rapid speed. As if he were afraid he wouldn't kill as many people as he originally wanted to.

The videographer had stood behind the baseball diamond, panning the field from left to right. Whoever it was, for some reason, panned past right field to Darren, who was just beginning to raise his rifle.

Why the continued pan? Did the person just want to get a wider view of the park, or did Darren catch the eye?

Darren fired the first shot. The camera shook and panned left, leaving Darren out of the frame momentarily. Understandable. A reaction to shock.

But the videographer must have sensed something needed recording, because the camera went back to Darren, where he apparently finished another shot.

Then Darren lowered the rifle to chest level and began spraying the field. She counted ten shots, based on the rifle's kick and the puffs of smoke that issued from the gun.

Darren lowered the rifle and turned and began to walk—not run, walk—away. A running man flashed past the camera, presumably toward Darren, and then the recording ended.

Lindy sat, silent, for a long moment. The reality of the crime hit her hardest. She actually saw her client commit the crime for which he was charged. That had never happened to her before.

"Pretty amazing, isn't it?" Sean said.

"What are you going to do with it?"

"Go exclusive. Then let Colby howl about it. He'll ask for a copy and get one, and then you'll get one. No doubt it'll go over the Net, so *everybody* who wants one will get one."

"Terrific. This doesn't help me at all."

"Maybe I can."

She looked at him.

"Give me something," he said.

"Give you what?"

"An insight, anything. First part of our deal."

"I guess you deserve it. You want an insight into me?"

Sean sat on a stool near his work desk. "I find you endlessly fascinating, which is why I am attracted to you."

"Can we keep things professional this time?"

"Suppose I try to mix in a little pleasure?"

"I will find a sharp instrument to jab in your back."

"In that case, I'll try to contain myself."

Lindy nodded. "Okay. Listen. Sometimes I do wonder if it's worth it to be a defense lawyer. Nobody likes you, especially clients. If you manage to get them off they're resentful about giving you any money. They figure they could've gotten off themselves. And if you don't get them off, you're the worst slime bucket in the world."

"Not like being one of those glamorous personal-injury attorneys, is it?"

"But there's something inside you that believes in what you're doing. When I was in law school I really started to believe in what they call 'the golden thread' that runs through the law: the presumption of innocence. You get rid of that, and everything falls apart. But everybody wants to moan about tricky lawyers, and criminals getting off scot-free. But let one of *them* get arrested on a false charge. They really are innocent, and they know it. The first thing they're going to want is a lawyer who cares as much about the case as they do. And they should get that lawyer. But after awhile, you get worn down."

"Maybe it's because you have to rub elbows with a lot of very bad people. Most people who are prosecuted are, in fact, guilty."

"So let's convict them, fair and square. The government has got to prove its case beyond a reasonable doubt. If it doesn't, the defendant walks. Because if you don't do it that way, you make it easy to convict the innocent."

"You see yourself as a hero?"

She rolled her eyes. "Back in the thirties, when white judges and juries in the South routinely convicted black men on flimsy evidence, the lawyers who came down from New York provided a real defense—

as opposed to the lazy crackers who didn't care one way or the other about their clients—they were considered heroes. Today, nobody considers a defense lawyer a hero. We're the dregs of the earth."

"Not to me," he said and then leaned over to kiss her.

She turned her head. "Not now, Sean."

"Then when?"

"I really don't know, okay? After the trial, we can talk."

"More than talk?"

"You never stop, do you?"

He smiled. "That's why I am where I am."

3.

But where was she, Lindy wondered as she drove back to Box Canyon. The video troubled her. Something about it. What?

Good thing the night was balmy, the sky clear. Lindy took Sunset to Pacific Coast Highway, one of her favorite routes, and then Topanga Canyon back to the Valley. She liked coming over the crest and seeing the Valley at night, sparkling below. There was no prettier sight in the world than her Valley at night.

When you could see it. Tonight a blanket of fog obscured the view. Something of a rarity, but there it was.

As she was about to head down, she slowed for just a moment. And had a crazy thought. She imagined herself on a flying motorcycle. Would that not be cool? Cruising right out into the sky and shooting all the way across to the Santa Susanna Mountains. She'd be able to see the major streets crisscrossing. Victory Boulevard, like in the Randy Newman song, and Ventura and Topanga and Sherman Way and Van Nuys. Getting the God's-eye view.

When she thought of God, that was when it happened. She'd remember later, when she could piece it all together. But it would take a long time for the pieces, any of them, to fit.

She saw lights coming her way. She looked right at them too, the way you're never supposed to. And when she looked away, and as the car passed by, she saw, from the corner of her eye, the lights flash. Like something was wrong.

She felt a sudden desire to be home. To curl up with Cardozo. To get out of the night.

She sensed a shadow on the left.

There were no cars behind her. The last set of headlights had turned away some half a mile back.

She slowed and pulled slightly to the right. There was a turnout just ahead. Maybe she'd—

The shadow was a car. It jerked toward her. *No headlights* she thought, and that was her last thought as the car hit her.

Bike, rider, lights, sky—a jumble, then a feeling of falling. Pain shooting through her body. A blow to the head, like a sledgehammer.

Blinding her.

THIRTEEN

† † †

1.

Leon Colby stepped out of the elevators on the eighteenth floor of the Foltz Building and gave his usual nod to the county safety police guard who watched the floor.

Another day at the office, though none ever seemed routine to Colby. That was the good part about being a prosecutor. No two cases were ever the same.

He punched in the three-digit code on the door, entered, said hi to a few people, grabbed coffee, picked up his phone message slips, and shut himself up in his office.

The DiCinni matter was rapidly approaching crunch time. Lindy Field was not blinking. She was not going to plead this out, which surprised him. The kid was not going to go to the funny farm. He was going to state. She had the chance to get him less time than a guilty verdict would allow.

Why wouldn't she take it?

Colby sat at his desk and ignored the phone messages and the stack of files that were also his business. He put his feet up and glanced out his small office window. He could see the field light towers of Dodger Stadium.

Maybe, as the new district attorney of the county of Los Angeles, he'd get a seat in the luxury section behind home plate. They actually had waiters who came out to take hot dog orders. A real L.A. experience. And they'd show his face on the Jumbotron. He'd wave. The crowd would give him a mixture of cheers and boos. Mostly cheers, because he was one of them. A few boos from relatives of the criminal element. But that was what DAs signed up for.

Back to the case at hand.

It wasn't that he didn't relish going to trial. That part never got old. His competitive nature was always on high alert, as the Office of Homeland Security might put it.

But with every trial came the risk of the major slip, the unanticipated event, the surprise sack that would take the most prepared quarterback out of the game.

That's why he had developed a poker face. Never, but never, let the jury see he'd been hit.

Problem was, the higher the profile of the case, the louder the reverb when the hit came.

One misstep and maybe the DA's office would not be graced with his presence.

Why wouldn't she settle?

There had to be a reason. Revenge? She couldn't give up the Marcel Lee ghost and wanted another chance at his prosecutor?

Somehow that didn't strike Colby as likely. Lindy Field had been a solid lawyer at one time. She was never petty. Of course, she went through that crackup after the Lee verdict. Maybe that had changed her.

She couldn't really think her client was crazy, could she? The legal threshold for insanity was just too high. Sure, he was relatively young, but—

A knock on the door. It was Lopez, here for the morning conference.

Something in Lopez's face told Colby all was not well.

"You don't answer your messages?" Lopez said.

"Just got here. You have my cell number?"

Lopez shut the door. "You heard?"

"What, they bringing back *Magnum P.I.*?"

"It's heavy."

"Tell me."

"Lindy Field. She's in the hospital."

Colby put his feet on the floor. "What?"

"Almost dead, man."

2.

The news came over the radio in Mona Romney's house while she was grating cheese for a quesadilla.

" . . . a major development in the mass-murder trial of Darren DiCinni. Defense attorney Lindy Field, who has represented DiCinni from the start, was nearly killed last night in a motorcycle accident on Topanga Canyon Boulevard. Early reports are that she is in critical condition at a local hospital. For what this means to the ongoing case, we turn to our legal analyst, Carl Sizemore. Carl, how is this going to affect the prosecution of Mr. DiCinni?"

Mona lost breath, sat down.

"Well, Gail, this is indeed a strange twist. If this had just been a momentary setback for the attorney, the judge would grant some leeway. But if the accident results in a permanent impairment of some sort, or a long delay, then there will be a substitution of attorney. That's got to be handled carefully, however, because everyone has the right to an attorney of his or her choice. Or if the attorney is assigned, has the right to keep that attorney. If that right is denied there's an issue on appeal. But if a lawyer is unable, really unable to carry on with the case, then that defendant has to hire, or be assigned, another lawyer."

She heard a knock on the front door. She ignored it. The killer's lawyer was in the hospital.

And I want her there, Mona thought. *I want her punished for what she's doing.*

The knocking persisted. She almost didn't answer it. Then she heard Syl Martindale's voice calling her name.

Dazed, Mona opened the door.

"Hi," Syl said with a forced smile.

"What brings you by?"

"I've really missed you, Mona. I just thought I'd—"

"Did Pastor Clark send you?"

Real hurt appeared on Syl's face. "It's not like that."

They sat in the living room in the fading afternoon sunlight. Syl danced around with small talk for several minutes, and Mona let her dance. Maybe she'd get tired and leave all the sooner.

But then Syl dropped her voice and stuttered. "Mona, do you . . . are you . . . in some way, are you questioning, at all, your faith?"

For some reason Mona had expected a question like this from Syl. "Don't you ever question it?"

"I did when it first happened, when Matthew was killed."

"And now you're all better?"

Syl did not seem to register the slight. "I only know it's at times like this we need faith most. We need to rely on God."

"Did that come from The Official Guide for Hurting Christians? Because I don't buy it. If God made me this way, then I'm this way. I can't manufacture feelings. I can't get over my doubts. Matthew is dead, doesn't anybody realize that?"

"Of course we do, and we want to be part of your healing."

"I don't want to heal. I want to stay sick."

"Nobody wants to stay sick."

"Don't tell me what I want, Syl."

"You're one of my closest friends in the world, and I can't stand to see you suffering like this—"

"All you have to do is leave, and you won't see it."

"But your relationship with God is hurting and I can't let that go."

"Let it go."

"You need to forgive this boy."

Mona glared at her, ice forming in her chest. "Don't tell me that."

"It's not me telling you. You know that. You know that we're to forgive, that Jesus commands it."

"You sound like Pastor Clark."

"Is that so bad?"

"He came to see me. Preached at me about forgiving. You know, I actually checked out the Bible on it. Did you know that? I looked it up. It's in Luke."

She got up and took a Bible from the bookshelf. She had a bookmark in it.

"Listen. 'If your brother sins, rebuke him, and if he repents, forgive him. If he sins against you seven times in a day, and seven times comes back to you and says, "I repent," forgive him.'"

"Yes," Syl said.

"First of all, it says *your brother.* Second of all, it says *if he repents.* That's what Jesus said. I don't see any repentance in this boy, and he is not my brother."

Syl swallowed, with a deer-in-the-headlights look. Mona had her high beams on.

"But what about Jesus on the cross? He asked God to forgive the ones who were crucifying him."

"It's up to God then, not me. If God wants to forgive that boy, fine. But I don't have to. I don't. And I'm not going to."

3.

"You got a message."

Darren looked out from his cell at the deputy. Hedgecock was one of the bad ones. From hell. *Don't listen.*

"You listening?" Hedgecock said.

Darren sat on his cot, looking down. Hedgecock was trying to get to him, like he always did.

"Your lawyer . . ."

Darren's head snapped up.

"Yeah, your lawyer. You interested?"

He wants me to talk. I won't.

"I asked you a question. You interested in a little news about your lawyer?"

What is it? Does she want to stop being my lawyer? She want to go away? I bet she does. They all do.

"Hey, I don't have to say nothin'," Hedgecock said. "You can sit and think about it."

He turned around and started walking down the corridor.

"Come back!" Darren stood up.

Another K–10 screamed an obscenity.

"Get back here!" Darren screamed.

The deputy laughed, turned back. "That's better, little man. You gonna behave now?"

Darren nodded.

"Your lawyer, she's in the hospital. Ran off a road. You're gonna need a new lawyer. Good luck."

Hedgecock walked away.

"Stop!"

Hedgecock ignored him. A voice screamed at Darren to shut up.

He screamed back. Then he threw himself against the wall. And again. And again.

The devils came in to stop him. Hedgecock was one of them, and he cursed at Darren while they tied up his hands.

4.

Lindy was being crushed under a boulder. It was night, no sound, only impending death.

As the dream faded she became more aware of the pain enveloping her. The night of the dream gave way to the glare of the hospital lights.

Bad shape.

Thank God I'm alive.

Darren.

Her lips felt like balloons. She tried to move her tongue and form a word, but everything wanted to stay just where it was.

She did not move. To move was to bring pain.

What had happened? She was riding, yes, she remembered that. Remembered the fog. The Valley. And something alongside.

A ring of some kind. What was it?

She groaned.

Darren.

What was the ring? Familiar.

Don't go back to sleep.

The ring.

"You awake?"

Roxy's voice. Lindy groaned.

"Girl, you look fantastic," Roxy said. "Frankenstein's got nothin' on you. The electrodes in your neck will go perfectly with your—"

"Don't . . . make me . . . laugh."

"I thought we were going to lose you. You were out, baby."

"How long?"

"All day. You can do a public service announcement now."

Lindy tried to figure out what Roxy meant, but thinking was painful too.

"Your helmet saved your life. Didn't do much for your face, but outside of the improvement, nobody's gonna know the difference."

Lindy fought off a smile.

"I prayed my knees off for you," Roxy said. "I want you talking to God about this."

"Later. My cat."

"Taken care of. Your neighbor, that funny old man, he's gonna feed him."

"Likes Fancy Feast."

"Your neighbor?"

"Cardozo."

"I knew that."

Hot slivers of pain shot through her.

Roxy's voice was anxious. "Need the doc?"

"No."

"What happened, Lindy? How could you have gone off like that? You know I've been telling you to get rid of—"

"Roxy."

"Yeah."

"Listen." Lindy motioned with her left arm. Her right was encased in plaster. Roxy leaned over the bed.

"Between us. Understand?"

Roxy nodded.

"I don't think . . . it was an accident."

"Huh?"

"Deliberate."

Roxy sat back slowly, pulled by an invisible string. "No way."

"Way."

"We have to tell the police, we—"

"No."

"Why not?"

"Gut feeling."

"That's crazy."

"I think it was a Mercedes. Dark color. No headlights. Moonlight. I saw the ring."

"Thing?"

Lindy sputtered impatiently. "Ring."

"Ring . . . hood ornament?"

"Yeah."

"What are we going to do?"

"How is Darren?"

"I don't know."

"Find out. Tell him I'm all right."

"But you're not."

"Tell him. And get Everett Woodard."

Roxy saluted, then kissed Lindy's forehead. Lindy took hold of Roxy's arm. "And while you're at it, pray some more, huh?"

"I've never stopped," she said, and with another smile she was gone.

Lindy pressed her body into the bed, trying to feel the points of pain. She couldn't count them all. Broken arm and ribs, seeming oceans of black-and-blue skin. Her fingers found a line of stitches along her cheek, and she could smell the treated gauze that, for all she knew, held her body parts together.

But she could move if she had to. She could stand up. She could walk and talk.

But could she be a lawyer?

Okay, God, why don't you tell me? If you're there. I'm not dead, I realize that. Did you keep me from dying? Thank you if you did. I'm not ready to die.

I need to get better. I need to help Darren. Can you hurry things along? Sorry if I'm being rude. I don't know how else to ask.

I need to know how to help Darren. No matter what people do, you love them, right? Isn't that the basic idea I've always heard about you?

Then love Darren and show me the best way to help him.

I need to know what's going on. I want to know you're there. I want to see my cat.

Show me you're there.

5.

Leon Colby met Everett Woodard in the courtroom, just as the deputies were bringing DiCinni in. Woodard had the same dignified look as Calvert Colby, the same sincerity. He'd look good to a jury. But he was a law professor. What were his trial skills?

"How's Lindy doing?" Colby asked after they shook hands.

"Pretty bad, but stable."

"Good. Tell her I said I hope she gets back on her feet soon."

"I will."

"You feel like talking any about a plea?" Colby watched the man's eyes carefully, trying to size him up.

"I think we should get the substitution settled first. We'll have time to talk."

Colby shrugged. "I'd be willing to—"

"Let's just wait," Woodard said. "First things first."

Sounds like Dad too.

"I can tell you one thing, Professor. This is not a winnable case. I tried to explain that to Lindy, but she has this streak in her."

"Called a will to win," Woodard said.

"You have to do what's best for the client."

"Thanks for the advice, and if you want some of mine—"

"No, thanks."

The judge entered, and everyone stood up.

Judge Weyer wasted no time. "Mr. Woodard, do you wish to make a motion to substitute in as counsel for the defense?"

Everett Woodard said, "I do, Your Honor. However, I have not received the assent of our client, Mr. DiCinni. He wishes to address the court."

Judge Weyer looked skeptical for a moment. "Very well, but I will ask the questions. Please stand up, Mr. DiCinni."

Darren DiCinni stood.

"You understand that your lawyer, Ms. Field, is physically incapable of continuing to represent you?"

The boy made a halfhearted nod.

"You understand that the trial must continue?"

DiCinni nodded again.

"You are entitled to the lawyer of your choice," Judge Weyer explained. "However, if that lawyer is unable to continue to represent you, in this case because of a physical condition, you do not have the right to delay the trial indefinitely. Mr. Woodard is a close colleague of Ms. Field and has volunteered to take over your defense. My advice is that you accept the offer. If you do not, this court will be forced to assign a lawyer to you."

"I want my lawyer back," DiCinni said.

"Mr. DiCinni, did you not understand me?"

"You don't understand," Darren said, his voice rising. To Colby it sounded very young. But the next words were not those of a normal young man. "You are all going to hell," DiCinni said quietly. "You're all against me. I know you. You are of the devil. You are—"

Judge Weyer rapped her gavel on the bench. "That's enough—"

"—devils. Every one of you—"

"Mr. Woodard, tell your client to—"

Before Everett Woodard could say anything, Darren bolted toward Leon Colby.

6.

Using the handset attached to the bed, Lindy clicked to the afternoon news on channel nine. Yes, this hospital life was terrific. A television! What more did a recovering lawyer need?

When was she going to get out of here? No one would give her a straight answer. These medical people, so careful. Why was that? *Lawyers. We've done so much to make the medical profession feel secure—*

Her ruminations stopped when she heard Sean McIntyre's voice on the TV. He was standing in front of the Foltz Criminal Courts Building in a live shot, saying "That's right, Peter. Stunning new developments in the DiCinni murder case, both inside and outside the courtroom. Just when you thought things couldn't get more dramatic, from the accident involving the lead defense attorney to the fireworks we seem to see in court every day, this case continues to make unbelievable twists and turns."

That's right, Sean. Milk the drama for all it's worth.

Lindy turned up the volume.

"The day's session just wrapped up," Sean said, "oh, about half an hour ago. But not before the defendant, Darren DiCinni, went into a rant about hell and devils, and then attacked Deputy District Attorney Leon Colby. Let's take a look."

Stunned, Lindy watched as the images unfolded. Darren calling everyone devils, and the judge trying to get order, and then Darren rushing Leon Colby.

He got his hands around Colby's neck.

Leon looked shocked, but his big hands grabbed her client's skinny wrists as if taking straws from a dispenser. And then the deputy sheriffs were all over Darren.

Sean came back on. "As incredible as that outburst was, it was not the most dramatic development in the case today. Hard to believe, I know, but I have obtained, exclusively, an item that could throw the whole case in a new direction."

Now what?

"I have just received this from a source who wishes to remain anonymous. It is the only known videotape of the shootings. This source was at the scene of the crime and just happened to take video of Darren DiCinni in the act of mass murder."

No . . .

"What you are about to see is the only visual evidence to surface so far. I want to caution any parents who are watching to use discretion if there are any children in the room. The footage here is very disturbing. I just want to make that clear. Here it is."

Lindy had not seen the opening of the video. Apparently Sean had chosen not to reveal that to her. A slow anger started up inside her.

The video showed the ball field as the game was going on. Parents yelled out encouragement; boys on the bench shouted to the opposing batter. The camera wobbled a little bit.

Then the sound of a gunshot.

A blur of an image as the camera moved. It came to rest on Darren as he sprayed shots wildly around the field. Then he stopped and began to walk away.

The report cut back to Sean, looking down soulfully at an unseen monitor. He turned back to the camera. "Horrific footage," he said. "Copies of the video have been turned over to representatives of the district attorney's office and to the defense, Everett Woodard, who we believe is representing Darren DiCinni at this moment, although the judge has not made a final determination. Again, an amazing day in court. Now back to you in the studio."

Lindy nearly broke out of her cast. She couldn't recall all the details of the video she'd seen in Sean's apartment, but she knew one thing for sure—the video clip she'd just seen on TV had been altered.

She grabbed the handset and buzzed for the nurse. When one finally came, which seemed like half an hour, Lindy sat up as far as her ribs would allow. "Get me a doctor, now. And while you're at it, my clothes."

7.

Leon Colby shook his head. To say that things were getting bizarre would have been an understatement. Attacked by a defendant! That had never happened to him in his entire career.

Not that the kid did any damage. Colby had peeled him off his body like a BandAid. More disturbing was the possibility that the kid might be crazy after all.

Then there was the matter of this reporter, McIntyre, showing up with key evidence. Seemed a bit too convenient, a perfect grandstand play. Why hadn't anyone in the vast web of the prosecutorial team discovered this?

Colby knew McIntyre, who always showed up to the high-profile cases, knew the guy would release footage of his own mother killing chickens if he thought it would help his résumé. This time, however, Colby suspected McIntyre was up to something more than publicity.

He was still puzzling over all this when Judge Weyer entered the courtroom and called the proceedings back to order.

Everett Woodard and Colby stated their appearances. There was one notable absence: Today DiCinni stayed in the lockup.

"Certainly is a little quieter in here this morning," the judge said, receiving laughter from the gallery. "Is there anything further from either counsel before I make a ruling on the substitution of attorney?"

"Not from the people, Your Honor," Colby said.

"I do have one thing," Everett Woodard said.

Colby looked at the man. What was he up to?

"There will be no need to substitute an attorney," Woodard said. "Ms. Field is going to continue representing Mr. DiCinni."

The judge did not look pleased. "How can she possibly continue?"

"Her doctor has cleared her, Your Honor. He advises the use of a wheelchair while she's in court, but that's not uncommon."

Judge Weyer sat back in her chair with a skeptical look. "Of course not. A lawyer in a wheelchair can represent clients in court, but from what I understand, Ms. Field's injuries are quite serious. Does she have the capacity to continue?"

"I assure Your Honor that Ms. Field will be able to defend her client competently."

"I want to finish the prelim today. Unless there is good cause to issue a continuance, which I don't see, I am going to appoint you as Mr. DiCinni's lawyer."

"May we continue this tomorrow, Your Honor?"

"No."

"Then I would request a recess until 11:00 a.m., at which time Ms. Field will be here."

With a sigh, Judge Weyer looked at Colby. "Any response?"

Colby stood. "I know that Ms. Field is a zealous attorney and cares very much about this case. But if she tries to do the job and is unable, later the defendant may make an appeal based on ineffective assistance of counsel. Perhaps the prudent thing to do is to have an in-camera hearing with Ms. Field to see if Your Honor is comfortable with her continuing."

"I think that's a good idea, Mr. Colby," the judge said. "Mr. Woodard, how long will it take for Ms. Field to get here?"

8.

Lindy felt a little like a washing machine on the fritz. The cast, which enclosed her right arm, and the brace around her ribs were imperfect attempts to keep her up and running. Even here, in the familiar confines of Judge Weyer's chambers, her mental and physical gears were knocking and wheezing, a double strain.

But she was not going to go down without a fight.

The way Judge Weyer looked at her wasn't promising. "I have to be honest with you," the judge said. "You don't look like you can represent anybody. What you need is recuperation time. And I can't stop this process while it happens."

"I feel better than I look," Lindy said. "I know that's not saying much, but there it is. I won't be playing handball anytime soon, but I want to continue representing my client."

"But that's not determinative in this matter. The law determines whether you shall continue, and I have great discretion under the law."

Everett Woodard said, "As Your Honor well knows, the presumption in favor of allowing a client to choose his attorney makes the exercise of your discretion narrow in its scope."

"Thank you, Professor. I do know the law. Now, Ms. Field, how can you assure me that you will be able to meet timetables?"

"I'm fully able to comply. I've already cleared this with my doctor."

"But you might require treatments, therapy, surgery perhaps."

"I really don't think so, Your Honor."

"Thinking is not good enough."

"What else can I do?"

"You can remember this is a court of law. This is not the Lindy Field show, no matter how many cameras are out there."

Bristling, Lindy said, "Your Honor, I assure you I'm not doing this for publicity."

"Nevertheless, if you continue in this capacity you are going to generate a lot of attention from the media. That could prove a distraction, to the ultimate detriment of your client."

Lindy looked at Leon Colby, who was standing by the judge's bookcase. "What about the publicity for Mr. Colby? Are you as concerned that he is using this trial as a platform from which to run for office?"

Colby put his hands out toward the judge. "Your Honor, please."

"I agree," Judge Weyer said. "Ms. Field, this hearing is about you. Let's try to stay focused."

"My client wants me. I want to continue. I am going to continue—"

Everett stopped her with a hand to her shoulder.

After a short pause, Judge Weyer said, "I know this has been a very stressful time for you. The accident, the attention of the press, all that. And I can see that it has caused you emotional upset. That's another factor I have to take into consideration here. I have to do what I think is right under the law to protect your client. Sometimes, clients need protection from their own counsel."

"Judge, let me—"

Weyer put her hand up. "No need. I know your position. Give me half an hour and I'll come out and make a ruling."

9.

"I blew it."

Lindy sat dejectedly in Judge Greene's chambers. Luckily he was not in trial. She needed to talk to him.

"Don't give it another thought," Greene said. "Weyer is good. She'll be reasonable."

"I don't know. She and Colby seem to be on the same wavelength. I don't think either one of them wants me around. I get the feeling they talked about this before I got a chance to make my case."

"Judge Weyer may have a point. If Darren is bound over for trial, which is likely, why not leave the trial with Everett? You have to take care of you for a change. There will be other cases."

"I don't want to think about other cases. I want to help my client."

Greene's face registered concern. "Lindy, you know how fond I am of you. I don't want to see you go down a road that will take another mental toll. I've been around a long time. And there was a time I used to think like Spencer Tracy in *Boys Town*. Remember that movie?"

"I think I saw it when I was a kid. Tracy played a priest or something."

"Yes. Father Flanagan. A real guy who set up a place in Nebraska for wayward boys. Back in the thirties. Anyway, the big line in the movie is 'There is no such thing as a bad boy.' And people used to believe that, and they shed a tear over Mickey Rooney reforming. But I don't believe that any more. By the time kids today reach your client's age, things are pretty well set."

Lindy felt a hollow place open up inside her chest. "We can't believe that. We can't just give up."

"It's not a matter of giving up. There will be exceptions. But they're rare. It doesn't seem to me that your client is one of the rare ones. But if you think he is and go all out, I just don't see that helping you."

"But Judge, it can't be about me, can it? I mean, isn't that the role of the lawyer? I sat down there in Judge Weyer's chambers while she all but accused me of using this trial for personal gain. Look at me! Do you think I need to be here? This isn't about me. This has never been about me."

The moment she said it, she knew it didn't sound convincing.

Judge Greene let the comment slide. She loved him for that. "Let's wait to see what Judge Weyer says."

10.

Mona chose to stay in the courtroom during the recess. The other VOICe members were out milling around. For some reason she did not want to be with them.

She hardly knew what she wanted anymore. Her insides knotted up every time she thought about the case, and she could think of nothing else. The killer, all this talk about forgiving him. Syl's and Pastor Clark's voices kept interrupting her own thoughts of justice.

And the killer's lawyer—how was it possible she was still involved, after what she'd been through? What was driving that woman?

Forty-five minutes dragged on like hours. Then, to Mona's relief, Judge Doreen Weyer entered the courtroom to make her ruling.

Lindy Field would no longer be the attorney for Darren DiCinni.

Everett Woodard then made his argument for dismissal. It took fifteen minutes. Then Judge Weyer ordered DiCinni bound over for trial on six counts of murder, with special circumstances.

FOURTEEN

✝ ✝ ✝

1.

A cheer went up from the members of VOICe as Benni Roberts held up her champagne glass. Mona held a glass, but did not cheer or drink.

They were gathered at Benni Roberts's house for the post-prelim celebration and strategy session. Benni looked flush with victory.

"This only goes to show, once again, what common people working together can do," Benni said. "It's the whole reason VOICe was formed. You are all doing a marvelous job."

Benni cast a quick glance at Mona, who forced a smile.

"And let's drink to the absence of Miss Lindy Field. She was beginning to divert a little too much attention from the real issues."

"She's a defense lawyer," someone said. "That's all they ever do."

Murmurs of agreement spread through the room.

Another woman said, "Now that she's off, George, what happens next?"

George Mahoney, sitting in the large chair in the corner, sipped his champagne. Mona thought he looked a bit like a king after a successful battle, gazing over the field of dead bodies, readying plans for the next fight. "This guy Everett Woodard is a professional. He'll do his job, Colby will do his, and justice will be done. Woodard won't make a lot of trouble the way Lindy Field did."

"You think there'll be a plea bargain?" Benni asked.

"I've let Colby know that the only plea that's going to be agreeable to us is one that puts that kid away for at least twenty-five.

211

Nothing less. And no insanity plea. He tries that, and we'll come down on that office so hard the Richter scale will register it."

Benni said, "On to the hors d'oeuvres!"

People began mingling, chatting, munching. Mona took an egg roll and sat off in a corner. Benni came to her almost immediately.

"Mona, you look out of it, if you don't mind my saying."

"Sorry. I don't feel very sociable."

"Something bothering you? About the case?"

"I don't know."

"Come on. You can tell me."

Mona hesitated then dove in. "I have the strangest feeling. For Lindy Field. I feel sorry for what happened."

"Oh sure, nobody wanted to see her get hurt like that."

"Didn't we?"

Benni just looked at her.

Mona said, "Maybe I'm just speaking for myself. But a lot of ill feelings are shared in our meetings."

"But isn't that part of the point?" Benni said, acting like a patient schoolteacher. "If we don't have anger and passion about these evil acts, they're going to continue. That's one of the reasons VOICe came into being. We are speaking for people who need us."

"I understand all that."

"Don't you hate what that monster did to your son? I'm sorry to be so blunt, but I don't think you should let go of that."

Mona shook her head slowly. "Is hatred right?"

"Sometimes, sure. Even the Bible says God hates evil."

"Then why don't I feel relief? Why don't I feel like God is in this at all?"

Benni walked Mona out to her car. Mona's four-year-old blue Hyundai sat like an unwanted neighbor at the curb in front of the expensive home.

"You just remember to keep relying on us," Benni said. "You're going to have all sorts of feelings pass through you. I know. I've been down that road before."

And then Benni hugged Mona. It felt awkward, a forced intimacy of strangers thrown together by mutual crises.

But Mona credited her disquiet to the stress of getting justice for Matthew. She told herself to give the whole process more time. As she drove away, she looked back and saw Benni giving her a wave. She was standing next to her beautiful, black Mercedes convertible, the perfect car for one of the leading real-estate agents in the Valley.

2.

It was nearly 8:00 p.m. when Roxy dropped Lindy off at Law Dogs on Reseda Boulevard. The hot dog stand was run by an old friend of Lindy's, Evan Moody. He had a network of lawyer friends who'd come down on designated nights, fill up on wieners and Coke, and dispense quick legal advice to Evan's customers.

Evan reserved one table in an enclosed, outside patio for private consultations. Lindy had given enough free legal advice at Law Dogs that Evan offered her the table for conferences any time she wanted.

It was here that she arranged to meet Leon Colby. Neutral territory, and not a place the press would be watching. He had seemed somewhat amused by her request, but he had agreed to come. That was the main thing.

Lindy parked herself on the bench facing the street. She could see more that way. What she expected to see, she wasn't quite sure.

Colby arrived just past eight, dressed in shirtsleeves, his tie loosened. The relaxed prosecutor, the one holding all the cards.

"Evening, Lindy," he said. "Nice office you got here."

"Let's get to the important stuff, shall we?"

"Like what?"

"Like do you want chili on your hot dog or not?"

Colby laughed. "Chili, cheese, and onions. And let me buy."

"In that case I'll have the same, with fries and a large Coke."

Colby went inside to order. Lindy watched him through the window, wondering what she'd think of him if he hadn't prosecuted the Marcel Lee case. He looked like a man people could trust. But could you fully trust a lawyer turned politician? She wanted to know what was going on inside his head.

He came back with the food and settled in opposite Lindy. "I want you to know," he said, "that I'm glad you called me."

"Glad?"

"Look, I know there's not a lot of love lost here. But I want you to know I respect you."

"Well. Thanks. I guess."

"That's the only reason I'm here. Respect. Most defense lawyers in this town, they call me, I'm putting 'em on hold. You I'll talk to. How's that arm?"

Lindy tapped her cast on the table. "I'm getting good with my left hand. Watch." She took a bite of chili dog, using her left hand to do it. A glob of chili dropped on her chin. Her other hand was useless for napkin grabbing.

Colby chuckled. "Yeah, you got it mastered." He reached over with a clean napkin and wiped her chin.

"Tell me something, Leon. Why is it you're not married?"

"You kidding?"

"I'm interested."

"Why?"

"Maybe I'm trying to decide if I'm gonna vote for you."

He paused a moment, then took a big bite from his dog. Half of it disappeared.

"Mmm," he said after some substantial chewing, "these aren't half bad."

"Answer the question."

"Was once. About two years' worth. But it didn't work out. Maybe because I was working all the time. I can't blame her for walking out."

"Nobody else after that?"

"Just why did you ask me to come here, Lindy?"

"You're not answering again."

"And we're not in court."

"I'm here because I think, down inside you, there's more than just ambition."

"What makes you say that? Not that I'm fishing for compliments."

"Oh, no. What politician would ever do that? But I know something about you, Leon."

"What's that?"

"Your father's a minister."

Leon paused with the last vestige of his hot dog halfway to his mouth. He looked at her with an astonished gaze. "You've been investigating me?"

"It's amazing what the Internet can do these days."

"So I have a father. He's a preacher. You want to connect this up for me?"

"You believe in God?"

"None of your business."

Lindy paused. "You're right. It's just that this case has God in it somewhere."

"And you think that place is DiCinni's head."

"Don't you?"

"No."

"I think you're wrong."

"Woodard can try to convince a jury."

Colby sipped his Coke, leaving Lindy to make more of a mess with her chili dog. This time she wiped her own face.

"Something tells me there's more to this meeting," Colby said. "Am I wrong?"

That Colby. He always did have good instincts. Lindy said, "Did you get a copy of the video yet?"

"I've seen it, yeah."

"The one that they showed on TV?"

"Sure."

"Or did you see the uncut version?"

"Uncut?" Colby raised his eyebrows.

"I saw it. When I went over to McIntyre's place."

"You and he still an item?"

"No. Stop distracting me."

Colby smiled. "Then how come *you're* not married?"

"Focus, will you?"

"What does it matter? They showed parts of a video on TV. We all saw it. We all got copies of it. It's not going to make a difference in the grand scheme of things."

"But why doctor it?"

"Who says it's doctored? There's a difference between editing and doctoring."

"That's the whole thing. It's different. Not just because of the editing."

"Different how?"

"I'm not sure. Not until we get the original. Which is why I want you to issue a subpoena."

"On McIntyre?"

"Exactly."

After a sip of Coke, Colby said, "Nobody can say you don't have chutzpah."

"What do you say?"

He shook his head. "I don't know. That would cause some ripples. I don't think I'll even use the video in court. Normally I wouldn't give away my little secrets, Lindy, but this one's not going to make or break either one of us."

"What if it did, though?"

"How could it possibly? It shows the kid spraying bullets. We have plenty of eye witnesses."

Lindy squeezed her napkin. "What?"

"What?"

"What you said."

"What'd I say?"

"Spraying bullets." An idea gripped her. "He wasn't spraying at first."

For the first time that evening, Leon Colby looked truly interested.

"Find out what the cops know about the tape, Leon."

"We've both got better things to do."

"Do we, Leon? Better than seeing what's really going on in this case?"

"I know what's going on. We both do."

Lindy shook her head. "Look a little deeper, will you?"

3.

Roxy picked Lindy up and drove her back to Box Canyon. When they came through the door, Cardozo regarded them with feline aloofness.

"Some watch cat you've got," Roxy said. "Why don't you come stay with me?"

"I'm not helpless."

"I mean, maybe you shouldn't be alone right now."

"I have a gun, Rox."

"You never told me that."

"This is Box Canyon, Roxy. People here understand guns."

"But you're a bleeding heart, get-them-off-on-a-technicality defense lawyer. What are you doing with a gun?"

"Thank you so much. I thought I had a mind of my own."

"You never cease to surprise me."

There was a knock at the door. "So who's home?" Mr. Klinger said.

Lindy turned. "Come on in, Mr. Klinger."

He was halfway in already. "Came to see how my favorite shyster is . . ." He stopped, looked at Roxy.

"This is my friend, Roxy Raymond."

"Hey," Roxy said.

"Two chicks and one rooster." Mr. Klinger clucked and bobbed his eyebrows.

"Watch him," Lindy said. "He's got moves."

"Like Red Grange, baby."

"Who?" Roxy said.

"Before your time, sister." Mr. Klinger, in his undershirt-and-suspenders ensemble, shuffled toward Lindy. "I hear you're off that case. That's a good thing."

Lindy shook her head. "I'm not ready to get off it."

"Now listen!" He wagged his finger at her. "You gotta take care of yourself. You've been in a bad accident. You need rest. You're no Jake LaMotta."

"Who?" Roxy said.

"Before your time," Lindy said.

"Now I just want you to know," Mr. Klinger said, "that I can look in on you from time to time. When I heard you were in sick bay, I made sure your place here was all right. I know where the key . . ." He stopped suddenly.

Lindy eyed him. "Key?"

"Key, sure, what key should I sing in?"

"You know where I keep my spare key?"

Mr. Klinger shrugged. "I'm your neighbor, I'm supposed to know."

"Have you ever used that key?"

"What's a key good for if it's not used?"

"Did you come in here a few weeks ago, at night?"

Now he looked caught, like the boy with cookie crumbs on his chin. "I just wanted to see if everything was all right."

"Why didn't you just knock on the door?"

"And scare you?"

"You scared me half to death anyway. I could have shot you."

"I'm sorry, Lindy." He looked at his feet. "I gotta have things to do, I guess. Nobody has anything for me to do."

Lindy sighed. "It's all right, Mr. Klinger. Thanks for thinking of me."

He smiled.

"But no more using the key, huh?"

"Deal," Mr. Klinger said, starting for the door. Then he stopped and nodded at Roxy. "Can I use her key sometime?"

"Good-bye, Mr. Klinger."

"I got my eye on you," he said to Roxy.

"*Good-bye*, Mr. Klinger."

After he was well out, Roxy laughed. "He's a feisty one, isn't he?"

But Lindy was barely listening. Something Mr. Klinger said . . .

"So where shall we go?" Roxy said. "Dancing?"

Lindy looked out the window. Night haze obscured the lights of the Valley she should have been able to see.

"Indoor volleyball?"

I got my eye on you.

"Come on, Lindy, focus."

She snapped a look at Roxy. "He was aiming at someone."

"Excuse me?"

"Darren's first shot, he was aiming. In the video. The part that wasn't on the news."

"Are you sure?"

Lindy nodded. "He looked deliberate at first. After that everybody says he was spraying bullets."

"Does that make any difference?"

"It might. Maybe he was after someone specifically at the beginning. Who was the first kid hit?"

"I think there were two kids," Roxy said. "One kid, Landis I think, was playing third base and the one named Matthew Romney was standing on the base."

"Two of them?"

"Yeah. You thinking Darren knew one of them? Had something against the kid maybe?"

"There's no indication he knew any of the kids." Lindy rubbed her left temple. "What about the adult, Dorai? He was coaching third base."

Roxy shook her head. "But it doesn't make sense that he was the target."

"Why not?"

"Because Darren went after the kids. Remember, he didn't even hit Jones, the first-base coach."

"Let's talk to somebody who knew Dorai," Lindy said. "He was a teacher at Coolidge High. Didn't you get a list of some teachers who knew him?"

"Yeah, and I made some calls. Nobody really knew him that well. Not like friends or anything."

"Who is the first name on that list?"

"I don't remember."

"Then find out. What am I paying you for?"

"You haven't paid me."

"Don't get technical."

4.

Leon Colby talked to Larry Lopez about the video over morning coffee at The Pantry. L.A.'s most famous downtown diner had been a fixture for decades and a favorite meeting place of professionals on their way to or from the high-rise offices that sprouted like iron and glass weeds between Temple and Seventh.

"Everybody in the world's seen it," Lopez said. "Can't put that genie back in the bottle."

"It's the doctoring part that bothers me."

Lopez waved his hand. "How can you take Field's word for it? She's kind of out there."

"But she's not a nut."

"Not what I'm saying. But she's been through a lot, almost killed. Got yanked from the case. And she and McIntyre were together once, remember that?"

"Yeah."

"So maybe she's out to make him look bad."

"I don't think she's the type."

Lopez shrugged. "But again, I'm saying what's the difference? The tape's not needed."

"I'll tell you what the difference is." Colby motioned to the waitress for more coffee. "Difference is I don't like being lied to, that's the difference."

The electric look Lopez gave him hit like a jolt of low amperage. Enough to cause a minor snap, make Colby look around for the cause. And he detected it immediately, in Lindy Field's voice. *Since when have you been so concerned about being lied to? You let things slide in court when it helps. Why get a conscience about it now?*

"You're working for me," Colby snapped. "So let's just get to the bottom of this."

"What bottom?" A little attitude in Lopez's voice.

"I want you to go see Mr. McIntyre, and I want you to get the original of this tape. Tell him we're not going to make a big deal if he just hands it over."

"Why should he do that?"

"Because we're the law. And if he doesn't seem inclined, tell him I'm more than willing to take it to the next level, maybe park his can in jail for withholding evidence."

Colby's voice was a little too loud for the setting. The waitress, holding the pot of coffee, didn't move.

"It's okay," Colby said, holding his cup for her.

After she left Lopez said, "Man, what's with you?"

"Don't go Dr. Phil on me, Larry. Just do what I tell you."

"Whatever," Lopez said.

5.

The door of the little house on Owensmouth opened a crack. A chain spanned the gap. Lindy could see half of the woman's face.

"Ms. Fambry?" Lindy said.

"Yes?"

"My name is Lindy Field. From the DiCinni case."

Pause. The darkness seemed to deepen. The nearest streetlight was half a block away and offered a poor excuse for illumination.

"You have to go," the woman said.

"Please," Lindy said, "I need to just ask you a few questions about Joel Dorai."

"I don't want to get involved."

"I won't involve you, I promise. This will just be between us."

"Please go away. Please. I can't . . . I don't want anyone to see."

"If you'll just let me in for a few minutes, that's all I ask. Then I'll go away and won't bother you again. No one will know I've been here."

The scared half-face turned. "Who's she?"

"This is my assistant, Roxy Raymond."

"Assistant? You're getting me involved."

"No, she's just here to help me move around. I'm a little incapacitated at the moment."

Kim Fambry looked Lindy up and down. "I heard about your accident."

"I got pretty banged up, as you can see."

"I'm sorry. Come in."

Kim had short black hair and a caring face etched with concern, the same look Lindy saw on so many potential witnesses through the years. People just didn't want to get involved in criminal cases these days, especially the high-profile kind. The three sat in the modest living room, Kim Fambry seeming ill at ease.

"You were a colleague of Joel Dorai?" Lindy asked.

"Yes, we taught at Coolidge together."

"What do you teach?"

"English."

"And Joel?"

"History."

"Did you know him well?"

"That's a hard question to answer."

"Why is that?"

"He wasn't very sociable. I don't mean in a bad way. I just got the impression he wanted to keep to himself. Some of the teachers thought he had an attitude. I didn't. Maybe that's why he talked to me now and then."

"Was this just passing conversation, or was there more to it?"

Kim shrugged. "Again, it's hard to know. He did say he trusted me, felt he could talk to me."

"Do you know if he was well liked by the students?"

"Some. A few were really fanatical about him, I remember that. He had a bit of a following, more than most teachers."

Lindy looked at Roxy, who scribbled a note on her pad.

Kim said, "I don't want you to write anything down, please."

"This is only for me," Lindy said. "I'm not going to use your name in any way."

"I don't want you to." The woman's voice was strained. "If you do I'm not going to say anything."

Lindy nodded to Roxy. Best to walk on eggshells. "Fine. No notes. What else can you tell me about Joel?"

"This was his second year at the school. I don't know where he was before that. He never said."

"The school would have records."

"Sure."

"Do you know if he had a family?"

"He didn't wear a wedding ring, never talked about having any family. Maybe he was divorced or something, starting over again."

"Maybe. But he coached a Little League team. Most of the time a coach is someone who has a kid playing. Not this time. Did he ever talk about baseball?"

"He never talked much about anything, he . . ." Kim's voice trailed off.

"You were going to say?"

"I don't know if I should."

Lindy leaned slightly forward. "Please. Anything. What you say remains confidential. I promise."

"Well . . . I think he was into some kind of pornography."

"What?"

"The day after he was killed, the police came to the school. They asked some questions. I talked to one of them."

"What did they want to know?"

"Same things you do, I guess. When they didn't get much from me or anybody else, they went ahead and took all the stuff out of his room. They put it in boxes."

"The police cleaned out Joel Dorai's room?" Lindy looked at Roxy.

"Yeah. That's why I think it was some sort of pornography deal. I mean, he's a single man, he keeps to himself, and then the police take all his stuff. That seems kind of strange, doesn't it?"

Lindy's ears started to tingle. "It's outrageous, is what it is. The prosecution never bothered to tell me about this."

Kim started rubbing her hands together.

"Is anything wrong?" Lindy asked.

"Could I get in trouble?"

"For what?"

"Is this really confidential?"

"I promise."

The teacher took a breath. "The police didn't get everything out of his room."

"What do you mean?"

"Joel . . . he gave me a box and asked if I'd keep it in my room, in the closet. Just for a while. It was taped up."

A skittering chill ran up Lindy's spine. "Do you still have it?"

Kim nodded. "I brought it here. I'm afraid to look in it. I'm afraid to give it to the police. They'll ask me questions."

"May I see it?"

"I'm afraid I'll get in trouble if I show it to you."

"Do you have a dollar?"

The teacher looked at Lindy, confused. "Of course."

"Give it to me," Lindy said. "That will be my retainer. You will have officially hired me to represent your interests. You will be absolved of all responsibility regarding the box. And I will not let anyone know how I got it. Fair enough?"

"Is that legal?"

"Rock solid."

Kim Fambry went to her purse, took out a dollar, and handed it to Lindy. Then she went and got the box.

6.

Leon Colby took lunch at the cafeteria. Normally he avoided the place as if it were a roach coach, but he was in a hurry.

The video thing was really bothering him. He hadn't been up-front with Lindy Field when he told her it didn't mean much. Maybe in terms of the case that was true, but it meant someone was playing with him. Probably McIntyre. And he did not appreciate that. No, he was not going to let him get by with that one.

He ordered chili and cornbread and took a table in the corner. Just before he dipped a spoon in the bowl of red, he thought about praying over his meal.

Now that was funny. He hadn't thought of returning thanks for a long time. It was something his dad always did. Maybe that was just because Lindy had reminded him—

"May I join you?"

Leon looked up at Judge Roger Greene.

"Well, Judge," Leon Colby said, "since I'm not up before you on anything, I guess the *L.A. Times* won't mind."

With a chuckle, Greene slid into the chair opposite Colby. He had an apple, a sandwich, and milk. A regular American.

"How goes the war?" Greene took a bite of his triangular half-sandwich.

"Keeping the world safe for democracy?"

"Or the streets at least."

"Fine."

"A lot of publicity on the DiCinni matter."

"What can I say?"

"Star-making publicity."

Leon wondered what he meant by that.

"I'm not looking to be a star," Colby said.

"Nothing wrong if it happens," Greene said. "You still running for DA?"

"This place is a lousy venue for secrets."

Greene smiled. "No worries. The case itself is taking most of the attention. Especially after what happened to Lindy."

Colby said nothing.

"I care very much for her," Judge Greene said.

"I know."

"She has some concerns about what's going on under the surface of this case. That videotape, for instance. What's going on there?"

"Judge, if you don't mind my asking, what's your interest in all this?"

"Besides Lindy? How about the truth?"

The word hit Colby like a fist. "Then we're in the same ballpark."

"Then you won't mind if I take an interest in the case, on a personal basis."

"Lots of people have an interest, don't they?"

The smile faded from Greene's face. "You want some free advice? Get a deal. Even if it's less than you want. Get this case done. Because I don't want to see any disrepute fall on the administration of justice."

"And you think that's what I'm doing?"

"Just some free advice." Greene stood up, having consumed one bite of his lunch. "I'll be seeing you, Mr. Colby."

Leon Colby's appetite left with the judge.

He was just about to head back to the office when his cell phone bleeped. Larry Lopez.

"You're gonna have to wait on that video," Lopez said.

"Why's that?"

"I'm here at McIntyre's apartment. His stuff is gone. Computers, cameras, all that."

Colby let out a breath. "And where's McIntyre?"

"Oh, he's right here, Leon."

"What's he got to say?"

"Not much. See, he's got two bullet holes in the back of his head."

7.

The scene Leon Colby encountered at Sean McIntyre's apartment was, in many ways, typical. A forensics team was busily doing its thing, taking photographs, gathering trace evidence. A team from Robbery Homicide Division oversaw the operation.

But in another more troubling way, this scene was not typical at all. Not for Leon at least. A citizen who had provided evidence turned up dead in what looked like a professional hit.

What *was* going on?

"Could've been anybody," Larry Lopez said. He had his arms folded over his wrinkled brown coat, looking down at McIntyre's body. A medical examiner with rubber gloves and a swab was leaning over the reporter's head.

"Not anybody," Colby said. "It looks professional."

"Remember, this guy liked to run with the criminal element, get their stories, sometimes exploit 'em. I wouldn't be surprised if it was some guy who wanted money for his video. McIntyre tells him to blow, and there you are."

"They have any idea when this happened? What time?"

"Too early to say yet. But this is how I found him. Me and the manager."

"He was with you?"

"Had to let me in. I made him. Showed him my shield."

Colby shook his head. "Nice illegal move."

Lopez raised a hand in protest. "I wasn't out to get evidence. I was out to talk to the guy."

"And maybe look around while you—"

"Yo, don't bust my bones, Leon. I'm on your side."

"Maybe I want my guys to follow the law from time to time."

"What's with you?"

Colby said, "Just stay here and get me a preliminary report. I want to know what time this happened and what was taken. Anybody who knew McIntyre, what was in here?"

"Yeah," Lopez said, smirking. "Lindy Field."

8.

The box Kim Fambry gave Lindy, at first glance, seemed to be a whole lot of nothing.

Lindy went through it at her kitchenette table. The box contained some marked-up history text, a few printed articles from the Internet on subjects like Lewis and Clark and the Treaty of Versailles. There were a couple of CDs—Cat Stevens's *Greatest Hits*, Huey Lewis & the News, *Piano Rags* by Scott Joplin. Joel Dorai might have had eclectic musical taste, but that wasn't going to solve any puzzles.

There was a baseball glove with a ball in it, the sort of thing a kid would have in his closet. A paperweight with a quote attributed to Winston Churchill: *Never never never quit.*

Some old *Newsweek* and *Time* magazines. And notebooks, with odd things scribbled in them. Blank verse. Attempts at poetry. Doodles.

What did it all add up to? And what was so important about his school materials that the police seized them? And the contents of this box, that Dorai would have asked someone to hide them?

She looked at Cardozo, sunning himself at the window. "Do you have any idea what's going on?"

Cardozo said nothing. He blinked when Lindy's phone bleeped. She almost let it go to voice mail, but something told her to pick up.

It was Leon Colby.

"To what do I owe the pleasure?"

"Not a pleasure call, Lindy."

The tone in his voice made her sit up. "What is it?"

"I have some bad news, and I wanted you to get it before the news does."

"Darren?"

"No. Sean McIntyre. He was murdered."

A hammer hit Lindy in the chest.

"In his apartment. Shot."

The surreal words pushed her to the wakeful edge of a nightmare. She wanted to cry out and make the words go away.

"I know you were close to him," Colby said.

She fought to say, "Why?"

"We don't know. We know he liked to get close to the crime element for his stories. He may have had a long list of enemies."

A hole opened inside her and she felt she might fall into it. Sean. Dead. She saw his face then, in her mind, smiling winsomely. She heard his voice. Her throat began to swell with grief.

"I'm sorry, Lindy."

She shook her head slowly.

"I have to ask you one question, just routine."

She waited, fighting back tears.

"You can account for your whereabouts last night, right?"

"You can't be serious."

"It's ridiculous, I know, but—"

Indignation overcame her sorrow. "No, it makes perfect sense! I broke into Sean's apartment with one arm and killed him."

"Like I said, it's just a question that someone might ask—"

"It's a stupid question."

"I know. I wanted to give you a heads up on it, that's all. Good night."

"Wait a minute, Leon." She paused and took a moment to compose herself. "Thanks for calling. I appreciate it, I really do."

"No problem."

"Now I want to ask you a question. How come you never told me about the police searching Joel Dorai's room at Coolidge High School?"

After a pause, Colby said, "First I've heard about it."

"What's going on with your office and the police?"

"They have their job to do. If they found anything relevant, they'd hand it over."

"Would they?"

"You've seen too many suspense movies, Lindy. But I'll make this deal with you. As soon as anything relevant comes across my desk, I'll get it to Everett. He's insisting on a speedy trial, and I'm happy to accommodate that."

"Are you still refusing to consider an insanity deal?"

"Yes."

"Darren needs treatment."

"Take care, Lindy. Again, I'm sorry."

And he was gone. Her trailer was suddenly very quiet. Box Canyon, normally alive with the whisper of night air, was still. As still as the lifeless place in her, where the broken memories of loved ones lay.

Then, quite unexpectedly, she was saying something out loud, and realized with a detached wonderment that it was a prayer for Sean McIntyre.

PART II

† † †

FIFTEEN

† † †

1.

"Nearly three months after the Capistrano Park killings, the trial is set to begin, and our panel of experts will be joining us later. First, though, we're going to hear from the mother of one of the victims, Mona Romney."

An eerie sort of calmness enveloped Mona. She had felt the calluses developing on her soul as the trial date approached. The calluses were tough and fibrous and protected her well.

Even being on TV with Hank Dunaway, who had a national talk show on cable, didn't faze her now.

"This can't be easy for you," Dunaway said. The avuncular man, a veteran of local L.A. news, was noted for his ability to relate to victims of crimes.

"It's just something I have to go through, as do the other parents," Mona said. She thought of Brad then, his face flashing before her mind even though she had not seen him since she had the divorce papers served. "But we do it because we're not willing to let injustice prevail."

"I should mention that you are a member of a group called Victims of Injustice and Crime, is that correct?"

"It's a support group that advocates for justice in the criminal courts. We've seen too many criminals get away with things because of technicalities in the law. We want to stop that."

"Your son, Matthew, was eleven years old?"

"Yes."

"Can you describe your feelings on that day, the day he was killed?"

"Hank, words can't begin to describe it. It was the worst thing I've ever gone through, or will ever go through. I just . . ." She shook her head. "I'm sorry."

"No, it's perfectly understandable. I'm sure everybody in our audience understands. Maybe you could tell us how you got through it. Did you rely on people, a religious faith? What was it that helped you deal with a trauma like this?"

Mona did not hesitate. "It's just an inner strength you have to have, or you fold. I just knew that if I wasn't able to go on I would be shaming the memory of my son. And I determined I was not going to do that."

"How has this inner strength changed you?"

"I just know that I have to fight for justice."

Hank Dunaway leaned on the desk, chin in hand, the way a concerned neighbor would talk over a kitchen table. "What's your feeling about the way the case has been handled thus far?"

"In what way?"

"By the press, the public, the lawyers. I mean, it's all over the place."

She was on national television. She should have been nervous. But something strong and sure and relentless had replaced the nerves with intoxicating confidence. Matthew's spirit and memory had brought her to this moment. She would not let him down.

"Hank, I feel this case is a wake-up call. We can't look away from these things anymore. Fortunately, the prosecutor in this case—"

"Leon Colby."

"Yes, Mr. Colby has assured me and the other victims' families that he is not going to compromise. He has been working closely with us. We feel that we can trust him."

"And the defense? They've had some setbacks. The motorcycle accident."

Mona's muscles tensed, like a rattlesnake had been tossed on the desk. "That doesn't concern me."

"The defense doesn't?"

"They have their job to do, and I'm sure they'll do it. But I'm also sure that any attempts to sway the jury with false sympathy will be stopped by Mr. Colby."

"What do you mean, 'false sympathy'?"

"A situation like this, where the defendant is a teenager, I'm sure they'll play that card. But we both know, Hank, that teenagers are capable of doing evil things, horrible things. Age doesn't matter. But they keep saying he's just a kid, and things like that. It does not *matter.*"

"Do you think he might be insane?"

"No."

"That's what the defense will try to show."

"Let them. He's not insane."

"You'd like to see him in prison."

"I'd like the law to be upheld. And as I understand it, when you shoot six people in cold blood, when you tear apart six families and a whole community, you must be punished to the maximum extent of the law. I for one am going to make sure that happens."

"I know it's hard, Mrs. Romney, to do what you're doing. You have tremendous courage. Will you be in the courtroom?"

"Every day."

2.

Finally here, Lindy thought. They were in trial. She practically vibrated with adrenaline. She sat at counsel table, her right arm finally out of a cast but feeling almost like a foreign appendage, a limb tacked on at the shoulder with duct tape. At least she could walk around now without severe pain.

She wasn't lead counsel. That was Woodard's role. He was the one being paid by the county now. But Lindy had come too far to bail on Darren.

He sat next to her, wearing the suit she had found for him. It fit loosely. He had been losing weight. Worse, he had withdrawn from her again. She could only imagine what was going on in his head as he sat in a cage at county jail. She hoped her mere presence would reassure him that he had one constant in his life, a lawyer who wouldn't abandon him.

Judge Lipton, an angular man with creases in his face that gave the impression of aged wood, reminded Lindy of the tree people in *Lord of the Rings*. Dark brown eyes burrowed twin knots in the deep bark of his face.

"Your Honor," Leon Colby said, "we are ready to proceed with our opening statement."

"Ready for the defense, Your Honor," Everett Woodard said.

"All right, let's call in the jury."

"One moment." Lindy stood up, giving a sideward glance at the gallery. "Your Honor, before we have the jury in, I would move that those in court wearing VOICe buttons be told to take them off, and keep them off when in the courthouse."

An immediate burst of groans hit the room. Lindy heard some voices behind her. Someone said *She can't do that.*

"Mr. Colby?" Judge Lipton said.

Colby spoke with assured calm. "These citizens have free speech rights, the same as any others. I don't see the problem."

"Of course not," Lindy said. "But the defense does. What's the jury going to think every time they look out here and see an interest group wearing their buttons?"

More voices, more outraged this time.

Judge Lipton banged his gavel three quick times. "I haven't had to use my gavel in ten years. And I don't want to use it for another ten years. Anyone who speaks out of turn in my courtroom will be escorted out." He looked over his glasses at the gallery. "I am going to grant Ms. Field's motion and ask that all badges be removed while in court, or in the building where they might be seen by jurors. I have no say about what happens outside these walls."

A few groans of protest, muted by the judge's previous admonition, was followed by the sound of buttons being thrown angrily into purses or pockets. Lindy half-expected to be hit in the back with one or two.

But calm prevailed and the judge called the jury in. The eight women and four men were about the best she and Woodard could hope for. Lindy thought two of the women and one of the men could be reached, maybe with enough conviction to influence the others. Maybe. By the longest shot of her career.

"Proceed, Mr. Colby," the judge said.

Leon Colby spoke without notes. "Ladies and gentlemen, on the morning of June 26, the defendant, Darren DiCinni, walked to Capistrano Park in West Hills, carrying a loaded rifle. You will hear from eyewitnesses about the horrible events that followed. You will hear about how five young boys and one adult man were killed by the gun fired by Darren DiCinni. What you won't hear, ladies and gentlemen, is any dispute about those facts. The defense is not going to try to prove to you that their client didn't do the killing."

Colby turned and looked at Darren. As he did, his eyes slipped past Lindy's gaze.

"What will be at issue, ladies and gentlemen, is what was in the mind of the defendant as he took a loaded rifle, proceeded to Capistrano Park, walked up to the field where a game was going on, and opened fire, spraying bullets, killing six people. We will present evidence to you, expert testimony, that the defendant knew that what he was doing was wrong. It's really that simple. If he did know, then he is guilty as charged.

"What we present to you will not be complex. You will hear from eyewitnesses what happened. You will hear the evidence that links the weapon found on the defendant to the bullets that killed the victims. You will hear evidence that the defendant, though a troubled teenager, nevertheless knew exactly what he was doing.

"At the end of the trial, when all the evidence is in, the judge will instruct you on the law. You are to apply the law to the evidence. And let me remind you that what I say to you as a lawyer is not evidence. It is not something that you are to base your verdict on. What I say to you is only to alert you to the evidence that will be coming in by way of testimony of sworn witnesses. That is what you are to consider. I say this because there may be an attempt on the part of the defense to elicit your sympathies by way of the arguments."

Fire ripped through Lindy. Every part of her body wanted to stand up and object. She felt Woodard's hand on her arm. *Steady*, he seemed to say.

She kept quiet.

"We can all feel sympathy for various parties here. Sympathy for the families of the victims, for sure. Perhaps even for the defendant. But you must not let that enter in to your decision. When the evidence is in and the law is presented to you, you will reach the only possible verdict: Guilty on all counts."

Leon Colby waited a dramatic moment, then sat down.

"Mr. Woodard, you may open," Judge Lipton said.

Everett stood, buttoning his coat as he did. "Your Honor, at this time the defense would like to proceed with the opening statement, delivered by Ms. Field."

A skeptical look flashed across the judge's oaken face. "That's not what the defense had proffered."

"Your Honor, it is a decision I have reached as lead attorney as I listened to the People's opening. Ms. Field left that decision to me. Our client has expressed his support for the decision. As I see it—"

"Mr. Woodard, I don't want any surprises of a procedural nature."

"And it will not be our practice, Your Honor."

"Any objection from the People?"

Leon Colby stood. "We are somewhat surprised too, as we were told Mr. Woodard would be speaking. But I have no objection to Ms. Field."

"All right," the judge said. "This is a decision that rests squarely with the defense. Ms. Field, you may proceed."

Lindy went to the podium. "Good morning, ladies and gentlemen. As you know, I represent Darren DiCinni. He's sitting right over there. He is thirteen years old. And he has been vilified and painted as a monster since the very first newscast about this case. This is my opportunity to give you another side of the story, the kind they're not interested in reporting.

"And I would remind you, as counsel for the People has reminded you, that certain things are not evidence. What you've heard in conversation or seen on the television or read in the papers, none of that is evidence. During jury selection you all said that you could disregard anything you have heard and be impartial. In fact you swore an oath to do so. I'm confident that you will be true to your oath.

"Mr. Colby said you could expect to hear expert testimony at this trial. Remember, you are the judges of the facts. Just because someone is an expert does not mean that you have to accept what they say as the gospel truth. You are going to watch them testify, and you are going to hear them be cross-examined. You will reach your own conclusions.

"You also heard Mr. Colby say that you should be suspicious of sympathy. It almost sounded like he was telling you not to be human beings—"

"And this," Leon Colby said, rising, "sounds like a closing argument, not an opening statement. So I'm going to object."

"Sustained," Judge Lipton said.

Lindy continued immediately. "I would like to remind you again of the presumption of innocence and the burden of proof. The People must prove beyond a reasonable doubt that my client, Darren DiCinni, was of sound mind when he fired those terrible shots on June 26. The defense, on the other hand, does not have to prove anything. We do not have to prove innocence. The law does not require us to do that. It requires the prosecution"—Lindy pointed at Leon Colby—"to present enough compelling evidence for you to find every single element required under the charges to be true, beyond a reasonable doubt. That is a very high standard, and it must be, for we're talking about a young man's life. Yes, he took the lives of six people. But mark this: Darren DiCinni's mind was not right. It's still not. He was legally insane at the time of the shootings, and that means that his mental state was not what is required for a guilty verdict.

"We do not punish people who are not responsible for their actions. We do not—"

"Counsel," Judge Lipton said sharply, "that is definitely a closing argument. Confine yourself to what you believe the evidence will show. I will instruct the jury on the law." He turned to the jury. "You will disregard any comment by the counsel for the defense on what the law says about mental state."

Lindy looked at the jury for an extended moment then said, "We trust you will do your duty."

3.

Mona's stomach clenched like a fist, a familiar reaction to the sight or sound of Lindy Field.

Especially when she was pulling another fast one.

Standing up like that, making a statement after her accident. A ploy to gain sympathy from the jury.

She wasn't going to get away with it.

George Mahoney, sitting next to her, must have sensed her physical distress. He put his hand on hers and patted it.

The way Brad used to.

She felt a pang, knowing Brad wanted to be here. He did not come, because it would upset her, or at least distract her. That was Brad. Mr. Noble. He needed a noble wife. She was not it.

She heard Janelle Thompson's name called. The first mother to testify.

She squeezed George Mahoney's hand. This was it. The lead witness, the setting of tone. Mona wished she were the one, but she was not on the witness list. She was ready, though, if things changed.

4.

"Mrs. Thompson," Leon Colby said, "you are the mother of Cody Thompson, one of the little boys who lost his life, is that correct?"

"Yes."

She was going to make a good witness, Lindy thought. A confident-looking woman, but not so much that her vulnerability was obscured. A woman who could be your best friend.

"How old was Cody when he was killed?"

"He was twelve."

"On the morning of June 26, can you tell us where you were at about nine o'clock?"

"I was at Capistrano Park for my son's baseball game."

"Your son was on the White Sox, that was his team?"

"Yes."

"Turning your attention to just before the shootings, let me—"

"Objection," Everett Woodard said calmly in his firm baritone. "Assumes facts not in evidence."

"Sustained," Judge Lipton said.

Colby looked annoyed, but only mildly. Lindy thought it uncharacteristic of him to be so sloppy in his initial questioning.

"I'll ask you this way, Mrs. Thompson. At some point during the game, did something unusual happen?"

The witness scowled. "Something horrible is more like it."

"Tell the jury, step by step, what happened."

She turned to the jury box. *Well prepared by Colby.*

"My son was playing shortstop for the White Sox. The other team, the Royals, was up to bat. There was a lot of good-natured cheering going on, as usual. I knew several of the moms and dads from the other team as well as our own. We were all having a good time. And that's when I heard the shots being fired."

"What was the sound that got your attention?"

"Like shots. *Bang bang bang.* Like that."

"What did you see?"

"I looked to my right and saw him"—she nodded toward Darren—"holding a rifle and just shooting at everything he could."

"May the record show the witness has identified the defendant?"

"The record will so reflect," said the judge.

Colby said, "What did you do in response to the shootings?"

Janelle Thompson took a deep breath. Now she appeared to be fighting for strength. "My first thought was for Cody. I thought, *Oh my God, he's shooting the children.* People started to scream. I was in the stands and I tried to get down. People were standing up all around me. It was terrible chaos. But I fought my way down, screaming Cody's name."

She paused. Stillness captured the courtroom.

"When I got to the field," Mrs. Thompson continued, "I saw Cody lying in the dirt. I ran to him. I dropped to my knees and screamed for somebody to help. He looked me in the eyes, but only for a second. That's how long it took him to go. That's how long I had with my boy before he died."

Colby nodded slowly. Not a sound filled the courtroom save the slight rustling of pencils on paper as reporters took notes. "How has your life changed since you lost your son, Mrs. Thompson?"

"Objection," Woodard said. "Relevance."

Judge Lipton said, "Yes, I will sustain the objection at this time."

But Lindy knew no objection could remove Janelle Thompson's expression from the jurors' minds. She fought back tears, and just as clearly held on to her dignity.

"Thank you, Mrs. Thompson," Leon Colby said. "I have no further questions."

"No questions at this time," Everett Woodard said.

"What?" Lindy whispered so loudly the judge snapped a look at her.

Judge Lipton said, "Mrs. Thompson, you may—"

"One moment, Your Honor," Lindy said.

Again, a sharp look. "What is it, Counsel?"

"May I confer with my co-counsel?"

"Regarding what?"

"Regarding cross-examination of this witness."

"Mr. Woodard said there would be no questions."

"I would like to confer with him on that," Lindy said.

Lipton shook his head. "I'm not going to have the two of you discussing these matters in open court. Mr. Woodard is the lead counsel, and therefore what he decides to do will be decisive. Now, I will allow it this one time, but from this point forward I want the two of you to get your act together, is that understood?"

"Understood," Lindy said.

Everett Woodard leaned down to Lindy and whispered, "What are you doing?"

"Ask her about the aiming issue," Lindy said.

"That crazy stuff about the videotape?"

"It's not crazy. Her story contradicts it."

"I'm not going to cross-examine on that issue. It doesn't help us either way. It's simply not relevant."

Still whispering, Lindy said, "I want to get this on the record. I want to know exactly what she says happened."

"Let this go, Lindy. I'm telling you."

The judge interrupted. "Have we got a decision or not?"

"May we approach the bench?" Lindy said, drawing a look of rebuke from her co-counsel.

"No," said Judge Lipton. "You may not approach on this issue. Are you going to cross-examine or not? Mr. Woodard, you may answer."

Woodard said, "We will not cross-examine this witness."

Lindy balled her hands into fists.

5.

Leon Colby addressed the next witness. "Officer Glenn, you were the arresting officer in this incident, were you not?"

"Yes, I was."

"You arrived at the scene after receiving a radio call, correct?"

"Correct."

"When you arrived at the scene, please tell us what you did."

Glenn turned slightly toward the jury. "My partner and I proceeded toward the baseball diamond. We encountered several people who were agitated. Some of them were crying. A couple of them were yelling at us to do something. I was finally able to ascertain from one of the people that the suspect had been shooting and had been apprehended over in the play area."

"About how far was the play area from where you were standing?"

"Not very far. I'd say about fifty yards."

"What did you do next?"

"My partner and I proceeded to the play area, where we saw several men holding the defendant down on the ground. A man who was standing close by held the rifle that was taken from the defendant."

Colby took the rifle from his counsel table and showed it to the witness. "Showing you now People's Exhibit Four, can you tell us if this is the rifle?"

"Yes, it is."

Colby put the rifle back on the table, in full view of the jury.

"Did you arrest the defendant?"

"Yes, I did."

"Did the defendant offer any resistance?"

"No, he did not."

"Would you describe the defendant as fairly passive?"

"Yes."

"Cooperative?"

"To a point."

Colby paused, frowned slightly. "What do you mean, to a point?"

"I mean that we read him his Miranda rights and he decided not to talk to us."

"So he did not request a lawyer or anything like that?"

"Nothing. He didn't say a word. He didn't have to."

Again, Colby paused. "Why didn't he have to?"

"Because he gives us, you know, an obscene gesture."

"An obscene gesture?"

"Yes. You can say a lot with one finger."

Colby nodded his head but did not ask another question. Which made Lindy all the more curious about this exchange. She leaned over to Woodard and said, "I want to cross-examine."

Perhaps fearing another outburst of bickering in open court, Everett held up his hands, shook his head, and said, "Fine."

6.

"Officer Glenn," Lindy said, leaning on the podium, "You testified in the preliminary hearing in this case, did you not?"

"Yes." His voice was clipped, formal, and aggressive. He had probably been waiting for this moment, hoping for it, since the prelim. Lindy told herself not to get too aggressive in return. This was going to be a showdown between two poker players.

Lindy had the transcript from the preliminary hearing on the podium. "I'm turning now to page forty-seven of the preliminary hearing transcript. I will ask if you recall the following exchanges. Mr. Colby asked you, 'Did you proceed to take the suspect into custody?' And you answered, 'I did.' Question: 'How would you describe the suspect's demeanor?' Answer: 'He didn't offer any resistance.' Do you recall being asked those questions and giving those answers?"

"If it's in the transcript, I guess I did. But since I don't have the transcript in front of me I can't remember exactly everything I said. It would be nice if you provided me a copy."

Clever boy. Make it seem to the jury that the big bad defense lawyer is not playing fair.

"Shall I have the judge explain the law to you, Officer Glenn? That this is a perfectly legitimate way of helping you to recall what you said?"

Before Colby could object, Judge Lipton, with only slightly muted sarcasm, said, "Thank you, Ms. Field. The court appreciates your concerns. Continue with your questions."

"I would have the court remind the witness to answer only the questions that are asked."

"The witness knows that, Ms. Field. Continue."

"Now that I have read these questions and answers to you, Officer Glenn, do you or don't you recall this testimony?"

"I recall it."

"By the way, when you testified at the preliminary hearing you testified under oath, did you not?"

"Of course."

"And when you swore to tell the truth, the whole truth, and nothing but the truth, that is the same oath you took here today, correct?"

"I know what the oath is."

"Going on with page forty-seven of the transcript, Mr. Colby asked you if the defendant was cooperative. At that point I raised an objection, which was sustained. Mr. Colby then asked you to expand on your answer that the defendant did not offer resistance. And you said 'He was cooperative.' Do you recall giving that answer?"

"Yes."

"Question: 'Did you advise the suspect of his Miranda rights?' Answer: 'Yes.' Question: 'Did he say that he understood his rights?' Answer: 'He chose not to say anything.' Do you recall being asked those questions and giving those answers?"

"Yes."

"You then stated in the transcript that you asked no further questions of the defendant. Do you recall saying that?"

"Yes."

Lindy closed the transcript. "Officer Glenn, at no time during the questioning by Mr. Colby did you ever say anything about the defendant giving you an obscene gesture, isn't that true?"

The witness leaned forward and Lindy thought she saw the start of a sly smile. "He never asked me about it. I only answer the questions that are asked."

A couple of the jurors laughed.

"Then I will ask you a question that you can answer yes or no, Officer Glenn. You did not mention this obscene gesture at the preliminary hearing, did you?"

"I did."

She could not believe his reply. "Excuse me, Officer Glenn. Can you direct me to the portion of the preliminary transcript where you mentioned the obscene gesture?"

He looked at the judge. "May I answer in my own way?"

"I'm interested in your answer too, Officer," Judge Lipton said.

"I mentioned it at the preliminary, but off the record. I mentioned it to Mr. Colby. He didn't seem interested, so I didn't push it. There was a lot going on, as there usually is when you're called in to testify."

"Officer," Lindy said, "I want you to listen very carefully to my next question. Can you do that for me?"

He smiled. "Sure."

"Here it is: Did you or did you not state while under oath that my client gave you an obscene gesture?"

"I did not state that while under oath, because I wasn't asked. I just thought—"

"That's enough," Lindy said.

"—Mr. Colby would ask—"

"Your Honor, I object to the witness carrying on."

"Sustained," Judge Lipton said. "The jury will disregard the last statement by the witness."

Sure. Right. Try to unring the bell. "Officer Glenn, so the jury understands"—Lindy turned toward the jury box—"and just so we're clear: You didn't make any statement about an obscene gesture under oath at the preliminary hearing. Was it mentioned in the police report?"

"No. I didn't feel—"

"Thank you. No further questions."

Leon Colby had only two questions on redirect. "Officer Glenn, you are testifying today under oath, isn't that correct?"

"Yes."

"Have your answers today been truthful?"

"Yes, of course."

"Thank you."

Yes, of course. Officer Glenn and Leon Colby are a couple of angels, flapping around the courtroom.

Lindy stole a glance at the jury. They seemed carved as Rushmore—twelve great, stone faces set in a mountain of disapprobation. Things would have to get better soon, or the rocks would come down on Darren DiCinni.

Sixteen

† † †

1.

Judge Lipton took Friday off for a "personal matter." Lindy figured it was a fishing trip. Lipton was known to throw three-day weekends into his schedule every now and again so he could chase bass.

Which almost gave Lindy and Roxy the day off.

Almost.

Roxy came to Lindy's at eight, bearing Starbucks. But Lindy noticed the twin venti cups shook in Roxy's hands.

"What's wrong?" Lindy asked.

"He called me last night."

"Who?"

"Travis."

"Oh yeah? Realized how good he had it, did he?"

Roxy's eyes watered as she went for a chair. Cardozo, who had been lounging there, jumped out of harm's way.

"What is it, Roxy?"

"He said he can't see me anymore."

"Can't or won't?"

"Who cares? He doesn't want to."

"How do you know?"

"Come on, Lindy! We know when a guy's giving us the backhand. You can hear it in their voice."

"What did he say, exactly?"

"That he *can't* see me anymore. That he's got a major *project* that will require *all* his attention. Yeah, I'd like to see what color hair his major project has."

"What about church?"

"He hasn't been there. How's that for a kick in the mush pot?"

"What exactly did you know about this guy, Rox?"

"I told you—"

"No. How did you meet him? I'm curious about that."

"We met. What's the big deal?"

"I don't know. This guy shows up in your life all of a sudden, then drops out. Gives us his story. How do we know anything he said was true?"

Roxy started to frown. "You saying I was conned?"

"I'm saying I don't *know*."

"It's almost enough to put me back on the stuff."

"Shut up," Lindy said. "Don't go relapse on me. You stay strong."

"Why are all the good guys in L.A. unavailable or gay or dead?" She put her hand to her mouth. "Sorry, Lindy."

"Forget it."

They sat in silence. Cardozo jumped in Lindy's lap. She put him back down. Her cell went off and she looked at the screen.

It was an unknown number. "Lindy Field."

"Hey, you shoulda leaned into the curve."

"Who is this?"

"A hog is not a toy."

The voice sounded vaguely familiar. "Again, who is this?"

"You don't remember your gun-toting Harley friend?"

"Wolf?"

"You remembered my name. You can bet I remember yours. Saw a thing on the news about you running your bike over a cliff."

"Sure. Why are—"

"You all right?"

"I'm in good shape for the shape I'm in. My hog isn't so good."

"Now that's sad."

"Thanks for the sympathy."

"You said to call if anything came up. I think something's up."

"Yes."

"Michael—what did you say his real name was?"

"Drake DiCinni."

"Yeah. He beat up Alice. After she took him in like a stray. I'm gonna blow his head off next time I see him."

Lindy was beginning to detect a theme here. "My advice to you is stop thinking about heads and blowing them up."

"Not why I called. He took off, and Alice told me he was trying to get back with his old lady. She told me who that is."

Lindy almost jumped. "You know who?"

"And where."

"Tell me, please."

A pause. "Maybe we can make a deal."

Deal? "Wolf, just tell me—"

"My brother's in the slam. He didn't do what they said he did. They planted the meth on him. He can't get a lawyer to help him do an appeal."

"There are indigent defense—"

"Would you talk to him?"

Darren DiCinni's fate dangled in front of her like a bowling ball on twine. Any moment it could drop for good.

"Fine, I'll talk to him. I can't promise—"

"You'll like him. He's a lot like me."

"Can we get back to—"

"Only not as friendly. But being in the joint'll do that."

"I understand. Who and where is Drake's woman?"

"I'm gonna hold you to this."

"Fine!"

"Her name is Charlene Little. She's a checker at a Wal-Mart in Duarte."

2.

The blue-vested Wal-Mart employee (his badge read Skip) greeted Lindy and Roxy. "Is there anything I can help you with today?"

"I'm looking for Charlene. Is she working today?"

"Charlene? Oh, I think I know who you mean. You a friend of hers?"

Lindy didn't blink. "At the moment, she's my favorite checker."

"Oh. Fine. Yes. Let me see. Oh, that's her." He pointed down to a register.

Charlene was a little thing. *Mousy* was the term Lindy's mother might have used. She had long, straight, rust-colored hair that hung down as if exhausted to her shoulders. Her face didn't hold much joy as she scanned items for checkout.

Someday a robot would be doing this, Lindy thought.

She got in the line with Roxy and picked out a pack of orange Tic-Tacs. The woman in front of her had a bottomless shopping cart. Finally, it was Lindy's turn. She handed over the Tic-Tacs.

"Charlene?"

The girl, about thirty, said, "Yes?"

"I wonder if I might talk to you on your break. My name's Lindy Field, and it's about Drake."

Charlene froze.

"I need to talk to you about him."

"Why?"

"It's a legal matter."

Suddenly aware that other people were waiting in line, Charlene quickly scanned the Tic-Tacs.

"I'll be waiting for you over at the Mickey D's," Lindy said. "I promise it won't take too long."

Charlene gave no answer. Roxy paid for the Tic-Tacs. They proceeded to the in-store McDonald's and set up at one of the plastic booths, Roxy in a position to watch Charlene's register.

"One nervous girl," Roxy said.

"Scared," Lindy said.

"Like us?"

"What do you mean?"

"The guy who tried to kill you, he's still out there. Maybe it was Drake DiCinni."

Lindy had thought of that, but the gears hadn't meshed. "Why would he?"

"Because he's nuts?"

"We don't know that."

"His kid is."

"You saying it may run in the family?"

"I can think of weirder things."

"Get us a couple of coffees," Lindy said.

"McDonald's coffee? Are *you* nuts?"

Lindy shot her a friendly glare. Roxy smiled, but it fell away from her face in an instant. She was looking over Lindy's shoulder.

"What's wrong?"

Roxy shot to her feet. "Our girl just ran out of the store."

3.

"Mind if I join you?"

Leon Colby sat down on the stool next to Officer Kirby Glenn. Glenn was having a taco at the stand on Olvera Street, right where dispatch told Leon he would be.

Glenn looked surprised.

"What, the DA need some free advice?" Glenn said, a bit of lettuce hanging from his lip.

"Looks pretty good," Colby said about the taco. He held up two fingers to the guy behind the counter and turned back to Glenn. "Gonna make you fat, though."

The officer did not seem in any mood to chitchat. "Just grabbing something on the run. Then I gotta get out of here."

"On duty, are you?"

"Soon enough. Keeping the city safe and all that. Just like you." Glenn put the crumbling remnants of the taco shell into the wax paper in front of him. He licked his fingers then grabbed a wadded up napkin and wiped them. "You come all the way down here to check my diet?"

The taco guy plopped a wax-paper–lined red basket with two tacos in front of Colby. Colby reached for the little bottle of picante on the counter, unscrewed the top, and doused the top of his tacos with it. "I like to clear out the sinuses," he said.

Glenn said nothing.

"Like to clear up my cases too." Colby took a healthy bite of taco.

"That a fact? Seems to me the one you're on is pretty clear."

"I wish that was so, my friend. Wish that was so." Colby dabbed at his chin with a paper napkin.

"What's not clear about it?"

"Things around the edges. I just get a bad feeling about things around the edges, you know?"

Glenn looked as if he did not know, as if he didn't want to know. In fact, Officer Kirby Glenn looked like he wanted to get out of there as fast as he could.

Which intrigued Colby. "What do you hear about the McIntyre killing?"

"Hear? Nothing. That's RHD."

"You know people. People say things."

Glenn shrugged and pushed the basket with his taco remnants to the side. "People say a lot of things. I don't always listen."

"So you hear anything on McIntyre?"

"Just what they say on TV. He was into some underworld stuff, right?"

"You tell me."

"I told you, Colby, I don't know anything other than what everybody else knows. What's up with you?"

"I told you. Edges. McIntyre was on the edge of this DiCinni case. He had an interest. An interest that may have gotten him killed."

"Or maybe it was totally unrelated."

"Maybe. But that's not clear." Colby took another bite, savored it, let Glenn just sit there and watch him. Finally he said, "What's your interest in DiCinni?"

"Don't have any."

"No?"

"I testified. That's as far as it goes."

"You puffed it."

"I did what?"

"Puffed your testimony. You put in a little more than was there. You recall that?"

Glenn half-smiled. "Since when have you been fired up about that, Colby? That isn't your rep."

Colby didn't have a response to that. He knew his rep, and he knew Glenn was right.

"Forget about it," Colby said. He got up from the stool.

"Hey, Colby."

"What?"

"Keep that rep clean, you know what I'm saying? Good things'll happen."

4.

Roxy had a pair of handcuffs on Charlene. Right there in the Wal-Mart parking lot. She had called Lindy on her cell phone to tell her she had the witness.

"Take those things off," Lindy said. Charlene looked like a wide-eyed doe with one leg in a trap, looking into the business end of a hunting rifle.

"I had to convince her to stay," Roxy said.

"When did you get those cuffs?"

"'You never know' is my motto."

"She's crazy," Charlene said breathlessly.

"You're a percipient witness," Roxy said. "We will do the talking."

Lindy shook her head. "I have to apologize for my associate. Take those cuffs off, Roxy."

"She was trying to get away. She knows something."

"The cuffs. Off."

Roxy reluctantly unlocked the cuffs. She looked like she might have had some words with the Wal-Mart checker.

"It's true you don't have to talk to us," Lindy said. "But it would help."

"I know who you are," Charlene said. "I seen you on the news. I can't talk to you 'cause of what he'll do if he finds out."

"Drake?"

Charlene nodded.

"He beat you?"

"It's none of your business. I just can't talk about things."

So she really was a doe looking into a hunter's rifle. Only the rifle was in the hands of Drake DiCinni.

"You understand that anything you say to me will be held in confidence. Nobody has to know we talked."

"I don't have anything to tell you. I don't know anything about the kid. Drake doesn't care what happens to him . . ." She put her hand to her mouth.

"What does that mean? Charlene, tell me what you're talking about."

She shook her head violently.

"Listen to me, Charlene. Drake isn't the only one who doesn't care about Darren. Nobody in the world cares about Darren. Except me, Roxy, and one other lawyer. That's it. That's all he's got. And if I don't do something soon, he's gonna end up in prison with a bunch of men who will take very bad advantage of him, if you know what I mean. I'm desperate here, and I need something, anything you can give me."

Charlene shook a little, then looked at the sky. Lindy thought for a moment she might cry.

Lindy waited.

"It's like this," Charlene said. "Drake doesn't want to have anything to do with the kid, okay? He told me so. He hates what happened. He said the kid was no good from the start. He did everything he could to make the kid do what he said. He did stuff to the kid that was stuff I wouldn't do, but it wasn't my place to say anything."

"Like what?"

"I'm not gonna say."

"Listen, if he beats you, you can get help," Lindy said. "We can help you." She handed her a business card. "This has my personal number on it."

Charlene wouldn't take the card. "I don't want any help."

"Yes, you do."

"Don't tell me what I want, okay?"

Lindy wanted to shove the girl in a car and get her to a safe house. Abused and wanting it. An all-too-familiar story. She settled for putting her card in Charlene's shirt pocket.

"Charlene, what did Drake do to Darren? This is really important."

"Stop trying to make me say."

"Did he beat him?"

The look in Charlene's eyes made it plain that Drake did all that and more.

"Why?" Lindy said. "Why would a man do that to his own child?"

"That's just it," Charlene said with a sudden defiance.

"That's what?"

"The kid. Darren. Whatever his name is. The kid isn't his."

SEVENTEEN

✝ ✝ ✝

1.

The district attorney for the county of Los Angeles, Jonathan "Iron John" Sherman, always reminded Leon Colby of the little quarterback who played for Cal when Leon was at UCLA. Wiry, fast, tough. Hard to bring down. Could kill you with a trick play.

Sherman had the same qualities—same intensity in his eyes, the same slight yet deceiving build, a build that had lulled many a defense lawyer into false security during Sherman's early years with the DA's office. But after a few poundings, word got around. Never underestimate Iron John—he got the nickname by refusing plea bargains. The man loved to go to trial and win.

As Colby entered Sherman's office, he wondered how much Iron John knew about Colby's desire to win something himself—this room. Colby thought he could fill the office nicely. He was even decorating it in his mind when Jonathan Sherman sat in his big, black leather executive chair and said, "Nice work so far on the DiCinni case."

It sounded exactly like what it was, a mere warm up, a prelude to the real reason he'd been called to Mahogany Row. "Thanks."

"No, I mean it. Really. You have that wild child, Field, in there. If this wasn't such a bad case for her, I'd be worried about a little sympathy factor from the jury."

"She may get it yet."

Sherman waved his hand. "I've seen a little on TV. You got nothing to worry about. *We* have nothing to worry about."

Sherman put his feet up on the desk. This bit of forced informality surprised Colby. Sherman never had a hair out of place or a suit with a superfluous crease. He looked like he was trying too hard to put Colby at ease.

"So what's the occasion?" Colby said.

"Just wanted to have a little strategy session with you, is all," Sherman said.

"It's a little late for strategy, isn't it? We've already had opening statements, the first wits—"

"I'm not talking about the DiCinni case, Leon."

Colby looked at him, tried to read the iron eyes. Couldn't. They glinted like polished stones, and then Sherman laughed and pulled his feet down. "Let's not get all fancy here, Leon. Cards on the table, what do you say?"

"What cards you got?"

"Here's what I know. I know that you have your eyes on this chair."

Colby opened his mouth but Sherman put his hand up. "Hey, listen, I'm not bent out of shape about it. Ambitious deputies, it goes with the territory. Shows a little moxie too. I'm not upset about that. If we were to go into the election, of course, I'd be sitting pretty strong. I'm a popular guy, did you know that?"

Colby knew it.

"Yeah, the *Times* even said I was the best DA in the last thirty years, and it's hard to please those people. They have this county-oversight complex that just drives me nuts. Hey, can I pour you a drink?"

"No, thanks."

"I'll just take a snort." Sherman had a wet bar in a rosewood cabinet. He poured some amber liquid—Scotch, probably—into a stippled glass. Then he turned to Colby and said, "What I have to say to you now is going to rearrange your brain."

2.

"Talk to me, Darren."

He stared blankly at Lindy, shook his head.

"Tell me about your father."

Now the eyes started to ignite. "No."

"Tell me what he did to you."

He shook his head.

"What did he do to you all those years, Darren? The beatings. Tell me what he did."

"Shut up."

"No, I'm not going to shut up. You need help. And you can get help, but you need to be up-front with me. Tell me now, tell me what your father did to you. How did he do it? Did he do it—"

"You don't know anything—"

"—with a rod, a wire, his hands? What?"

"—you don't know what you're doing—"

"Why, Darren? Do you think you deserved that?"

"Yes!"

The answer brought her up short, like a seat belt locking on a hard stop. "Nobody deserves that, Darren. Especially not a child."

"Yes, I did!"

"No."

"You don't know anything."

"Why did you think you deserved that, Darren?"

He looked at his hands as veins began appearing under the skin of his neck.

"Why?" Lindy demanded.

"To get the devil out," Darren said. He looked up at her. Tears were forming in his eyes. "He's still in there and I have to get him out."

"Darren, you're just a boy."

"Shut up!"

The on-duty sheriff's deputy hurried over. "That's it."

"Wait a minute," Lindy said.

"Make her shut up!" Darren cried.

"On your feet." The deputy began to unshackle Darren's table cuffs.

"I'm not finished here," Lindy said.

The deputy pulled Darren to a standing position. "You are finished," he said, pushing Darren ahead of him.

"Stop!"

They did not stop. She was losing him. She had tried to force things, and now she was losing him.

Oh God, don't let me lose him.

God. Darren. The devil in there.

She jumped off the hard jail bench.

3.

"What I want to tell you, Leon, is the following." Jonathan Sherman sounded like he was about to deliver one of his famous closing arguments. Rock-hard logic that few defense lawyers ever had the legal jackhammer to crack. "I don't like being the DA."

"You could have fooled me," Colby said.

"I fool a lot of people. That's why I'm here. But this is too much flesh pounding, too much time with city council members with sweaty foreheads and receptions with money men and their plastic wives. It's not very satisfying, not as satisfying as putting some drug dealer in the can for the rest of his natural life."

Leon nodded.

"But I clearly cannot go back to being a deputy. Which leaves me with private practice, some cushy rainmaking job at a big firm. But the problem is, Leon, I don't like those people either. I'm sort of a loner, if you want to know the truth."

He paused, looked out at his panoramic view of downtown L.A. "What I really want to be is attorney general." He turned back to catch Colby's reaction.

"That's not a bad thing," Colby said. "Sacramento is a nice place to—"

"No," Sherman said. "A.G. of these United States of America."

"Isn't that an appointed position?"

"Sure is. And if the national election goes like the polls say, I've been assured from the inside that I'm their guy. See, Leon, I can play politics when I have to."

"I would say so."

"But what I don't need is a big black eye before that day comes. One lousy case, as you'll find out, can make your life miserable up here."

"What do you mean, as I'll find out?"

With a big, political smile, Sherman said, "Why, Leon, you're going to be the next DA. I'm going to hand the office to you."

"I'm not sure I—"

"You're going to come off big after the DiCinni conviction. It'll be a good way for me to go. I am not going to run for reelection."

A shocker.

"It's all part of the big picture," Sherman said. "Here's what I get: I go out a success, I take time off to be with my family—and I make sure everybody knows about that—and then I sponsor the first African-American DA in the history of Los Angeles. The party will love that."

It was a good political plan, cynical and effective.

"So how does that sound to you, Leon?"

In truth it sounded very, very good. It sounded like a dream on a silver platter. "You've put in some thought on this."

"That's the secret of any trial, isn't it? Preparation. There's just one thing . . ."

Colby's prosecutorial antennae went up.

"Judge Greene came to see me," Sherman said.

"Greene? What for?"

"About DiCinni."

"He doesn't have anything to do with DiCinni."

"Yeah, but as presiding judge he naturally takes an interest in the judges he supervises and what goes on in their courtrooms. And he has expressed a concern."

"About what?"

"About the integrity of the police witnesses you've got. He came to me because he wants to keep it quiet, for the sake of this office and the whole administration of justice. So I'd kind of like to know what you know."

Colby cleared his throat. "Are you asking me if every one of my witnesses is squeaky clean?"

"If I asked you that, I know what the answer would be. So that's not what I'm asking. I'm asking if anything is going to leak out of this trial that could be potentially embarrassing to me. To us."

Colby thought long and hard. A political question like this deserved a clever answer. But nothing clever came. Which bothered him more than he thought it would.

"There's been some expansion, shall we say, of certain facts," Colby said. "I don't see it as any big thing."

"Lindy Field, is she a big thing? Is she going to make trouble like she did on the Marcel Lee case?"

"She might."

"And what do we do?"

"We do our job. We fight back."

"That's not good enough. I want a win. A slam dunk. What I don't want are a lot of embarrassing questions dogging me after I leave this place. And Leon, I want to know if I can count on you, or if my confidence is misplaced. Because if it is, I'll look around for someone else to take my place."

Colby rubbed the burnished-wood arms of the leather chair. They were clean and smooth and a whole lot nicer than the arms of the chairs in his own office. He said, "You have not misplaced your confidence."

Iron John smiled.

4.

"Drake is God," Lindy said.

She sat in Roxy's car in the jail's parking structure. The cement edifice cast dark shadows across the lot, even though the L.A. sun was bright and the sky blue. Only thin shafts of light made it between the columns and cars.

"Drake is God to Darren. I'm sure that's it. Drake beat him, telling him all the time he was getting rid of the devil. And that left him to be God."

"You got all that from Darren?"

"Not in so many words. I'm reading between the lines here. Maybe Darren was listening to Drake when he says God told him to shoot up the field."

"You think?"

"Let's chase that for a minute. The question is why? Why would Drake tell Darren to shoot up a baseball game? And if Darren was aiming at Joel Dorai, what was it Drake had against him?"

Roxy chewed her thumbnail. "Darren won't tell you?"

Lindy shook her head. "Not yet. He's scared."

"But if you get this in front of the jury, we might be able to create reasonable doubt on mental state, right?"

"That's the question. How am I going to prove it?"

"Maybe I can help."

Lindy said, "Go for it."

"While you were inside I finally got a call from the homicide detective in Vegas who handled the death of Darren's mother, Trudy."

"Right. She was a hooker, wasn't she?"

"Yes."

"And died of a drug overdose?"

"No."

"No?"

"At least not according to this guy, Walsh. He thinks Drake killed her."

"Why didn't he arrest him?"

"They never had enough evidence. The DA told him to forget about it."

"The district attorney in Vegas?"

"Right."

"Told this guy Walsh to forget about making it a murder?"

"That's it."

Lindy said, "That's nothing! What relevance is that information going to be? We can't use it in trial. Unless Drake DiCinni takes the stand, which he's not going to do."

"The guy said something else that was interesting."

"What?"

"He said there was a community activist going after the DA on some corruption deal. Shortly after they dropped Drake as a murder suspect, this activist winds up dead. And Drake winds up out of town, never to return."

"He thinks Drake killed the guy?"

"More than that, he thinks the DA got him to do it."

5.

Leon Colby knocked softly on the door of his father's house.

Rosa answered with a big smile. "Good, you're here. He miss you, I think."

The house, as usual, smelled like old shoes and Mexican spices. Rosa was always in the kitchen, cooking something up not just for his father but the visitors from church who always stopped by.

And there his father was, in his favorite chair, staring at the TV. The picture was on—a game show—but the sound was muted.

Reverend Colby glanced up as his son sat next to him on the sofa.

"How you doin', Pop? Lookin' good."

His father's look did not register the usual signs of recognition. Colby felt a rush of despair and fought it back with words. "Let me tell you, Pop. I've been real busy with this case. You've probably seen me on the news a few times, right? Look pretty good, don't I? The Colby good looks. You gave them to me, Pop."

His father put his head back slightly. His mouth quivered in what looked like an attempt to form a smile.

"Yeah, you'd be real proud of me, Pop. Working hard. Getting the job done, you remember? Like out on the field? Remember how you used to tell me to get the job done? And then I'd go out there and do it for you, Pop. For the team."

What else did his father used to tell him? There was something else.

"Remember that night against Manual Arts?" The biggest night of Colby's high-school career. "We got the job done that night, didn't we? Went to the city championship." Where they were whupped, but that was okay. Colby had been the star of the game.

Rosa came in with lemonade. She handed a glass to Colby. She held the other glass, with a straw in it, up to Reverend Colby's mouth. He took a feeble sip.

"That's pretty good, huh, Pop? That Rosa, she makes a good glass of lemonade, doesn't she?"

"And he is eating Milky Way today," Rosa said. "His special treat."

"That's great." Clearly though, no amount of candy or anything else was going to get his father's weight back to where it should be. His father was wasting away, looking worse every time Leon came.

"Oh, I find something," Rosa said.

"What's that?"

"In a closet. I think maybe your father like you to have it."

She put down the glass of lemonade and left the room.

"You got a present for me, Pop?" Colby said. "Well listen, you just get better and that's present enough, okay?"

His father looked at him with cloudy eyes, though behind the veil he could see a spark, a bit of the old light that the Reverend Colby used to shine on his congregation when he preached.

Rosa came back holding something. When Leon saw it, he almost fell backward.

"You recognize?" Rosa said.

"I don't believe this." Colby took from Rosa's hands a small rubber football. The one he used to sleep with. The one family legend said he once threw from his crib into his daddy's forehead. It was brown and faded. The white seams were barely visible. But he could still see in pale ink the words his father had inscribed. On one seam was written, *Play hard*. On the other, *Play fair*.

The memory engulfed him. That's what his father always told him. *Play hard. Play fair.*

Colby looked at the football, completely encased in one big hand.

When had he put this ball away for good? Was it when he was ten years old and he talked back to his father for the first time and got a good old-fashioned spanking?

He tossed it in the air a couple of times, spiraling it up to the ceiling. "Yeah, I remember this old thing, it—"

Colby stopped. His father's cheeks had streaks on them.

"Hey . . ." Colby slid off the sofa and took a knee. He put his hand on his father's arm. "Hey now, Pop, no need for that."

But his father's tears kept coming, not in diffuse streams but small, incessant rivulets. And then he felt his father's hand on his, grasping feebly.

6.

Another sleepless night.

Mona was used to it now. She'd heard about the dangers of sleep deprivation, all that. She even knew that something was happening to her body, the weakness of it. But that was only a small part of what she thought.

Mostly she thought about the killer and his lawyer, and why she was not hating them like she wanted to.

Why not?

As she watched television, the images flashed before her unseen, the sounds of the commercials melding into one big indistinguishable sound.

Was she going to go crazy? Maybe that would be a relief. Crazy people were happy in their own heads.

No. Hang on for Matthew.

What could she do? What could she possibly do?

Hang onto the anger. Like they told her. Anger is good. Hate the evil. Hate the killer.

Don't worry, Matthew, don't ever worry.

Her stomach flared, hot and sharp. That was happening a lot too. Mona went to the bathroom and got a few Rolaids. That was the only sure answer she knew these days.

7.

The morning's chief witness for the prosecution was Dr. Daniel Tucker, a psychologist of stellar reputation. Around sixty, trim, and bereft of ostentation, he possessed complete command of his area of expertise.

Lindy and Everett had readied a double-barreled response to his report. Judge Lipton posed the only potential obstacle. How would he rule when Colby's objections came up, as they inevitably would?

She watched Leon, who huddled with his investigator, Lopez, at the counsel table. Was it just her imagination, or did Colby's expression register more concern than usual?

Probably imagination. Wishful thinking. The big wish being that Leon would do the right thing. She had seen a flash of decency in him. *Just go with it, Leon.*

The doctor took the oath and sat on the witness chair. Colby asked him the usual introductory questions about his education, qualifications, and experience. Lindy watched the jurors' faces carefully. They looked impressed.

Then Colby went to the meat of the testimony. "Dr. Tucker, did you examine the defendant in this case?"

"I did."

"And how many times have you examined the defendant?"

"Twice. For one hour each time. The first examination occurred three weeks ago and the second eight days ago."

"Was counsel present during these examinations?"

"Mr. Woodard was present."

"Did you prepare a report on your examinations of the defendant?"

"I did."

"Would you please tell the jury what your conclusions were?"

"Certainly." The veteran witness turned toward the jury box. "I found Darren DiCinni to be of average to slightly above-average intelligence. He did not have any trouble understanding my questions, nor communicating his answers, though he was not entirely forthcoming with me. He chose to remain silent much of the time. This I found to be consistent with feelings of deep guilt. I found also that his physical and emotional reactions were similar to those of a young teenager with normal troubles at home. Mr. DiCinni did show positive reaction to the Hunt Battery of questions regarding knowledge of right and wrong, good and bad."

Woodard stood. "We object to any consideration of the Hunt Battery as being outside the Daubert test for scientific reliability."

Judge Lipton looked as if he had been expecting this. "The court will overrule the objection. Counsel is free to present contrary evidence at the appropriate time. You may continue, Mr. Colby."

"Thank you, Your Honor." Colby returned to the witness. "Will you briefly explain to the jury what the Hunt Battery is intended to show?"

"Yes. This is a series of questions designed to elicit both verbal and nonverbal responses in young adults regarding certain behavioral norms. An observer trained in the Hunt Battery response will listen to voice inflection as well as observing gaze nystagmus—that is, movement of the eyeball—and other nonverbal indicators. From this the observer uses a scale to determine both understanding of and conformity with said norms."

"Where on the scale, in plain English, did the defendant fall?"

"Again, he was in the average to above-average classification. That means his understanding of norms is precisely where it should be for a normal thirteen-year-old."

"Is your conclusion consistent with someone understanding the gravity of a crime?"

"Yes."

"At the time of your examination, then, was your conclusion that Darren DiCinni understood, or had the capacity to understand, the wrongful nature of a criminal act?"

"Yes."

"Thank you. No further questions at this time."

"Who is going to cross-examine?" Judge Lipton said.

"I am," Lindy said. At the podium she faced the witness. "Just a few questions for you, Doctor. Your examination of the defendant took place months after the events in question, isn't that true?"

"True."

"You have no idea what happened to the defendant prior to the events, do you?"

"By use of a backward extrapolation, I can make an educated guess about—"

"Whoa. Slow down. I don't want any educated guesses here."

"Your Honor," Colby said, standing, "that is what an expert witness does. That's one of the reasons he is called an expert. Since Ms. Field has opened the door to questions on the day of the killings, I must ask that the witness be allowed to walk through that door and state his opinion."

"Objection sustained," Judge Lipton said. "The witness may complete his answer."

Tucker said, "All I was trying to say is that looking back from this point to the point of the events, one can make an educated judgment about the defendant's capacity to understand right from wrong and the like."

This wasn't helping, not with the judge being cheerleader for junk science.

"Dr. Tucker, on direct examination you mentioned that my client was not outside the normal range of teenagers who, I think you said, had troubles at home. Is that right?"

"That's part of what I said, yes."

"Then is it psychologically possible that a teenager might receive enough mental trauma *in* the home to affect his mental state *outside* the home?"

"Objection," Leon Colby said. "No foundation."

Before the judge could speak, Lindy said, "Your Honor, as Mr. Colby knows, when you open a door, you need to let the witness walk through it. On direct, his witness mentioned home life, specifically trouble at home. I want to explore that a little bit more."

"I will see you in my chambers," Judge Lipton said.

8.

Lindy felt the focused ire of the judge before he said a word. He threw his robe onto the back of his chair but didn't sit down.

"I've been very patient with you, Ms. Field. In part that is because of my soft, good Samaritan heart, which wants to give you a break. But I've just about had it. Mr. Colby made an objection out there, perfectly proper, and you used it as an opportunity to make a quick speech to the jury. Now if I rule against you, the jury will wonder what Mr. Colby is trying to hide. That kind of ploy is beneath you, Ms. Field."

The judge paused, folding his arms.

Lindy said, "I'm sorry, Your Honor. You're absolutely right. It was not my intention to do that, make a speech. It just came pouring out of me."

"You learn in first-year law school not to let things pour out of you, especially in court. And in a trial of this magnitude and attention, controlling yourself is even more important. Now why don't you tell me the basis for these questions?"

Lindy gave Colby a brief glance, wondering if he knew exactly what the basis was. "We have reason to believe that Darren DiCinni's father engaged in the repeated physical and psychological abuse of his son."

"Do you have an offer of proof?"

"We have a reluctant witness. My investigator and I interviewed her, but she is unwilling to testify."

"You have the power of subpoena."

"She's too frightened. I think she would deny everything in order to protect herself."

Lipton sighed and shook his head. "Then on what foundation can I allow you to ask questions?"

"May I offer a citation?" Woodard said.

"By all means," Judge Lipton said. "It would be nice to have a little law enter the discussion."

"It has long been held," Woodard said, "that the defense has wide latitude in the cross-examination of prosecution witnesses in a criminal case. The case is *People v. Ormes*, 1948. It's one of the cases I use in my class on trial procedure. Further, in the case of *Gallaher v. Superior Court*, it was stated that a prosecution witness testifies to facts tending to establish guilt, but defense is entitled to cross-examine on all relevant and material matters relating to those facts."

Judge Lipton turned. "What do you have to say, Mr. Colby?"

"The question is whether her cross-examination is material," Leon Colby said. "Your Honor asked for an offer of proof, and she does not have one."

Lindy bristled. She *knew* what she had. "I have given you an offer, Your Honor."

"No, you haven't," the judge said. "You don't even have a written statement to offer me."

"Well, that's just wonderful! Why don't we let witnesses for the prosecution say whatever they want and make the defense jump through hoops?"

"Ms. Field!"

Lindy stopped.

"I'm going to ignore that as a mark of your zealous representation, which is admirable when it is under control. I will remind you that we have a camera in the courtroom. That's not supposed to matter, but we all know that it does. Everybody out here in Hollywood Land is waiting for us to make a spectacle of ourselves. We are not going to do it. I'm going to rule that you cannot ask that question, or any question that deals with hypothetical evidence of the defendant's home life. If you come to me with an offer of proof, I will reconsider. If your client takes the stand and testifies to conditions at home, I will allow you to recall the present witness for a brief cross-examination."

"But, Your Honor—"

"I'm not interested in discussing this further. Now let's go back into court and act as if we are really lawyers."

9.

With the teeth kicked out of Lindy Field's questioning of Tucker, the rest of the morning was uneventful. But Lindy Field had something. Colby knew her well enough to know that when she said she believed a thing, she really believed it; if she said she had some witness, she was not lying.

So after Tucker's testimony, Colby requested an early lunch hour. And ordered Larry Lopez to his office.

"Do you know anything about Drake being abusive to Darren?" Colby asked his investigator.

Lopez shook his head.

"Why don't I believe you?"

"I don't care if you believe me or not."

"I think you're holding back. I want to know why."

"Lay off, Leon. You got your job to do, I got mine. There's nothing gonna get this kid off, you know that."

Yeah, he knew that. He knew it was the ol' slam dunk. A notch, a victory, another step toward Mahogany Row.

So why didn't this victory taste sweet?

10.

"I'm going to take a deal from Colby," said Woodard quietly.

Lindy stepped back from him as if pushed. "You can't."

"Listen to me." He looked at her sternly, not like a professor, but like a parent. "If Colby will offer less than twenty-five years, we need to take it. The case is getting away—"

"But—"

"And the best interest of our client demands the least amount of prison time we can get."

"We can't do that." She tried to keep her voice down. The courtroom was slowly clearing out. Darren had already been removed.

"What do you suggest? Have you been watching the jury? They are not buying insanity, not in the slightest."

Chill desperation grasped Lindy. "We can't. I won't do it."

"Lindy," he said softly, "I want you to listen. The worst thing a defense lawyer can do is lose objectivity. That's what's happening here. You're attached to this case in an unhealthy way. You need to step aside and let me make the call."

"Step aside?"

"Leave it to me—"

"No. I won't."

"Lindy—"

"I won't do it. I won't sell him out."

Woodard frowned. "If you think that's what's happening, then you truly have lost your ability to serve your client."

"We have to keep going."

"It's not your call, Lindy."

She looked into his resolute face. "I won't go along with this."

"I am the attorney of record, remember?"

Lindy braced herself against the counsel table. "You'd do this over my objection?"

"If I think it's in Darren's best interest. That's the only thing either one of us should be thinking about."

Her legs felt weak. "Everett, please . . ."

He put his hand on her shoulder. "We've got till Monday. Go home and think about it. But think about it like a lawyer. Think about it dispassionately. Will you do that for me?"

She swallowed hard, her nerves starting to feel like frayed wires. "All right, Everett. Till Monday."

"Good. Come on, I'll give you a lift home."

"Roxy's meeting me. You go ahead."

"Get some rest." He swept up his briefcase and walked out.

Absently, Lindy packed her own briefcase with scattered notes and tried to find the light in this dark scenario. There was none. Woodard was right. The jury was not on their side. Maybe a couple of them, and so maybe they could get a hung jury.

That would only mean doing this all again. But if so, she could buy some time and try to find . . . something, anything that would help.

On the other hand, if this jury returned a guilty verdict, Darren would be slapped with the upper limit of a prison sentence.

There was no light.

Lindy clasped her briefcase shut, turned, and looked into eyes staring directly at her.

It was that woman again, Romney. She was fixed in the center of the courtroom, unmoving.

And Lindy thought, if there's insanity going on, this woman might be right on the edge.

Lindy looked away and started up the aisle. But she felt the woman's eyes on her all the way out the door.

EIGHTEEN

✝ ✝ ✝

1.

"Things aren't going so good, are they?" Roxy asked.

Lindy closed her eyes. "Everett wants to plead Darren out."

They were driving back to the Valley from the courthouse. The afternoon was L.A.-hot, and Roxy had the windows rolled down. Her air-conditioning wasn't working. Sweltering air streamed through the car, doing no good at all.

"Maybe that's the right thing to do," Roxy said.

"Not you too."

"I can see his point. Colby wants the max and he may get it."

Lindy snapped her eyes open. "You remember that girl surfer a couple years ago who got her arm bit off by a shark? And she was back to surfing a few months later?"

"Yeah."

"Leon Colby wants to bite off my head. He doesn't care if I ever practice law again, after this case is over. But I won't have my head."

Roxy laughed. They were on Victory Boulevard now, beating the freeway traffic by taking surface streets.

"What's so funny?" Lindy said.

"I just had a vision. Your head, sitting on Colby's table, shouting, 'Objection, Your Honor!'"

"You're sick."

"I am." Roxy looked in the rearview mirror and her expression changed. "And unless I'm totally gone, there's somebody following us."

"What?" Lindy looked at the side-view mirror. Several cars stretched out behind them. "You sure?"

"I'm pretty sure. That blue number, a couple cars back."

"When did you pick this up?"

"I noticed it a few blocks from the courthouse, but thought it was just my imagination. Now I'm not so sure."

"Speed up a little."

"I'm not going to do a chase scene here."

"Relax. Just a little. Let's see if he keeps up."

Roxy complied, giving the car a little extra gas, changing lanes. Lindy saw in the mirror that the trailing car changed lanes too. And sped up.

"Now what?" Roxy said.

"Keep it steady."

"Red light coming."

"No sweat."

"I'm the one driving. I get to sweat."

Over the next few blocks, the blue car kept an irregular but discernable distance between them.

"I don't like this," Roxy said.

"Let's circle back around and drive to the West Valley police station, on Vanowen."

"What if this guy's a cop? Ever think of that?"

"Then he'll feel right at home. Let's go."

"Can I wait for the light to turn green?"

When it did, Roxy proceeded to the next corner and turned right. The blue car followed.

"I don't believe this," Roxy said.

"Keep going."

Roxy turned right on Vanowen. Lindy saw the blue car in the mirror, still tailing.

"Persistent sucker," Lindy said.

They approached the West Valley station.

"Go up the driveway halfway. Let's see if he pulls in with all those black and whites."

Roxy did as ordered. Two uniformed officers, in an act of impeccable timing, came out the front doors as Roxy screeched to a halt nearly on top of them.

Lindy looked in the mirror. The blue car whizzed by without turning in. Lindy caught a flash of the driver's face.

And knew who it was.

2.

Leon Colby was in his office when he took the call from George Mahoney.

"How goes the war?" Mahoney asked.

"Fine." Colby didn't want to add anything to that. From what he knew of Mahoney, the less information you gave him the less could come back to bite you. Even though he was for the prosecution and could be of enormous political help, there was something about him Colby didn't like.

"Any updates?" Mahoney asked.

"Nope."

"A little inside info for your friends at VOICe."

"And as always, we appreciate your support."

"Ah, come on, Leon. You're sounding like a politician already."

"My door is always open."

"You're the master of the runaround."

"What have I got to run around?"

"Many a thing, if past history is any example. Sometimes we have to fight a little harder depending on who the district attorney is. Before Sherman took over, we had to deal with a pretty closed shop up there, and that came back to bite the previous DA."

"It's a little early to be influence peddling, George."

"The fact that you want to be DA is one of the worst kept secrets in this town. It's like Cher and silicone."

"Is there a reason for this call, other than to tell me Hollywood jokes?"

"Well, I was wondering if your relations with the law enforcement community will be an issue in this upcoming race. You know, the support of the Police Officers Guild was the big advantage for Sherman last time around."

"I like the police."

"That's what I thought. But I hear things, you know? I'm sort of the central clearing house for the health and morale of this city's good officers. They trust me. What can I say? I've earned that trust over a long period of time. And I know if you earn trust, and then lose it, you can't get it back."

"I think I can guess. Kirby Glenn called you. Or was it Larry Lopez?"

"I don't reveal names, that's part of the trust factor. What I want to know, Leon, is whether you're turning up the flame on the good guys a little too high. The DA has enough trouble cooking the collective goose of the criminal enterprise. He shouldn't be increasing the heat on the home team."

Tread carefully here. George Mahoney was a definite power in city politics. Get on his bad side and watch the tide turn in a close election. "Thanks for the call."

"Then I take it I've been of some help to you, Leon?"

"Always helpful to talk to the good citizens of L.A."

Mahoney laughed. "You are going to be great in that office, Leon. Just great."

After hanging up, Colby sat in silence for several minutes, mulling over what he knew about George Mahoney. Ex-cop. Now active for victims' rights. His group, VOICe, was gaining influence.

And before that?

Colby thought about doing a little Internet search on Mahoney, see what came up. He'd start with the *L.A. Times*, maybe expand via the LexisNexis database.

Then he asked himself why. He had things well in hand. Mahoney was on his side, that much was plain. He could use Mahoney in his corner during the campaign.

But unease needled him, pricked at his insides. And he found himself wondering what his father would counsel him to do.

3.

"No way," Roxy said.

"He had that long hair, that goatee," Lindy replied.

"Why would *Travis* be following us?"

"You tell me." They stayed in front of the police station. The two uniforms who had walked out the front doors apparently decided Roxy would not run them down and were proceeding slowly toward the parking lot.

"It's too weird," Roxy said.

"Follow him then."

"What?"

"Go!"

Roxy shifted the car and backed out. Lindy heard the squeal of rubber. And saw the two policemen look at them again.

Roxy burst onto Vanowen, headed east. A car screeched behind them, the driver laying heavy on the horn.

"Sorry," Roxy said. She shifted, put foot to pedal, and burned more rubber.

"Easy!" Lindy held on to the dashboard with both hands.

"You want me to go or not?"

"Go!"

The blue car was well ahead of them, past the Wilbur intersection, cruising by the YMCA.

"Make this light," Lindy said, as the red *Don't Walk* sign stopped flashing. The streetlight turned yellow. Roxy gunned it. The light turned red just before she reached the intersection. She sped through as a chorus of furious car horns protested.

"How was that?" Roxy smiled.

"He's at Reseda."

The blue car was completing a left turn at Reseda Boulevard, at least half a mile ahead. Lindy caught a look at the speedometer. Roxy was doing fifty, a healthy fifteen above the speed limit. But this was the Valley after all, where thousands of drag racing kids did twice that.

Some justification.

The light turned red when they reached Reseda. They sat in the left-turn lane behind a black pickup.

"The slowest light in the world!" Lindy said.

"Actually, Orange County is much slower. I remember—"

"Go!"

The light turned green, but cross traffic held them up. Finally Roxy shot up Reseda, past a string of fast-food joints—Subway, Jack in the Box, Arby's. Ahead, Lindy thought she saw the blue car turn right on Sherman Way.

"There's a string of stoplights up there," Lindy said. "He may have made a mistake."

Roxy gave the car an extra dose of gas. It seemed to Lindy that they were driving through mud. Every moment out of sight gave the blue car an opportunity to cut down a side street.

Approaching the corner, Lindy saw the light about to change to green. "Don't slow down!"

Roxy slammed on the brakes.

Lindy jerked forward. Her seat belt locked and kept her from putting her head through the windshield. Her heart made a vertical leap to her throat. The smell of burning rubber and scorched brake fluid filled her nostrils.

"What're you—" Lindy stopped when she saw what had caused the stop. A large Hispanic woman was pushing a baby stroller in the crosswalk.

The woman wagged her finger at Roxy and said something hot and Spanish.

"This is nuts!" Roxy was breathing like she'd seen death too close.

"Keep going!"

"You're crazy."

"He's getting away."

"Let him!"

"What's wrong with you?"

A siren answered her question. Lindy saw the cop car in the side-view mirror, the red and blue lights flashing.

"Great!" Roxy said. "We're Thelma and Louise now. Happy?"

Lindy recognized them as the officers from the station. They must have hunted them down after Roxy's less-than-smooth exit from the driveway.

"Relax now," Lindy said. "Let me do the talking."

4.

Iron John Sherman glared at Leon Colby from the door of his Hancock Park home. "What're you doing here? I don't recall you're being invited—"

"This can't wait," Colby said.

"I have guests—"

"Five minutes."

Sherman sighed, took a sip of his drink, and walked past Colby. Ice clinked in Sherman's glass as he led Colby halfway down the walk. "I'm schmoozing, Leon. It's a fine art and one you need to get good at. Coming to somebody's house unannounced is not the way to do it."

"I didn't want to use the phone."

"That's odd. Sort of *All the President's Men* by way of South Central."

"What do you know about George Mahoney and VOICe?"

"Good group to have on your side."

"What do you know about *him?*"

Sherman shrugged. "Not much. Active in the community. Something of a ladies' man, I hear."

"Did you know he used to be a cop?"

"I think I may have read that somewhere."

"Do you know where he was assigned before he left the force?"

"Leon, get to the point."

"Rampart."

Sherman did not flinch. Instead he took another drink. Then he said, "He got out before the scandal hit."

"I thought you didn't know much about him."

In the dim light from the windows, Colby saw Iron John Sherman smile. "Leon, you are going to make it big. You saw right through me. I held back. That's another thing a great prosecutor does. Holds back as much as he can from the other side, or they just might use it in ways that will be, say, harmful."

"You think I'm going to use it that way?"

"Not if you're the man I think you are, Leon. I don't think you would, because you need me in your corner. I know that." Sherman smiled. "I don't pick dumb people to back."

Colby felt the coolness of the words as he would a stiff breeze. "I just don't like being unaware of things I should be aware of."

"Who needs awareness? You're whacking at Lindy Field and Everett Woodard like they were piñatas. Just keep whacking."

"That's not good enough."

Sherman stared at him. "What's that mean, Leon?"

"I want the truth."

"Will you just can that cheap patter? Please, Leon? Use that in a campaign speech, but don't let's get all Mother Teresa here. You have a job to do. Finish it and move on. Forget about George Mahoney—"

"And a police officer named Glenn."

"You've never had trouble with the police before. Why start now?"

"I'm a prosecutor. You're the DA. We're the ones keeping the system balanced between—"

"Balanced?" Sherman spat the word. "Don't go back to law-school fantasies, Leon. You think it's balanced that every time a cop sneezes funny an Internal Affairs suit knocks on his door? You think it's balanced the city council, with their coffee and croissants, gets to hold the chief's head in a vice? It's not a balancing act out there, Leon, and you know what? The people don't want it to be. They want the cops to win. They're tired of gangs and graffiti and drugs and people sleeping on the sidewalks. So don't ever get it in your head that balance is what this system, or your job, is about."

A woman stuck her head out the front door. "Jonathan? What's going on?"

Sherman turned. "Office matter. I'll be right in."

"We're going to play Balderdash."

"I said I'll be right there."

The door closed. Sherman said, "Leon, you'll have plenty of time to find out about everything. I'll brief you myself before you take over. But my advice to you is don't dig any deeper. I've learned that what I don't know about what happens on the street with certain parties doesn't hurt me one bit."

Colby shook his head.

"Welcome to politics, Leon. There's plenty not to like." Sherman poked Colby's arm with his finger. "The secret is not to let it get the better of you. Because if it does, things happen."

"Things?"

"You're not the DA yet. You're on the fifty-yard line, heading for the end zone. If you make it, you have a great career ahead of you. But if you trip, or get tackled . . ." Sherman shrugged his shoulders. "Now, I've got to go play some Balderdash," Sherman said. "Learn to do the same, Leon."

5.

"I've been concerned about you," George Mahoney said. "I just wanted to stop by to see if there was anything I could do."

Mona shifted in her chair. Mahoney had made a special trip out to her house, at night. It was a caring thing for him to do, but she did not want him to see her this way. She knew she looked terrible. Lack of sleep and stomach pains were wreaking havoc on her face and body.

Especially tonight. She'd started having visions of Matthew, seeing his face everywhere, like he needed her.

"Is the killer going to get off?" Mona said, hearing the desperation in her own voice. "Are they going to say he was insane?"

"No," Mahoney said, his voice reassuring. He was sitting on the sofa next to her, his eyes full of compassion and concern. "If I can read the jury, I don't think they're going to go that way. Colby's doing a good job."

"They can't let him go, they can't."

Mahoney put his hand on her knee. "Don't worry. I'm here. Trust me and let me help."

Could he help? "I think I need to get a little rest. I haven't been very good for VOICe this past week."

"It's perfectly understandable to go through times like this," Mahoney said softly. "It happens all the time."

"It does?"

"Sure. Like you, many people jump into the group as a way to cope with loss. It can help, but it's not the whole answer. If I've misled you in that regard—"

"Oh no."

"—in any way, I apologize. If you feel you have to step back for a time, no harm done."

"No, no. I just don't know what to do next." It was as true a statement as she'd ever made. "But I have to do *something*."

"First things first," Mahoney said. "Your husband?"

How much did he know? "We're divorcing."

"I'm so sorry."

Mona shook her head. "It's better that way."

"Sure, sure. I just want you to know that this too is common. I went through a divorce myself at a particularly stressful time."

"I didn't know that."

Mahoney nodded. "I used to be a cop, as you know. Back in '94 my daughter was sixteen, and she fell into some bad company at school. My wife and I, I guess we were in denial. Anyway, at a party she was drinking pretty heavily. Her boyfriend gave her some pills, and the mix killed her."

"Oh . . ."

"We tried to get the DA to prosecute for murder or manslaughter or something. But they said my daughter's conduct would make it impossible to get a conviction. Can you believe that?"

Mona shook her head.

"Anyway, the stress of this on my marriage, plus my job, took its toll. The divorce happened." He paused. "But every cloud has that silver lining, they say. Through that time I met Benni, and we were even together for a while."

"You're not now?"

"Not romantically. We're still great friends. And we started VOICe. That's our legacy. So you see what I'm saying?"

No, she didn't see anything. Her head was starting to ache. "I just want this to be over. Oh God, when will it be over?"

Mahoney slipped off the sofa and knelt by her. "It will be over soon, and then you'll go on." He put his arm around her shoulder. "You'll go on with VOICe, because you need us, and I need you."

She swept some cobwebs out of her brain, but it left only trickling dust. Did he say *I need you*?

"Thank you," she said.

"No, thank you. For your passion for justice." Mahoney pulled her toward him, pulled her head to his chest.

He held her.

She was doubled over, her stomach throbbing.

His hand stroked her hair.

"There's always a silver lining," he said.

Now his hand was under her chin, tipping her head up.

She looked into his eyes. And suddenly his lips were on hers.

She tried to pull back, but his hand was behind her head, holding it.

6.

"Thanks for coming in so late, Doc."

Colby showed Dr. Tucker into his office. Only one or two deputies were around, and none of the support staff. Colby usually liked this quiet time of evening, a good time to prepare for the next day at trial.

"I assume you're wanting me back on the stand tomorrow," Tucker said.

"No."

"Then how can I help?"

The doctor sat. Colby remained standing. "Forget you're my witness for a second. Forget that you're an expert we use a lot. And forget what I'm about to say to you, just like I'll forget what you say to me. This is between us, off the record. Clear?"

"All right."

"This boy, Darren DiCinni. How is he?"

"Do you mean can he distinguish right from wrong?"

"Forget that. Forget the legal part. Just tell me in your own words."

The doctor shifted around in his chair. "Mr. Colby, I thought my testimony was clear. Were you not happy with it?"

"My happiness is irrelevant."

"Is it really?" Tucker's experienced eyes homed in on Colby.

Colby felt the look slice through him. "Suppose I tell you I want you to make me unhappy? I want you to tell me the truth."

"Now listen—"

"Just between us."

Dr. Tucker cleared his throat. "The truth? The truth is forever beyond us, just around some corner. We can't know for certain what's going on in anyone's head. It's like I said in court. The most we can make are educated guesses, and the ones with the most education get paid the most to guess. Right? And when we are presented with the data, we can make it do little dances, this way or that, depending on who's paying the band. You know that and I know that and that's the way it's always been done around here. So tell me again, Mr. Colby, why am I here?"

Colby sat in his chair. "Let's say I'm putting together a whole new band. Let's say I want you to give it to me straight between the eyes. And let's say this kid was abused for years by his father. Physically and psychologically. What would you say about that?"

Tucker sighed. "You don't need an advanced degree to know that's the worst thing that can happen to a boy."

"Is there any way somebody could recover from something like that?"

"Depends on the individual. The fact that this one's only thirteen offers a little hope. With the right treatment, of course." He paused. "What are you thinking, Mr. Colby?"

Colby shook his head. "I'm thinking life doesn't get any simpler the further we go along in it."

"I agree. And people seem less and less equipped to deal with it. The increase in depression and anxiety disorders in recent years is monumental."

"My dad said that years ago."

"He did?"

"And he predicted it would get worse." Colby remembered the sermon exactly. He was eighteen at the time, riding high on football glory, thinking life couldn't get any better. So his father's words shook him. "He said the more people give up on God the more the drug companies will prosper. Pills were going to replace prayer, he said."

"Your father was a prophet," Tucker said.

Nineteen

† † †

1.

Roxy flailed her arms like a swimmer without a pool. *"Let me do the talking,* she says. So I let her do the talking. And I'm the one who gets the ticket for reckless driving."

"Can you get off that already?" Lindy tossed her a can of Diet Dr Pepper. It was late, but Lindy would not be sleeping tonight. "I told you, I'll help you fight the ticket."

"The way you sweet-talked those cops?"

"I wasn't prepared."

"I'll say. The minute they found out who you were, they couldn't write a ticket fast enough."

"I'll pay the fine. It was my fault. There, I said it."

"I accept." Roxy popped her second can open at the same time someone knocked on the door.

"It's Klinger," said the voice outside.

Lindy opened the door.

"What are you doing up so late?" he said.

"What is it, Mr. Klinger?"

"Ah, my ticker. She ticks when she oughta tock."

"I have someone here."

Emil Klinger leaned past the open door. "That hot pastrami mommy?"

"Mr. Klinger, please—"

"Okay. I thought you should know some guy was out here today, driving around."

"Guy?"

289

"He looked interested in your place. Say, you're not sweet on someone, are you?"

"What do you mean he was interested in my place?"

"Because I'm the jealous type."

"Tell me what he was doing, Mr. Klinger."

He shrugged. "Drove up the drive about halfway, stopped, looked, drove away."

"Did you get a look at him?"

"You think I'm some shmoe? I got a look. 'Course, the eyes ain't what they used to be."

"And?"

Mr. Klinger snapped his suspenders with his thumbs. "He had hippie hair and a beard."

Roxy came up beside Lindy.

"Hello, baby," Klinger said.

"Beard or goatee?" Lindy asked.

"Yeah, one of them little chin things."

"What color was the car?"

Klinger frowned. "This is twenty questions?"

"What color?"

"Blue. So there, Miss Quiz Show."

Lindy looked past him, out into the darkness. Was he out there? Was Travis Kellman watching them right now?"

"Go home, Mr. Klinger."

"The night is young!"

"Go home and go to bed."

"Some neighbor!"

Lindy shut the door. She went to the bedroom and got the gun. Cardozo watched her from the bed.

Roxy came in. "It could have been anybody."

Lindy shook her head. "Anybody with long hair and a goatee in a blue car." She placed the revolver on her nightstand, then sat at her computer. "Let's do a little Googling."

Roxy sat on the edge of the bed next to Cardozo.

"First, our friend Travis Kellman." Lindy typed in the name in quotes and hit return.

No results.

"Figures," Lindy said. "That's probably not his real name."

"Okay, I'll just be running along—"

"Stay here. We're going to keep going through the haystack."

"What haystack?"

"I'm going to jump around on Google. The box that teacher gave us is over there." She pointed to her closet. "Go through it again. Go through those crazy notebooks page by page. Find me something. Anything."

"Lindy, you need to get some sleep. I need some sleep."

"Just do it, please. "

As Roxy grumbled over the box, Lindy typed VOICe into Google and hit return. A moment later the results came back: 41,700,000 hits.

"Oops."

Google was not case specific. It had found every page with the word *voice* in it. She added "George Mahoney" to the search box. Two hundred ninety hits came back.

"Better."

"What are you mumbling about?" Roxy said.

"Nothing." Lindy started scrolling. She found some recent stuff from the *Times* and *Daily News* related to cases where VOICe had been involved in some way.

For the next half hour she read, linked, jumped back and forth between pages, learning a lot about George Mahoney's group and activism. Sometime in there Roxy made tea. As she served it she said, "How about a little Cat Stevens?"

"Hm?"

"We need a little music in this place. It's like a funeral parlor."

"I don't have any Cat Stevens."

"No, here," Roxy said. She was holding the Cat Stevens album from Dorai's box.

"Why not? Pop it in the CD player."

Lindy went back to reading. She heard Roxy mumble what sounded like *weird*.

"What's wrong?"

"He has two CDs in this case. Cat Stevens was on top of this one, but it isn't marked."

A tiny alarm, like a car's security system kicking off a block away, sounded in Lindy's mind. "Bring it here."

Roxy handed the CD to Lindy. It was a gold Maxell CD-R, 650 MB. But no label. "Let's check it." Lindy opened the CD drive on her computer and put it in.

"Music?" Roxy asked.

"Wait a second. No. There's a whole bunch of—" Lindy stopped. It felt like a hand grabbed her throat. "I don't believe it."

"What?"

"A bunch of these files have the word *Hawkstar* in them."

Roxy bent over to look at the screen. "Were these downloads or something?"

"Roxy, I've been checking that Hawkstar conspiracy site. You know he didn't post anything after June 25."

"That's the day before the killings."

Lindy stared at the screen, at the list of files. "What if Dorai was Hawkstar?"

Roxy looked at Lindy. "You think?"

"I don't know, but you have this quiet teacher type, not many friends. Coaches baseball, but had no kids on the team."

"That makes him a conspiracy nut?"

"Why did the police seize a bunch of his stuff?"

Roxy shrugged.

"He was into police conspiracies," Lindy said.

"You think there's some connection?"

"Let's find out. Is there more in that box?"

"Some."

"Have you gone through everything completely?"

"Well, that depends on your definition of *completely*."

"Back to the box."

"I was afraid you'd say that."

Lindy started reading the Hawkstar files. It was mostly fluff and nonsense about extraterrestrials, Cuban infiltrators, Skull and Bones moles in the government, and speculations about movie stars and plastic surgeons. Her eyes were starting to burn with fatigue when she opened one last file.

Hawkstar Notes
Saturday, September 9, 2000
Here's some inside dope on the Rampart fallout.

"Bingo!"
"What?"
"Cop stuff."

There's a hot disagreement, and I mean HOT, among the fifteen-member council that's repping the city in negotiations with the U.S. Department of Justice over police reforms. They do not speak with one voice on this. Big issues remain, like should the city enter into a consent decree to prevent the Justice Department from filing a federal civil rights lawsuit against the city over the LAPD's conduct? (A consent decree is a binding settlement whose implementation is overseen by a monitor and federal judge.)

Other issues unresolved by the sharply divided panel of negotiators include:

Whether a federal monitor should be appointed to oversee a lengthy list of reforms in the problem-plagued police department.

Whether the LAPD should be required to compile statistics on the race of individuals subjected to warrantless searches and pedestrian stops.

Whether the department should have to undertake a study of how it treats mentally-ill suspects.

Lindy's skin tingled. *Mentally-ill suspects*. The Department of Justice was scrutinizing this? Where were they now that she needed them? She read on.

For more than four years, federal officials have been investigating allegations that the LAPD routinely employs excessive force and infringes on the rights of minority residents. Their inquiry accelerated amid the allegations growing out of the Rampart scandal.

The hot part involves at least two highly placed members of the council, who have threatened to resign if the city caves. I haven't got the names, but my sources say shouting was heard within the chambers where the last meeting was held!

Lindy could almost hear the click of mosaic tiles dropping into place, starting to form a picture. The color scheme and the outline were taking shape.

The next installment was dated a couple of days later.

The dam has burst!

We know this much. A representative of the Department of Justice's Civil Rights Division was in a heated exchange with at least four members of the council, including the mayor's chief of staff, Orrin Martin, and the LAPD Deputy Chief, Palmer Kelly, as well as a former police officer, George Mahoney.

Lindy threw her hands in the air, spooking Cardozo. "Roxy!"

"What, *what?*"

"Get your car keys." Lindy broke out of her chair.

2.

It took half an hour for Roxy to drive to Judge Greene's house. A thick blanket of fog covered the coastline and made the darkness more impenetrable than usual.

The lights pouring from Judge Greene's windows filled Lindy with relief. She knocked on the front door, rang the bell. She heard footsteps inside, then the porch light went on. In the pause that followed, Lindy waved at the peephole.

The door opened. Judge Greene was in a bathrobe and slippers. "Lindy, what on earth—"

"Judge, please. I'm sorry to surprise you. But I didn't want to say anything over the phone."

"What is it?"

"It involves the police," Lindy said. "And I need help."

"Come in." Greene led Lindy and Roxy through the house to the outside balcony. He left the sliding door open. The curtains floated on the soft breeze. Lindy could hear the nearby ocean, encased in a bubble of heavy mist. Greene sat down. "Tell me what you've got."

Lindy took a moment to gather her thoughts. "Let's start with Darren DiCinni. His mother is a prostitute, someone Drake DiCinni, using a different name, has taken an interest in. Whether Darren is really his son or not, we can't really determine right now, but for some reason Drake gets it into his head that Darren isn't his. And he kills the mother."

"How do you know all this?"

"I've got several sources. I just want you to tell me if you think I'm crazy."

"I know you're not crazy, Lindy."

Lindy paused, then said, "Drake comes out here to start a new life, bringing his son along. Only he doesn't treat him like a son. He brutalizes him. But not without purpose. He wants his son to literally think he, Drake, is God."

The judge nodded. "I think I know where you're going. Drake is the one who actually put his son up to the killings."

"Yes."

"So when Darren said God told him to do it, in his own mind that's what he believed."

"That's exactly what he believed," Roxy said.

"Question," Greene said. "What was the motive? Why would Drake DiCinni want Darren to kill a bunch of innocent kids? Was it his way of getting rid of Darren? That seems an awfully complicated way to do it. Besides, what if Darren eventually implicated him?"

"That much he could probably cover. He could say—and in fact he did—that Darren was always a troubled kid, and even all the discipline he meted out couldn't keep him in control."

"Why the kids then?"

"It wasn't the kids at all," Lindy said.

"What?"

"The kids were just cover. Darren was really going after one man, the one adult who got shot, Dorai."

Greene frowned. "How do you figure?"

"I saw the uncut version of the videotape. On the first few shots, Darren was clearly aiming his rifle at the third-base side, where Dorai was coaching and was the first to go down."

"So somebody altered the videotape?"

"Exactly. Because they didn't want anyone to know Dorai was the target."

"Why do you suppose Dorai was the target?"

"Dorai was a conspiracy nut. He had his own Web site dedicated to this stuff. He updated it daily. One of his theories involved a conspiracy within the Los Angeles Police Department, a small group that didn't care about civil liberties or inconvenient things like the Constitution They just wanted to get rid of bad people. Dorai was actively soliciting people to email him with any information. I emailed him, but of course I never heard back. I did, however, get run off the road one dark night on Topanga."

"Run off? You didn't have an accident?"

"That's what I wanted people to think."

"I've got to tell you," Greene said finally, "this is about the wildest story I've ever heard."

"But it's true," Roxy said.

Greene shook his head. "Then we are in a lot of trouble."

Lindy saw something move behind the curtains. Immediately the movement became a shadow, the shadow became a body, and the body held a gun.

She looked up at the face silhouetted by the back lighting. She knew that face.

Drake DiCinni held the gun calmly, pointed directly at her.

3.

Mona's thoughts were not her thoughts.

She knew this. She was in a hospital room—*tomb* her mind said. Her stomach, they said something about the lining, her insides churning and acidic.

She had collapsed, or something like it. Where? She had a vague memory of arms reaching out, hers, and arms reaching for her.

George Mahoney's arms.

That was it. He had kissed her. Hard. And then she must have blacked out, the pain and the confusion and the ugliness of it, too much.

She had failed Matthew.

Yes failed yes failed yes failed. And there was no turning back, no rewind option.

Oh Matthew, forgive me, I let you down, I failed, I am no good for anyone—

She stopped, hearing voices—small, scattered voices agreeing with her. One of them sounded like Matthew's.

No! Oh God, no. Don't let that be him, God. Not Matthew. He would never have said that to her. He couldn't be saying that to her now. *No no no.*

Voices. The killer had heard a voice like this, hadn't he? Heard the voice of God, they said, the lawyers said, some doctor said. God telling him what to do. And they said his father had hurt him, made him insane . . .

Insane.

Was she insane? Was this what it was like? To have no thoughts certain, nothing to trust in, to never know any peace, ever again?

Was this what it was like to be the killer?

God, please don't let it be.

Jesus, please don't let it be.

"Jesus." She said it out loud, heard the name and for a brief moment there were no voices in her head, there was no torment.

And in that moment of stillness there *was* a knowing.

4.

Lindy thought, *We're all dead.*

How had DiCinni found them? Did he follow her all the way from the Valley? Was he the one who had been watching her?

He'll kill us all. Roxy was behind her, at the balcony rail. The judge was in a chair. They were all sitting ducks.

DiCinni's eyes were calm as he looked at Lindy. "You're a smart one, aren't you? That's too bad."

Lindy expected the gun to blast. But then Judge Greene spoke with a firm, measured tone. "Put the gun down, DiCinni. I'll handle this."

Lindy's heart dropped inside her, a dead weight. Her mouth went dry when she looked at Greene.

"Tell her," DiCinni said with a wicked smile.

Greene looked at Lindy. "I didn't know anything about the attempt on your life. You have to believe me. You have to understand the whole."

No. There could be no understanding, no *whole*.

"After the federal consent decree, crime went up," Greene explained. "It's brutal out there. Good people, good cops, getting killed because we can't bring killers down. We know who they are, but our hands are tied."

"So you plant evidence?"

"Not always."

"Against Marcel Lee?"

"Lindy, please try to see the big picture."

"And this guy, Dorai, caught on. That was why you had him killed. And Drake DiCinni works for you?"

Greene sighed. "In a war against the devil, you can't always use angels."

Lindy felt the world swirling like a crazy kaleidoscope. "And you picked me to defend Darren because you thought I didn't have much fight left in me."

"I didn't want you to get dragged into this thing," Roger Greene said.

"You thought"—she almost choked—"you thought I'd just roll over. You wanted a lawyer who wouldn't push too hard. You thought I couldn't handle another Marcel Lee case."

Greene nodded slowly. "It would have been best, and you know that."

"How deep does it go?"

"What goes deep," Greene said, "is evil. Evil in this city. Allowed to prosper because the city sold out to the Justice Department on police reform, because politicians don't have to sit in a courtroom day after day and look at victims' faces, or the faces of the families of dead people. Listen, Lindy, Rampart was—"

"You were on the council." Lindy's mind clicked pieces into place. "You were opposed to the reforms. You were the angry one who resigned."

"It was a kangaroo commission. It was a farce."

"So you organized your own Rampart division. You were the one behind Marcel, weren't you?"

"You know Marcel Lee is guilty as sin."

She shook her head. "Not unless he is found guilty by a jury in a trial without lies."

"The city is better off with him in prison."

"It's wrong."

"We're in an awkward situation here, Lindy," Greene sighed.

"*Awkward?*"

She looked at Drake DiCinni, who just stood there, gun in hand. "But why him?" Lindy said.

Greene opened his mouth to speak, but DiCinni cut him off.

"That's enough," DiCinni said.

He shot Roger Greene in the chest.

5.

Leon Colby looked out the window of his apartment, at the lights of Ventura Boulevard below. The reds and greens and blues of the street signs and restaurants gave the night a celebrative glow.

What was there to celebrate in this town anymore?

What was wrong with his ambitions? Where did they go all of a sudden? It was strange and unsettling. Ever since he could remember he had been charging, always going forward, head down, with all his might.

Had he ever identified what he was charging toward?

Darren DiCinni heard voices in his head, telling him to do bad things. Were they any different from the voice of ambition in Leon's own head? An ambition that got him to turn a blind eye sometimes, to cut corners, to justify?

How different?

He let the curtain go and sat in a chair, putting his head back in the darkness. *This is what life is like for so many people. Darkness. You keep moving because you're afraid something might be sneaking up on you.*

What was sneaking up on him?

He flicked on the lamp.

Pills, prayer. How his father had believed in prayer. How he could preach about it.

Colby remembered something. In his bookcase. Where was it? He searched the bottom right shelf and found it. The Bible his father had given him when Leon was in high school.

It had his name in gold letters on the cover.

But it showed little sign of use.

Colby took it back to the chair and sat with it on his lap. He had known this book as a kid, as a star of vacation Bible school. Even then he wanted to be the best. He had memorized all the books in order and could recite fifty verses.

They started coming back to him in random order.

Trust in the LORD with all thine heart; and lean not unto thine own understanding.

In the beginning God created the heaven and the earth. And the earth was without form, and void; and darkness was upon the face of the deep. And the Spirit of God moved upon the face of the waters. And God said, Let there be light: and there was light.

Blessed are the poor in spirit: for theirs is the kingdom of heaven.

Colby put his hand on the Bible. It had been a long time, a long time since he was nine years old, at his father's old church in Inglewood, coming forward to be baptized.

A long time.

Another verse his father had taught him came to him again. *If any of you lack wisdom, let him ask of God, that giveth to all men liberally, and upbraideth not; and it shall be given him. But let him ask in faith, nothing wavering. For he that wavereth is like a wave of the sea driven with the wind and tossed. For let not that man think that he shall receive anything of the Lord.*

Colby opened the Bible to James, found the verses in chapter one. Yep. Just like he remembered them.

6.

Oh God, oh God, oh God.

Lindy moved. She pivoted, getting between Roxy and DiCinni.

She heard a shot, felt a hot fist in her side. The impact knocked her forward. She went down on top of Roxy. Then another shot.

She tried to move, was weighted down, splayed oddly. There would be no getting away.

She heard two heavy steps behind her.

Oh God.

Bullets to the head.

God help us.

Lindy's side burned and she felt the oozing of blood. She kept Roxy under her, protecting her.

Something heavy fell on the deck.

Lindy turned her head. A body.

Drake DiCinni. His eyes were wide, shocked. And, Lindy realized in a second, dead.

What?

Then a hand was on her shoulder, and a voice called her name.

7.

Mona put her left hand on her stomach and with her right she reached out for the phone. Where was it?

There.

Picked it up, laid the receiver on the pillow next to her ear. Punched in the number.

Heard the first ring.

Oh God, be there be there.

A second ring.

Oh God, let him pick up. God let him.

A third. A fourth.

Dear God, dear God, dear God, forgive me . . .

"Hello?"

His voice was soft, distant, empty.

"Brad?"

"Mona." Surprise there now, longing.

"Brad, come get me. I want to go home."

8.

Travis Kellman held a revolver in one hand. "Are you hit?"

Lindy was too stunned to answer.

"You're hit," he said.

Roxy stirred under her. "What's happening?"

Lindy had no idea. What was Kellman doing here? With a gun?

Kellman put the gun down and helped Lindy get to her knees. Roxy scurried out. "Travis?"

He was taking his shirt off. "We've got a bullet wound. Hold this on her, Rox."

Lindy saw him hand his shirt to Roxy, whose mouth was hanging open. "Why are you here?"

"Followed you."

"But why—"

Travis took Roxy's hand and made her apply the shirt to Lindy's side. "Keep it there. I'm calling 911."

Lindy's head was light now, swirling. "How you doing?" Roxy whispered.

"I'm totally confused, is how I'm doing."

She heard Travis talking to the 911 operator. And then she heard a groan.

It wasn't Drake DiCinni. He hadn't moved. It was Greene, still in his chair, his arms out to the sides.

She moved a few feet toward him. Roxy followed, still holding the shirt on her wound.

"We have a shooting here," Kellman said in the background. "A woman, early thirties has been hit, needs an ambulance."

"And a man, late fifties," Lindy called over her shoulder.

Greene looked up at her, his eyes obscured. He moved his mouth. Lindy put her hand on his shoulder. "Don't say anything, Judge."

His lips moved again. "Lindy . . ." he said, barely loud enough for her to hear.

So this is what it's really like to lose a father, one you loved, trusted. Lost not to death or distance, but deceit. The enormity of it, the chasm of sadness inside her, threatened to swallow her. Her loss of blood was nothing. The loss of Greene, of trust, of certainty, that was everything.

"Forgive me, Lindy . . ."

She looked into the hurt and uncertainty of his eyes.

Oh God, forgive us all.

TWENTY

† † †

1.

Leon Colby got the message from reception at 8:37 a.m. A guy from Internal Affairs to see him on an urgent matter related to the DiCinni case.

Which was on the calendar for nine.

Colby did not know the man who introduced himself as Travis Kellman.

"I thought I knew all the faces at IA," Colby said, shaking his hand.

"Special assignment," Kellman said. "I'm from San Diego. It was undercover."

"Undercover? What for?"

"Because it involved cops who didn't need to know what I was looking at. By the way, Lindy Field was on to it."

Colby cocked his head. "What does Lindy have to do with it?"

"She was shot last night, at the home of Judge Roger Greene."

Colby stared at him in disbelief.

"I followed her there. She was with her investigator, Roxanne Raymond. I was keeping an eye on them, mainly for protection. I was late getting into Greene's house. Almost too late."

"How is Lindy?"

"She's going to be all right," Kellman said. "The bullet took a chunk out of her side but didn't do any permanent damage. But Greene is hanging on by a thread. He gave me a full statement at four this morning."

Colby was having trouble forming words. "Who shot who and why?"

"Drake DiCinni shot Greene and Lindy. I shot DiCinni. DiCinni was hiding out at Greene's house."

Colby's mind failed to produce a complete picture. "How does Greene figure in this?"

"He ran a network of rogue cops. A star chamber, if you will. Judge and jury and executioner rolled into one. I've got names, dates. Drake DiCinni was part of it. He worked out of Vegas originally. Got recruited by the DA there to do dirty work in order to avoid a murder charge. The DA had served with Greene in Vietnam. They had similar views, shall we say, of how the law should operate. The DA there actually sent DiCinni to work for Greene."

Colby looked at the clock on his wall. 8:40.

"You might want to ask the judge for a continuance," Kellman said. "Until you can talk to Greene."

"And Lindy. I'd like to see Lindy."

"Greene said it was George Mahoney who ran Lindy off Topanga. We're picking him up now."

Leon almost asked how this could happen, but he knew how. With a sudden clarity he knew very well how it happened, and his part in it.

The office door opened. Larry Lopez came in. "You ready to go? We got—" He stopped when he saw Kellman.

"This is Larry Lopez," Colby said, "my investigator."

"I know Mr. Lopez. Judge Greene mentioned his name."

"Greene?" Lopez said.

Travis Kellman removed his gun and pointed it at Lopez. "Hands on your head, please."

Lopez stared. "What's this?"

"Now," Kellman said.

"Better do it, Larry," Colby said.

For a moment Lopez looked like he might bolt. But then a resignation swept his face. He put his hands on his head. "You sold me out, didn't you, Leon?"

"I sold myself out," Colby said. "A long time ago."

Kellman disarmed Lopez, pulled his hands behind his back, and cuffed him.

"You are under arrest for the murder of Sean McIntyre," Kellman said. "You have the right to remain silent . . ."

2.

"Where is Ms. Field?" Judge Lipton was on the bench, ready to get started.

"I'm sorry, Your Honor," Everett Woodard said. "There was some trouble last night."

"Trouble?"

"Lindy is in the hospital again. There was a shooting and—"

"Shooting? What is going on here?"

"Excuse me, Your Honor." Leon Colby stood. "Let me try to explain."

"I don't know if I want to hear this. I want to bring in the jury and I want to keep this case moving."

"There won't be any need for the jury."

"I beg your pardon?"

Colby looked at Everett Woodard, seeing the surprise on his face. He knew it was nothing like it was about to become. He also knew that the numerous VOICe people in the gallery were about to go ballistic.

"At this time," Colby said, "the People will accept the plea that has been offered by the defense, in their previous memorandum." The plea that would send Darren DiCinni to a mental facility and not prison. The plea he had previously refused even to consider.

He was right about Woodard and VOICe. The defense lawyer's face became a neon sign of shock, then elation. At the counsel table, Darren DiCinni's eyes registered confusion. Behind Colby, the grumblings in the VOICe section rose like a wave of auditory outrage.

Judge Lipton said, "Approach the bench."

When Woodard and Colby were in front of him he leaned forward. "Do you know what you're doing, Leon?"

"Absolutely."

"Does your boss know what you're doing?"

"He will."

"Do you want a few minutes to—"

"No, Your Honor. We are ready to proceed."

"You know," Judge Lipton said, "there are going to be some very upset people around here. And I'm not just talking about the people in this courtroom."

Colby nodded toward the courtroom wall, at the bas-relief of Justice holding her scale. "Yeah," he said, "but she's good with it."

3.

Iron John Sherman was not good with it. Leon Colby took a clue from the blue vein swelling under the tight skin of Sherman's forehead.

"Are you completely insane?" Sherman shouted. "Do you know what you've done?"

Sherman's arms flailed wildly, like he was conducting the *1812 Overture*.

"You're toast," Sherman said. "Kiss this office good-bye. You big dumb—"

Colby shook his head. "Don't say it, chief. Wouldn't want word to get out that you're prejudiced."

"Don't threaten me, Leon. You don't know who you're dealing with here."

"Yeah. I do. Anything else?"

"I hope you like Compton. Because that's where you're going. You can do traffic cases the rest of your life."

Colby felt light, flying for the first time in years. He reached in his coat and took out the letter, tossed it on Sherman's desk.

"My resignation," Colby said.

"Then get out of my office."

Colby took one last look at that office, the place he would never occupy. Plush carpet, fancy desk, expensive artwork.

Some words came back to him then, sounding out in his head like his father's voice when he was in his prime, pacing at the pulpit. *I count all things but loss—*

He saw his father raising his hands toward heaven.

"I said get out, Leon."

"So long, chief. Just wanted to leave you with a thought: Play hard and play fair."

"What?"

Colby left without another word.

TWENTY-ONE

† † †

1.

Sundays.

They were different now. Sundays were church days. Lindy would usually meet Roxy and Travis and they'd go together.

Travis finally explained his behavior. He had introduced himself to Roxy as a way of getting information on the Marcel Lee case. He hadn't expected to fall for her, but when he did, he felt he had to pull away so as not to involve her further in the investigation.

Roxy seemed more than happy to forgive and forget.

As did, remarkably, Mona Romney. She approached Lindy tentatively at church, then asked Lindy to forgive her. Unreal, the way God worked in people. They even embraced.

But that wasn't, to Lindy's way of thinking, the most astounding thing.

Most astounding was this man standing in front of her, here at another church, a church that rocked with gospel music and pulsed with people who sang like none she'd ever heard.

Leon Colby filled the pulpit with his presence. Six-and-a-half feet of him, the former trial lawyer, preaching for the first time in his father's own church. He'd called Lindy to invite her.

Shortly after Darren's sentencing, Colby officially quit the DA's office. He also unearthed all sorts of records on the Marcel Lee case, which he handed over to Marcel's appellate lawyer. This time Lindy was sure Marcel would get a reversal. The real story would come to light. And Colby's testimony before a federal grand jury would help bring indictments against the last vestiges of the underground unit once headed by Judge Roger Greene.

Her heart still ached for Greene. He'd been a good man, she really believed that. But good intentions can lead to bad ends. Street justice was not justice at all. Maybe Greene knew that and decided not to fight for life. He died a couple of days after being shot.

When Leon Colby sermonized, he mesmerized, just like he had with the juries of Los Angeles County. "You all have been so kind to me," he said, "after my years of wandering. You never forgot about me in all that time. I know you were praying for me too. I know Dad was praying all the time, even when he could no longer speak . . ."

His voice trailed off for a moment.

"But I'm here, and I'm humbled you've allowed me to be here, to hear my testimony. I'd like to come back."

A chorus of voices shouted, *Amen!*

Then another surge of singing and waving hands filled the place, and Lindy thought heaven would certainly be filled with a joy like this.

After church Colby stood around, talking to well-wishers. He asked Lindy to wait, and when they were finally alone he said, "Thanks for coming. I was hoping you would."

"To be honest, I had to see this with my own eyes. I don't know if I would have believed it otherwise."

Colby smiled, a nice easy smile that Lindy had never seen on him before. He looked at his feet for a moment. "And I was wondering if you were doing anything for dinner tonight."

"Leon, are you asking me out?"

"Guilty."

"I don't know what to say."

Colby laughed. "That's got to be a first for you."

And for a moment, she really didn't have the words. Then she said, "Is this one of those times when the Lord is working in mysterious ways?"

"And it won't be the last."

Of that Lindy was certain. "Okay, Leon. You're on."

She was smiling as she got on her Harley, which Wolf had fixed up in return for some legal work on his brother's case. She pulled out onto the Inglewood streets and then the 405 freeway.

But she didn't go straight home.

2.

"How are things today?"

Darren looked at Lindy with soporific eyes. "My head feels squishy."

His voice was still. Not a voice that had known horrors beyond most imaginings.

When he spoke, he did not gesture. His words had a numb dispassion about them. Lindy knew this was because of the meds, which would be a part of his world, probably forever. His head would always feel squishy.

They were on a bench in the sun yard. The state hospital in Lancaster was, all things considered, the best Darren could have hoped for—if he knew how to hope. He wore a white cotton jumpsuit, a definite improvement over the stiff orange of the K–10 jail inmate.

"Anything I can get for you?" Lindy said. "I can bring in books and—"

"When do I get out?"

That question again. He asked it every time she came. He had no concept of time, nor of the likely duration of his sentence. "Just keep getting better," she said, "and we'll see."

At least he was better off here than in prison. One reason she came once a month was to check the conditions. If this state institution messed up, which it had in the past, she'd be ready for them with a civil action.

But the main reason she came was to see Darren. He'd been here eight months now, after the agreed-upon plea. He'd be here for years before his first limited-release hearing and the inevitable public outcry. And Lindy would be there to speak up for him. She'd be there because she was his lawyer.

A light stirred behind his eyes. "Where's God?"

It was the first time he'd mentioned God since the trial.

Lindy didn't answer at first. The doctors warned her not to upset the delicate structures they were building up in his mind.

Darren's tone grew more insistent. "Where *is* God?"

Careful. Careful.

"There's no need to be afraid, Darren. Ever again."

"Where is God?"

"Darren, you don't have to be afraid."

"Where?"

Lindy silently prayed for the right words. "The one you thought was God, the one who told you to do the bad things, he's not going to hurt you again." Drake DiCinni had been convicted a month ago for the murder of Roger Greene and was on his way to death row at Quentin. Lindy's own testimony had sealed the conviction.

Darren looked confused, but in a new way. His mental faculties were being mashed around by the psychotropics, so his expressions usually had a chemical sameness about them. Not now. He was straining toward something.

"Why does God do bad things?" Darren asked.

"God doesn't do bad things."

"How do you know?"

"Because God is always good."

"He's not." He frowned, as if trying to understand.

"I have never lied to you, Darren. Do you know that?"

He nodded tentatively.

"And I never will. God is always good." She paused. "I want to tell you about God, Darren. Really tell you. Do you want me to?"

He nodded again.

"I'm learning all about God. And Jesus. Okay?"

Another nod.

"All right then. I'll keep coming back and we'll learn about Jesus and God and all of that. We'll learn it together."

"Together?"

"Yes."

He looked at his hands then. Like he was studying them. He looked at them for a long, silent moment.

Then, suddenly, he began to shake. At first Lindy thought he was going into some sort of seizure. She was about to call for help when Darren said, quietly but firmly, "I did bad. I did bad."

He paused a moment, quivering in his coveralls. "I did bad. I—" A sob smothered his words. He sucked in a labored breath, his face clenched in palpable anguish. And then he put his head in his hands, muffled wails surging.

Lindy put her arm around him, absorbed his trembling. And knew he'd experienced a breakthrough. She didn't need a doctor to tell her that. So she wouldn't wait to tell Darren. When he calmed, she would tell him about the love of Jesus, about God the Father, the true Father to them both. She'd tell him all she knew, and stay until he understood.

"Together," she said, stroking his hair. "You and me."

ABOUT THE AUTHOR

† † †

James Scott Bell is the bestselling author of *Deadlock, Breach of Promise,* and the historical legal thriller series the Trials of Kit Shannon. A winner of the Christy Award for Excellence, Jim is a columnist for *Writer's Digest* magazine and teached fiction at Pepperdine University. He live with his wife, Cindy, in Los Angeles.

Visit his website at *www.jamesscottbell.com.*

ACKNOWLEDGMENTS

† † †

I owe an enormous debt of thanks to the following people:

Cindy Bell—my wife, first editor, and best friend.

Karen Ball and Erin Healy, for their insightful editorial help.

Sue Brower and "Team Zondervan," an absolute joy to work with.

The lawyers who go into criminal courtrooms every day seeking justice for the accused and victims alike, especially the public defenders and prosecutors who do the often thankless work of making our constitutional system work.

The men and women of the Los Angeles Police Department, who struggle long and hard to keep our city safe.

We want to hear from you. Please send your comments about this
book to us in care of zreview@zondervan.com. Thank you.

GRAND RAPIDS, MICHIGAN 49530 USA

WWW.ZONDERVAN.COM